PRAISE FOR J. M. DONELLAN

KILLING ADONIS

★ This first mystery from Donellan will remind many readers of Tom Robbins's work: cleverly crafted and overflowing with idiosyncratic characters and mordant humor. A most unusual mystery, indeed.

—*Kirkus Reviews,* Starred Review

"Donellan has a gift for witty turns of phrase and dialogue that jumps off the page and makes you smile."

—*Publishers Weekly*

SIX COLD FEET **PODCAST**

"A hypnotically immersive story… *Six Cold Feet* has become one of my favorite recent listens."

—*Wil Williams Reviews*

"The writing for this podcast is incredible, you will love every single second. I cannot wait for their next season."

—*audiodramarama*

"Smash the sh*t out of the subscribe button."

—*Aidan's Audio Reviews*

ALSO BY J. M. DONELLAN

NOVELS
A Beginner's Guide to Dying in India
Killing Adonis

FOR YOUNGER READERS
Zeb and the Great Ruckus
19½ Spells Disguised as Poems

POETRY COLLECTION
Stendhal Syndrome

PODCAST SERIES
Six Cold Feet

RUMORS OF HER DEATH

RUMORS OF HER DEATH

A NOVEL

J. M. DONELLAN

Poisoned Pen
PRESS

Copyright © 2023 by J. M. Donellan
Cover and internal design © 2023 by Sourcebooks
Cover design by theBookDesigners
Cover images © Perepadia Y/Shutterstock
Internal design by Tara Jaggers/Sourcebooks
Internal images © Adobest/GettyImages

Sourcebooks, Poisoned Pen Press, and the colophon are
registered trademarks of Sourcebooks.

The characters and events portrayed in this book are fictitious or are used
fictitiously. Apart from well-known historical figures, any similarity to real
persons, living or dead, is purely coincidental and not intended by the author.

Published by Poisoned Pen Press, an imprint of Sourcebooks
P.O. Box 4410, Naperville, Illinois 60567-4410
(630) 961-3900
sourcebooks.com

Cataloging-in-Publication Data is on file with the Library of Congress.

Printed and bound in the United States of America.
VP 10 9 8 7 6 5 4 3 2 1

1

I feel euphoric, which doesn't bode well. Serotonin floods my mind. I examine the room: clinical white walls, sharp angles, the heavy scent of industrial cleaning chemicals. The word arrives in my mind like a raindrop striking my skull: "hospital." Okay then, that's a step up from the morgue (or a short walk at least). An IV drip leads to my left arm. I wrench the cannula out, unleashing a tiny geyser of blood. I press the crisp white sheets to the wound, turning them a muddy red-brown as I try and shake the drug haze. I lift the sheets and examine the damage, immediately regretting my decision. I wonder if the scarring will be permanent. That could be a problem. People tend to notice scars, and I'm not sure I can survive an Australian summer in long pants. Also, my left wrist is handcuffed to the bed.

So there's that.

I touch the bandaged flesh, and the pain, though morphine-muted, is still severe enough to catapult me back into the memory of *screeching steel and howling horns. They say that when you approach death your whole life flashes before your eyes. But as I sailed through the air towards oblivion, I didn't see my whole life, just the one moment ad infinitum. You in that dress, the things you said, flashing over and over until finally I struck the ground and was enveloped by the all-consuming roar of the infinite l—*

"You're awake!" The doctor's voice wrenches me out of my memory. She picks up the chart from the end of my bed.

"Evi-dently...yes." The words stumble out of my mouth like wounded soldiers. A cop pokes his head around the corner, then disappears again.

"Please ignore our uniformed friend. Can I start with your name?"

"It's..." I come up blank for a few terrifying moments, then finally manage to pluck a name from the detritus-littered wasteland of my psyche. "...Eric. Eric Blair."

"Great to meet you, Eric! My name is Dr. Jill Sandersen. Do you mind if I ask you a few questions?" She has the kind of perky, educated voice that belongs on a kids' science program where they explain wave-particle duality over hip-hop beats.

"Sure."

"Can you tell me what month it is?"

"September."

"Great! What city are we in?"

I feel like I'm on the world's most depressing game show. "Sydney."

"Very good, who is the current prime minister?"

"Some underqualified populist muppet who'll soon be kicked out in a leadership spill, if history is anything to go by."

"Also correct, unfortunately. Do you remember what happened to you?"

"I was in an accident. A car swerved and braked in front of me. I ran into the back of it and was thrown off my motorcycle."

"Good. Your speech and memory seem clear and ordered. That's an excellent sign. It's a good thing you invested in proper safety equipment. You wouldn't believe how many motorcyclists we get through these doors who hit the road in shorts and thongs."

Even after nine years, I still can't get used to the Australian usage of "thongs" to describe footwear.

"Your gear saved your life. Mostly." She looks over my chart, glances up at me. "You were *technically* dead for a few minutes there. You had cardiac arrhythmia as a result of blunt trauma to your chest when you landed. The paramedics were able to restart your heart. Feel free to shower them with praise and adoration."

"I will. Thank you."

"I see you've removed your cannula? I assume you would've been very disoriented when you woke up, but we'll need to get that reconnected or the pain is going to be—"

"No morphine!"

She tips her head, waiting for an explanation.

I could tell her I have allergies? No, there'd be some sort of reaction already. "I'm an addict. Recovering. Two years sober. Can't touch opioids."

She glances at my arm, checking for track marks.

"Not heroin, oxy."

She tenses and shifts her eyes back to my chart, clearly not reading so much as buying herself some thinking time. I use the opportunity to glance at her watch. It's a little after eight p.m., which means I've been out around two hours. My delivery is overdue.

"Well, that is going to complicate your pain management somewhat."

"I'll get by." The only pain management I'm worried about right now is making sure Saklas understands there's a good reason his package hasn't arrived yet.

"We're not talking about a sprained ankle here. You're going to be experiencing—"

"I have a high pain threshold, I can take it. Where's my bag?" She shoots me a look of bemusement.

"The package I was carrying. It's important."

"Your personal effects are there on the table, but I'm afraid your courier bag and its contents have been confiscated by the police. Hence the handcuffs. Apologies for the discomfort, all part of these draconian new laws. Anything they can tentatively link to terrorism lets them do this, and thus far I've seen them justify any crime above jaywalking as a direct line to ISIS. It's a barbaric practice, if you ask me."

I choke down a gasp of horror. I've got a few bags of cash in the storage unit I could offer up as compensation, but it's difficult to guess the opening bid for an unknown object. Saklas is going to want reimbursement in either money or blood. I'm not sure I have enough of either. My heart races; the room lurches and sways. "'Scuse me. Gotta use the bathroom." I clock the confused expression on her face and realise I've slipped back into my real voice. I switch gears back into Eric's English accent and murmur, "Ah, still a lil' foggy. In my head. And voice. 'Cos it comes out of my head."

"I see. There's a wheelchair here if you'd like to—"

"I'm fine. I think."

There's a sigh from outside the door as I pull off the sheets. The cop enters, unlocks the cuffs, and fixes me with a steely glare. "Make it quick. No fucking around in there. Got it?"

"Understood. Won't be a minute." Sandersen lowers the bed railing, and I slide my legs over and place my feet on the floor. I stumble to the bathroom door, ignoring the doctor's pleas for caution. My legs feel like Jell-O in an earthquake. I slam the door behind me and sit down on the toilet seat, head reeling. I realise I actually do have to piss. I lift the seat and sit down again, too weak to stand. There is a mirror directly opposite. What kind of sadist positions a mirror opposite a hospital toilet? My eyes are tired and sunken. Bruises cover most of my body. The scar you gave me cuts a sharp line across the stubble on my chin, a cleared zone in the follicular forest of my face. At least I look like the addict I'm pretending to be.

I stand up and wash my hands, practicing the accent in my head so I don't slip up again. I open the door and the cop greets me with a weary frown, sweeps his hand back to the bed. "Right this way, Mr Blair." I nod and take a step forward. The strength vanishes from my legs. I tip towards the floor, and he catches me, throwing my arm over his shoulder. I liberate the cop's keys from his belt as the doctor grabs me from the other side and they help me back onto the bed. The officer cuffs me and resumes his post at the front door.

Sandersen flashes me a professional smile and says, "You've sustained major injuries; two broken ribs, substantial blood loss…" She whips out a torch and shines it in my eyes. "Possible concussion. Over the next few days we'll need to do some testing and get you to see one of our physical therapists—"

If I disagree with her there will be forms, waivers, signatures, explanations. Better to just lie and comply. "If that's what you think is best, consider me a temporary guest of chateau de… whatever hospital this is."

"Great. I need to keep on with my rounds, but tomorrow we'll come up with a pain management plan. You can contact the nurses if you need anything urgently."

"Will do."

She departs. I lie back on the bed as the click-clack of her shoes fades into the distance, enjoying the momentary calm and comfort. My meagre possessions huddle together on the bedside table; my wallet, some chewing gum, and the wooden ring you gave me in Santa Clara. The phone must've been confiscated by the police, but it's a cheap burner with no saved contacts or call history, so no big loss there. My keys will be somewhere in the river, along with my beloved bike. They must've taken the ring off me during one examination or another. I slip it back on and feel slightly restored, then remove the cash from the wallet and toss the wallet in the trash. The "Eric Blair" persona has been burned now, so his cards won't do me any good anyway. I use the keys I lifted from the cop to unlock the cuffs and then shove the money into my socks. I study the map of the fire exits on the wall. My legs move like they've only been recently acquainted with my body.

I turn out the light and wait for my eyes to adjust to the semidarkness, then use the cuffs to smash the mirror and flatten myself against the wall. The officer charges in and I shove him to the ground then slip out the door. I pull it closed and clamp one side of the cuffs to the door handle and the other to a nearby railing. He yanks the door open but only gets it wide enough for his fingers to claw impotently at me through the gap. His screaming recedes into the background as I follow the hall-way around to the left and duck into the elevator, hitting the button for the second floor. A trio of nurses dashes towards my room as the doors slide closed and I ascend.

The elevator opens, and I duck around the corner, attempt-ing to appear like a garden-variety invalid as I pass patients and visitors on my way to the stairs. The sound of the nurses pursu-ing me is cut short by the stair door closing as I make my way back down to the ground floor. A couple of nurses are chatting around the corner, and a heavily bearded man is snoring in the ugly green plastic seats in the waiting area. I take casual steps towards the glass doors of the exit, acting like I'm just heading out for a cigarette. The TV screen above the bearded man's head is displaying scenes of yet another American senator embroiled in sexual misconduct. I still find it strange how much news from back home is scrutinised in the media here compared to the smattering of dispatches from Australia's much closer Asian neighbours. But what really catches my eye isn't the news itself, but the time and date displayed in neat white text in the bottom right corner.

I haven't been out for two hours, it's been *twenty-six*. Saklas will already have people out looking for me. I quicken my pace as I reach the exit, but as soon as I make it outside I'm blinded by a flash of white light. For a second I'm thrown back into the memory of *the light the heat the infinite everything swirling corus-cating consuming—*

"Hey! You okay?" Two teenage girls glare at me. The one on

the left is withered and worn, under the thrall of what I assume must be leukemia. A nasal cannula dangles from her nose, leading down to the oxygen tank at her feet. She's clutching her phone in her hand as though it's far more precious than mere medical equipment.

"Did you take a picture?"

The girl on the right replies, "...yeah? Cassie just finished her last round of treatment and we were—"

"Hey that's great congratulations I'm really excited for you pleasedeletethatphotoimmediately."

"Ex-*cuse* me?" Cassie demands. "Dude, you can't tell me what to do with *my* phone!"

I step closer, holding my hands up and implore, "It's really important that—"

"Step the fuck back, psycho!" The other girl squeals. A police siren wails somewhere in the distance.

I lower my voice and say, "I'm sorry, I didn't mean to alarm you, but I think I was in the background of that picture you took, and I'd really like you to delete it."

"If you're in public, you waive your right to privacy. It's like, the fifth amendment or whatever," Cassie's friend proclaims confidently.

I resist the urge to address the multitudinous errors in that statement and say in sotto voce, "I'm in witness protection. The cops told me I can't have my face anywhere on social media. If the people I'm running from find out where I am..." I let their imaginations fill in the blanks.

Cassie considers this and replies, "Ok. We won't post it." She purses her lips, aims a manicured black fingernail at me. "If you give us $500."

"WHAT?" I yelp. The squad car is maybe a block away now.

"If it's that important, you can make it work. I need the money, dude. Being sick is fucking expensive."

Her friend looks slightly aghast at the suggestion, but then holds up the screen and says, "Yeah, it's geotagged and everything, so they're gonna know exactly where you are. Probably worth $500 to skip that, hey?"

"I don't have any cash on me."

Cassie shrugs. "Bummer. Okay then, say hi to my 7,398 followers…"

The squad car tears around the start of the long driveway that leads up to the hospital entrance. The teenage extortionists glower at me. "Okay. I've got some money in my socks." I move to bend over, feigning like I'm reaching for the cash, then pull my hand up and snatch the phone, taking off at as much of a canter as my violently remixed legs can manage. The cop car screeches to a halt in the pickup zone as I run through the carpark entrance. Behind me, voices scream for me to stop running, accompanied by the infernal shrieking of a teenage girl deprived of her cell phone.

I yank the door to the carpark stairwell open as wide as it'll go, then hit the ground and roll under the nearest car. The world oscillates wildly around me. The urge to puke rises in my gut. The cops enter the carpark just as the stairwell door slams closed. They take the bait, open the door, and run down the stairs. I wait a few seconds until their footsteps have disappeared, then delete the picture and smash the phone on the cement next to me. I wonder what you would you say if you saw me lying in an oil stain, staring at the rusty undercarriage of an old Toyota, after robbing an enfeebled young woman? I can hear your voice in my head now:

"¡Mentiroso! ¡Embustero! ¡Fabulista!"

Everything was sweat and drums and liquor. I remember the way your satin dress sent glistering red rays around the room whenever the light caught you. The way you moved like your flesh was an extension of the music itself, a corporeal manifestation of rhythms and melody. Our eyes locked, delirious smiles painted across our faces, brains addled with lust and adrenaline and tequila, words stumbling inelegantly out of our mouths.

I remember looking at you and the word "forever" piercing the boozy haze of my brain. That solitary word, over and over, with the same urgent insistence as the drums behind you.

Forever.

Forever.

Forever.

2

I hand the driver a fifty-dollar bill and hope he doesn't notice
the faint aroma of feet it now carries. He assesses me with a wary
gaze. Using cash is fast becoming cause for suspicion in an age
of digital transactions. It could also be the fact that I'm wearing
ill-fitting jeans and a *World's Best Dad!* sweater stolen from the
clothesline of some poor bastard who's going to spend the next
week scratching his head over their mysterious disappearance.
He drives away, and I walk over to the entrance of the storage
facility and punch in my PIN. The keypad responds with an
angry bleat. My head is a Slavic mob disco of pain and dizziness.

The first digit is definitely 6. Or possibly 9. I type the numbers in again, and the keypad repeats its refusal. I close my eyes,
shuffle through the debris of my memories. I type the number
in, and the door bleats its greeting as it opens. I did a lot of
research to find a storage facility that would grant me twenty-
four-hour access with nothing but a PIN; no keys, no swipe

card. I'd reasoned that I wanted to be able to get in even if I'd been stripped naked and thrown out of a moving car, mostly due to the time that a potential client I'd refused to work with had stripped me naked and thrown me out of a moving car. Once something like that happens to you, you tend to factor it into all future planning scenarios.

The motion-sensing halogens flick on, blinding me with cold white light. I throw my hands up to shield my eyes. My consciousness goes into conniptions, and I'm flung back into the memory of *imploding exploding inverting reverting infinite everything—*

I shake myself out of the memory of my cursory brush with death, take a breath, and continue down the hall. My footsteps echo cavernously around the cement-lined foyer. I pass rows and rows of luminous orange doors, each hiding a hoard of hidden secrets and sundries, until I reach mine. I stare at the keypad, once again rummaging in the dilapidated palace of my memory. This personal keypad I programmed myself; with your birthday—October 11—as the PIN. I type the numbers in, and the keypad bleats its refusal.

"FUCK!" I slam my fist against the shutter door. Behind me, a roller door shudders open, and a light flickers on. I wait for a moment, but there's no movement. I approach cautiously, keeping my back to the wall, glancing around for anything that can be employed as a weapon. The storage unit is stuffed floor to ceiling with a pointillist clusterfuck of pastels. Racks of floral dresses tetrised on antique chairs on top of an upright piano beside cross-stitched cats sandwiched between plastic flowers, porcelain gewgaws, and plaster gimcracks. The smell of dust and decay is overwhelming. I take a step closer, equal parts intrigued and horrified, and hear the unmistakable cocking of a rifle.

She's at least eighty years old, her face illustrated with a complex interlocking series of wrinkles and liver spots, a shock of white hair radiating out from her skull. Her eyes (like mine) are sunken from sleeplessness. I calibrate myself into the Declan persona; he usually does well with the elderly. I let my shoulders drop a little, tilt my head, slow my breathing.

"Don't you touch none of my things, unnerstand?"

My eyes flick over her mountain of miscellany. "I shall attempt to restrain myself."

She glares at me, eyes filled with hate and mistrust. "So you say. This is *my* stuff. Mine! No one's gettin' their filthy paws on it. Not my kids, not my grandkids, not my fat fuck of an ex-husband!"

I stare at her, unsure of what she's expecting of me.

"And *that's* a fuckin' lie!" She tilts her chin at me.

"I'm afraid I don't follow."

"That rot on your jumper. 'World's Best Dad,' my arse! World's best dad wouldn't be clompin' around storage units in the middle of the night, still smellin' of the cheap perfume his tart of a mistress wears!"

"I bought it from a thrift store."

"You're a *liar*," she snarls. She's correct, but not for the reasons she imagines.

"I'm simply here to grab my things and then depart. Is that alright?" I flash her Declan's winning smile.

She considers this for a moment, then nods, reaches for the light switch. It clicks off, and for a moment she's just staring at me from the darkness, like some deranged Dickensian ghost.

"Would you like me to…close the door?"

She grunts. I take this for a yes and pull it closed. I walk back over to my unit. The confusion has revealed the number amongst the fog of my postmortem memory. October 12. Your birthday is October 12. The door bleeps open, and I duck inside. My bug-out bag is stuffed with a little under fifty grand in cash. Hopefully, that's enough to cover the cost of Saklas's package plus a hassle fee. I'll be completely cleaned out, but I'd rather be dead broke than dead with every bone in my body broken. I grab a couple of boxes of painkillers and shove them into the bag, then change into a spare set of clothes.

My backup motorcycle is in worse shape than I remembered, but it should get me where I need to go. Good thing about bikes is they're cheap and reliable, especially an old Yamaha like this. It might not have any bells and whistles, but it's got brakes and wheels. I sling the bag over my shoulder and wheel the bike towards the entrance, hoping not to wake Grandma Storage Wars.

I pull my bike to the curb. It's been maybe six months since I last used it. Really should've taken it for a spin around the block now and then, just to keep the battery in shape. I offer up a silent supplication to the god I sometimes pretend exists when I'm in trouble and then turn the key. The engine sputters to life and then dies again. On the second attempt it begrudgingly shudders into wakefulness. I pull my helmet on, secure the bag to the back of the bike, and take off towards Saklas's, praying he'll be lenient. *You always said prayer was only for the stupid, the pious, and the stupidly pious. Hopefully, for once, I can prove you wrong.*

3

Saklas's house is a cubist sentinel rendered in glass and steel, gazing out at the wine-dark sea. One of his Demons stands at the door, I forget his name; Muzza? Bazza? Gazza? One of those classically Australian monikers that sounds like a normal name after a run-in with a combine harvester. He calls to someone inside and holds his hand up for me to wait. All the Demons look more or less identical; shaved heads, prodigious beards, mirrored shades and—oddly enough for a motorcycle gang—no visible tattoos. It's Saklas's strategy to make identification and prosecution as complicated for the authorities as possible. It's smart, and it works. It also has the added benefit of creating a cultlike uniformity amongst gang members.

Goldie appears in the door, his lips peeled back to reveal the ludicrous golden grill that grants him his nickname. His oral ornamentation illustrates the fact that he's high up on the food chain. One of the perks of his seniority is that he's granted a modicum of individualistic flair. He leans in close enough that I can smell the hummus on his breath and whispers, "Yer fucken' fucked Leach." Not the most artfully phrased statement, but in terms of candour, it has an almost Shakespearean quality to it.

"You've got something in your teeth," I whisper back. Thing about having a post-death death sentence is that it tends to make you a little reckless.

He grunts and motions for me to lift my arms, proceeds to pat me down. "Boss has been waitin' on you. He don't like waitin.'"

"I'm aware."

"He's as mad as a cut snake."

I've been in Australia almost a decade, and I'm still not even close to wrapping my head around the relentlessly absurd slang. "I'm aware of that too."

"You might've been better fucken' off to Thailand. Had a bloke did that last year, ripped us off then had a luverly little holiday on Koh Samui. I mean, we found him after a month or two and strung him up from a coconut tree, but by then he'd got himself a nice tan and a cute local girl to keep him warm at night. Not a bad way to go out."

"But if I moved away, I'd so miss our little chats. I don't think we could capture this chemistry via Zoom."

He snorts a laugh and motions for me to follow him. The interior is a surreal pastiche of bikie clubhouse iconography (southern cross flag, hunting trophies, dartboard, beer cartons) and bizarre esoterica (books on demonology, archaic weapons, Nepalese thangkas). A handful of the Demons are playing cards and smoking in silence. A couple more are counting cash, weighing baggies; one of them is doing a crossword. "Vestigial!"

He yelps triumphantly. "Eight across, v-e-s-t-i-g-i-a-l!" His colleagues whistle in approval.

I follow Goldie down the hall, and we pass a Viking helmet, a pile of welding equipment, and an enormous bonsai tree. Goldie throws open the heavy oak double doors of Saklas's living room. Saklas is sitting in his leather armchair, the sea is a vast and imposing panorama framed in the floor-to-ceiling windows beyond him. You'd love this place, aside from the occupants and accoutrements, of course. You always dreamed of living somewhere with an ocean view. I've never been here in daylight, but I can only imagine the sunsets are glorious. It's a mark of Saklas's great wealth that he spent all this money on a premium seaside view when he could just as happily be facing a brick wall. It's a full moon, which is good because it means I can actually see well enough to make my way across the room to sit opposite him. Saklas never has the lights on in the living room because he doesn't see the point in wasting money on his power bill. Grievous bodily harm is very much par for the course in this line of work, but I often wonder if the Demons' frequent bruises and broken bones are a result of stumbling over furniture while wandering around dark rooms in aviator sunglasses.

Saklas is wearing a pair of gigantic Sennheiser headphones. He's a notorious audiophile; he has a new pair every other time I see him. He holds up his index finger indicating I should wait. We sit in silence for a few minutes, my stomach performing a series of acrobatic manoeuvres as he strokes his beard and murmurs quietly. I consider following Goldie's advice, running out the door and finding some tropical paradise to disappear to, starting over again. Third time's a charm, right? But Saklas would find me, eventually. And I'm already running from—well, I don't need to remind you.

After a tiny eternity he removes the headphones, inhales, and strokes his Ned Kelly–esque beard like he's trying to find a lost set of keys in there. "Sardinia," he says at last. I'm not sure if it's a statement, question, observation, or threat. Possibly all of the above. "I was listening to a podcast about Sardinia. Funny thing about that little island? The have the world's highest proportion of centenarians, people over the age of 100. Some of 'em as old as 120. Know what their secret is?"

I shake my head, then realise for the hundredth time this is a useless gesture in this scenario and say, "No, I don't."

"There is no secret. There's no magic in the water, no mystical practice. They just do all the shit you're supposed to do. It's mountainous, so everybody's getting their daily ten thousand steps; they got plenty of fresh air, trees, nature, and shit. And they got strong social connections. Loneliness is the new smoking, right? Kills more people than cancer. But these Sardinians have got their shit together. They do alla the stuff you're supposed to in order to live a long 'n healthy life. *You*, on the other hand, have been doing shit, or rather failing to do shit, which will see you dismembered and dumped into yonder ocean." He gestures casually towards the vast and voluminous sea.

"Mr. Saklas, you have my most sincere apologies."

"Can't do much with fucking apologies, Leach. Goldie, what's the going rate for an apology nowadays?"

"Fuck all, boss."

"Yeah, that's what I figured. Market rate on apologies has been somewhere between nada and zilch for a while now."

"I understand. But please consider, in all the years we've

been working together, how many times have I delivered a package late?"

He pauses and thinks for a moment then says, "Goldie? Pull up the stats for Archie Leach in our system."

Goldie marches over to his laptop and begins tapping keys.

"I can explain—"

"I feel much the same way about explanations as I do about apologies."

"Understood, but this is an extreme situation. I was hit by a car and hospitalised. Everything's still very...gelatinous. That might not be quite the right word. My vocabulary's still a bit remixed on account of the concussion. Also temporary death."

He pauses and leans in close, "Death, you reckon?"

"Yes. I was clinically dead for a few minutes."

"That right? So, what's the John Dory then?"

"The what?"

"The story. What did ya see?"

Infinite white infinite light endlessly recursive autonomously regenerating karmic compounds creating a— "Nothing. Just a black void."

He throws back his head and laughs, the sound bouncing off the vaulted ceiling. "Fuck, that's a relief. You hear that Goldie? There's no eternal torment. We're off the hook!"

"Glad ta hear it. Got the records here. Looks like...557 jobs over seven years aaaaaand...one late delivery."

I clear my throat. "I think you'll find that was a clerical error. I thought Fieldsy was going to fix that up?"

"Ah, yeah. He was. But he was the one I mentioned who took a little trip to Thailand. Turns out his accounting errors were largely intentional. Bazza took over on the books; I'll have a word."

"For fuck's sake, Goldie! How many times have I told you that effective task handover is fucken' imperative to the efficient management of any organisation? Did you even read *Nineteen and a Half Secrets of Great Leaders and Innovators*?"

"I...started it. Still makin' my way through. Been busy an' that."

"It's barely 300 pages. Get it done." Saklas shakes his head and leans in close, "Honestly, sometimes I wonder if I shouldn't just go legit, you know? Most of these clowns couldn't organise a root in a brothel. Well, except McClaren. He's doing a pretty good job of running the whorehouse portfolio, truth be told." He leans back, sips at this coffee, places it back on the saucer. "Righto then, taking your exemplary record and temporary death into account, I think it's only fair..."

I exhale with relief.

"...that we kill you quickly. No torture or mucking about."

"*Wait!* I have money. I can compensate you."

He grimaces and says, "I'm listenin'."

I unzip my duffel bag and place it on the table. "I have fifty thousand dollars here. I'm hoping that covers the cost of the package, plus the hassle fee."

Saklas considers this, then snaps his fingers. "Goldie! Get a count on this cash." Goldie picks up the bag and starts running the bills through the money counter.

"Fifty should cover it," Saklas says.

I exhale with relief for the second time.

"And by 'it,' I mean the hassle fee. The package was worth a couple mill."

A horrified gasp erupts from my lips. "A couple *million*? Are you serious?"

"Yeah. That's why we had someone with a stellar record

handle the delivery. Bad day to have your first fuckup, hey?" He takes another sip of coffee, smacks his lips. "Y'know, Leachy, when we first started working with you, a lotta my boys said you weren't to be trusted. They said we shouldn't put our faith in someone who hasn't been patched yet. Truth be told, I think a lotta them just don't like Poms. But there's a reason why I got where I am today. I started from nothing. And now..." he gestures around the room. "I'm a god. I got politicians and police chiefs who do what I tell 'em to. I got property and street cred and more money than I know how to spend. I went from street brat to kingpin. But I am a jealous god. And almost everyone out there, from babies to bartenders, has got something I don't got, and I can't fucken' stand it. The package was supposed to fix all that."

"What was in—"

"MY EYES!" he roars. He slams his hands down on the coffee table, feels for the edge and flips it over. The porcelain mug shatters into tiny white shards floating in a pool of coffee. They look like ice in an oil spill. "Fucken' cutting-edge tech, had to cut a few tech-heads to get ahold of it. Brand-new bionic retinal prosthesis. Lean forward."

"I...what?"

He cocks his head, triangulating the sound of my voice and grabs me, pulling my face into his. "I was going to *see* for the very first time. Can you imagine my disappointment when you didn't show up? I sat here, like a fucken' jilted groom at the altar, as the hours ticked by. Hour one, I'm tense. Hour two, I'm fucken' ropable. *Five hours* go by, you're still not here. I had one of the world's finest surgeons flown over from Germany, no expense spared. Set him up with a lavish hotel, his pick of hookers, our finest-quality blow (on the proviso he not snort up until after the job, obviously). He spends six fucking hours here twiddling his very expensive and highly trained thumbs before I gotta send him away."

Saklas shoves me back into my chair and continues. "He went back to his penthouse and had the time of his fucken' life. He'll be in Zurich by now. Had some keynote to present to a bunch of boffins, meant we couldn't keep him by carrot or stick. People would've noticed if he didn't show up."

"Mr. Saklas, I'll do anything to—"

"Yeah. I reckon 'anything' is exactly what I'm going to need you to do."

I stare at my twin reflection in his aviators. I look like a terrified corpse.

"Let me explain the first of many anything's you'll be doing from here on in. One of our warehouses got raided recently, we're a little light on storage space. You northside or southside?"

"I don't see why that's—"

He growls; a low, primal sound that makes my hair stand on end. I think about lying, about running, but the only way I'm going to make it out of this alive is if I tell the truth (for once).

"South."

"House or apartment?"

"Apartment."

"You live alone?"

"Yes."

He calls out to Goldie, "Sounds like we found our new storage unit!"

"Nice one. Okay, count's done. We got 51,450 dollars here."

"Great. Take the fifty K and give Mr. Leach his change. He'll need it to get a few things fixed up in preparation for our arrival."

I shuffle in my chair and say, "I really don't think—"

"Lean forward."

"Mr. Saklas, surely we can—"

He backhands me, the pain piercing the fading fog of the morphine. Imminent bruising aside, I can't help but be impressed with his accuracy. I spit blood onto the floor, where it joins the pile of shards and coffee. Goldie sniggers to himself in the corner. Revenge fantasies would be blossoming in my mind if not for the fact that its entire bandwidth is currently occupied with terror.

"Moving forward: As of now you owe me two million, loaned at three percent interest. We'll pay you a five-hundred-dollar-per-week storage fee; you can pay off the rest in instalments of twenty-five K a fortnight, for as long as it takes to pay it off. You got all this, Goldie?"

"Yeah, boss."

"But I don't make anywhere near that kind of—"

"Not my problem. Get it sorted. You'll need to give Goldie a set of keys. Might have the odd chinwag there as well. Make sure you keep the place clean. Get some candles; sandalwood. Or cinnamon. But no fucken' lilac! Plays hell with my allergies. What size we talkin' about?"

"One bedroom, about ninety square metres total."

He mulls this over, whispers some calculations under his breath. "Righto. Probably a bit small for a cook-up or a training facility, but we'll stash some stuff there. Maybe use it for the Tuesday yoga session. You got aircon?"

"Yes?"

"Good. This lot smells like a bucket of fish-heads in a heat-wave after they've done a couple of downward dog poses. I know some of the other shot callers around town make fun of my yoga policy, but I think the results speak for themselves. My boys are more centred, more focused, recover from injury faster. That last one alone makes it worthwhile in terms of ROI. In any case, Goldie will sort the details with you. You have any questions, run them by him. But a word in advance, nine times outta ten the reply is gonna be 'because the boss fucken' said so.' You got all that?"

"Yes, Mr. Saklas. Thank you for your time." I stand on rubbery legs and try to focus on the fact that I'm still breathing rather than the fact that this may well only be a temporary state of affairs.

He grins. "Goldie, there's a lot to be said for British manners, no? Old Leachy never forgets his Ps and Qs, does he?" He pauses. "Wassat stand for, anyways, 'Ps and Qs?'"

"Ah...I believe there's a few different theories. It might stand for 'pints and quarts,' but it might be short for 'please and thank you's', because the latter sound rhymes with 'Qs.'"

Saklas treats us to his demented laugh again and says, "Fucken' wealth of knowledge, our British friend here! 'Knowledge is the key that opens infinite doors', that's from chapter seven, Goldie. I'm going to be grillin' you on this shit. I want it read by next week," he calls over his shoulder, before turning back to me. "We're done here, Leach, for the moment. Here on in; let's keep things Sardinian, yeah?"

"Yes, Mr. Saklas."

"Righto. Fuck off then. I'm gettin' back to my NPR." He places the headphones back on and reclines.

Goldie winks at me and says, "Text me your address, I'll pop around soon."

"Can't wait." I hurry down the hall, out the front door, and back to my bike. I turn the key and the engine thrums to life underneath me. The predawn streets are quiet and empty. I pass the occasional car, a couple of taxis, a handful of late-night revellers screeching and stumbling. I stop at a red light and listen to the engine rumble, not sure if I should be grateful to still be alive or if I should just get it over with and plunge towards oblivion.

A flash of motion in my peripheral vision draws my gaze to the apartment verandah on the corner across from me. There on the first floor is a woman in a silk nightdress. She lights a cigarette, the orange star of its lit end flaring, fading, flaring again. My eyes adjust, and I realise her face is familiar. It's a face I've spent countless hours contemplating, a face I've enshrined in the hallowed halls of my memory.

It's you.

My heart spasms, and I call your name in a desperate howl. You turn your head to look at me and...

...it's just a trick of the light. The nose is too large, the eyes too narrow. You could be distant relatives, at a stretch, but it's clear that my longing has simply subdued my vision to its will. This kind of thing used to happen all the time when I first moved here. I'd see you in coffee shops, on street corners, in bookstores, at the beach, but this is the first time in years I've been so sure it was you that I actually stopped and called out.

The car behind me beeps; the light has turned green. I accelerate and disappear into the darkness, cursing myself for being so stupid. What would you think of me still hallucinating you after all these years apart? I should've heeded your warnings.

You always said that if I told a lie for long enough, I'd start to believe it.

I remember looking at you and the word "forever" piercing the boozy haze of my brain. That solitary word, over and over, with the same urgent insistence as the drums behind you.

Forever.

Forever.

Forever.

We stumbled back to your apartment, tripping over each other, laughing and howling at the moon. Making it up the stairs took a solid fifteen minutes. We opened a bottle of wine and toasted the full moon. It looked like someone had cut a perfect circle in the night sky, revealing an ethereal portal to unknown realms.

4

The scream pulls me from the same dream I always have. My nerves are an infernal chorus of agony. At least now that I don't have to worry about letting secrets slip in the presence of medical professionals, I can properly dose myself up with drugs. I reach for the pills next to my bed and inhale a couple, then drain the rest of the water in my glass. There's another scream, louder this time. I put the pillow over my head and try and ignore it, but the screamer is persistent. I walk out onto the balcony and look up at him; one floor up and to the left, hands stretched to the sky, mouth open wide like he's trying to inhale the stars. I don't know what his real name is, but at some point I started referring to him as Edvard Munch.

You'd probably find that pretentious, or insensitive. Then again, you're not around to chastise me anymore, are you? Munch has a carer with him most nights—a procession of sallow-faced, sleep-deprived men and women who can usually calm him down—but some nights he's all on his own. His condition is called aphasia; he can scream, grunt, cough, sneeze, howl, but never talk. Imagine reaching the third act of your life and reverting to the linguistic capabilities of a helpless newborn child.

Sometimes I try and picture what the inside of his apartment is like. If I could somehow astrally project inside at the times when he is not screaming, would I find him in the calm repose of a Buddhist monk, or inscribing arcane symbols on the wall, lit by candles? Or maybe scrawling a vast array of mathematical equations revealing the secrets of the universe? Or perhaps he just sits in front of the television, languorously masturbating with one hand and ingesting Doritos with the other.

He screams again. Sometimes I'm jealous of that scream. That raw, primal release. I can't remember the last time I screamed as an act of emotional expression, rather than a mere vocalisation of pain. Someone—my upstairs neighbour Reese, I think—yells at him to shut up. He might as well be firing bullets at a hurricane. The clock displays the time in iridescent green digits; 6:49 p.m. This is around when I wake up most nights anyway. Might as well get my evening started.

It won't be long before one of the Demons shows up and starts creating chaos. Maybe I could leave town, create a new alias. I could get plastic surgery; see if that helps keep me hidden. After all, you always said my nose was my weakest feature (joke's on you, it's clearly my lack of moral integrity).

A car pulls into the central driveway, followed by the sound of slamming doors and the shuffling of boxes. I sit cross-legged on the floor and draw in breath, attempting to enter a blank state, but that ethereal white light keeps flooding my mind. I can't forget the feeling of *every atom in my being effulgent with limitless unknowable transitions my consciousness a colony rather than a discrete ego my—*

The drawer in the kitchen buzzes. I slide it open; it's filled with a cluster of burners. Declan's phone vibrates, jarring its brethren. I pick it up and check the text message.

> Hey Dec! Just checking to see how yr recovery is going. Im here ready to resume training my fave student whenever yr up for it! PS I know you said you werent interested in a setup, but just in case Im sending you a pic of my friend Heather. I think youd rlly hit it off! Shes a psychologist. CRAZY smart. Great laugh. Feel better soon!

My sensei is a kind person, and I'm sure he is genuinely concerned about my well-being. I'm also certain he's missing the exorbitant cash fee I pay him for private training at his very quiet dojo. He gets on well with Declan, probably knows that persona better than anyone else, but I wish he'd stop trying to set us up. Declan's backstory is that he's a widower. That kept him off our back for the first few years, but now every other week there's a Jenny or Aiko or Svetlana he wants to introduce me to, not to mention the constant dinner invitations I have to keep refusing. He's taught me enough to help me fight my way out of a few tight spots when running hasn't been an option. Maybe it's time to just practice on my own; cut another thread that threatens to pull me back into the world. Heather has gorgeous skin and kind eyes, but she has the same problem as every other woman on earth. She's not you.

I delete the picture, turn Declan's phone off and put it back in the drawer. The door next to my apartment slams closed, a woman's voice swearing as she drops something. The apartment has been empty for the last few months, but this idyllic situation wasn't going to last forever. There's a knock at the door. I think about not answering, but if the Demons are about to be stomping around the place, I should try and get on good terms with my new neighbour. I unbolt the deadlock but leave the chain in place as I pull it open.

"Hi. I believe this is for you?" She's tall, early thirties, Indian. She holds up a manila folder. "I'm your new neighbour. This was outside my door." She has an articulate hybrid accent that suggests she's both well-educated and well-travelled. I run a few quick heuristics and decide Sam is going to serve me best in this situation. I let his smile colonise my face, draw my spine up straight, and inject a little effervescence into my voice before unlocking the chain and opening the door.

"Ohhhh, thank you! Welcome to the building." I grab the envelope from her. "I'm Sam Clemens." Sam greets her with a vigorous handshake that makes the bracelets on her arm jingle.

"Nisha Mukherjee. I just moved here from Brisbane."

"Well it is a *plea*-sure to meet youuuu! Thanks so much for this. Quick heads-up, I'm a bit of a night owl, so I don't mean to be unneighbourly, but I don't usually open the door to strangers. I'm *just* in the middle of something at the minute, but I'll see you around soon no doubt. You have yourself a *love*-ly evening!" I start to ease the door closed, but she slams her hand on it and says,

"Wait!" Fuck. She's really not making this easy. I'm starting to realise maintaining Sam's verve is exhausting in my current state. Maybe I should've gone with Declan. "Sam, I know I'm a stranger, but, ah, a stranger is just a friend you have not met yet, right?" In my experience, a stranger's just a meeting you'll soon regret. "Well, I moved here because of a breakup. A bad one. I don't know if—"

"Oh, honey! I have been there, done that and got the T-shirt." And the scars and the trauma and the fake passport.

"Okay then. So you understand. And I am all alone in this city. I work from home, also strange hours, so I do not even have any colleagues here. If it is not too much trouble, could I ask you to help me with some of these boxes? I would love to cook you a meal as a thank-you? I make an excellent palak paneer."

"Aw, shucks. I am sooooo sorry, Nisha, but I have the *worst* slipped disc. No lifting, that's doctor's orders! And I *always* do what a handsome man with a stethoscope tells me to." I take out the bottle of pills from my pocket and shake it as evidence. She looks confused, and I realise I've overdone it.

"Perhaps my dog Dante could hang out with you for a little bit while I move some things? He is not used to the place yet, and with all the excitement, he keeps digging into all the boxes and—"

"Sooo sorry, I really gotta go I'm right in the middle of—" Edvard screams again and Nisha shoots me a terrified look. "Oh, don't mind him, poor thing. He's harmless."

"But…he's screaming?"

"Yes. He does that. Quick word of advice? Get yourself a nice pair of noise-cancelling headphones. Cheerio!"

I slam the door closed and turn the dead bolt, then lean my back against it and slide down to the floor. Nisha shuffles back and forth on the other side of the door. I feel a tiny twinge of sympathy, not an emotional muscle I've flexed in quite some time, but I've got enough problems of my own right now, and I have the feeling that whatever's in this envelope is only going to add to that list. It's labelled simply "APARTMENT 3." No stamp, no return address. Clearly hand-delivered then. That's not a great start. The packages I deliver for Saklas and my other clients are either picked up from them directly or from a dead drop. Until last night I hadn't given my address out to anyone. The apartment is paid for in cash under the name Samuel Clemens to a landlord who was more than happy to ignore the usual checks and balances in exchange for a healthy up-front sum. No one should know where I am. None of my aliases list this as their address.

I tear the envelope open. At first it appears empty, then I realise it contains a single large-format photo, pushing against the side of the envelope. I take it out and the breath leaves my body. There you are; that unforgettable face, bright brown eyes, wearing that incomparable red dress.

5

People often claim "there just aren't enough hours in the day," but recent years have taught me that if you isolate yourself from any kind of meaningful vocation, creative pursuits, and social interactions, then the days go by as slowly as geriatric tortoises on ketamine. Having taken myself off the delivery roster for a few days while I recover, I'm deprived of any significant activity at all to fill the hours between waking and sleep. I swallow some more pain pills and meditate for half an hour, then make a meal of okonomiyaki. I've found cooking to be a quiet, satisfying, and meditative practice, and over the last few years I've managed to slowly master the key dishes of a range of cuisines from across the globe. I started out by making Chicago-style deep dish pizza, since my hometown's signature dish is pretty hard to come by here in Australia. From there I started picking a country at random and attempting to master its culinary offerings one by one. For the last few weeks I've been fixated on Japan.

When I'm finished, I clear the table, lie on the floor, and listen to Nina Simone while trying not to think about the massive debt I have hanging over me or the photo I shoved into the drawer. I take another couple of pills then continue my work on a three-thousand-piece jigsaw of Bosch's *Garden of Earthly Delights* I've been assembling over the last few weeks. I relish the way the pieces snap easily together, find their home, and then rest. Putting together a puzzle is a methodical, linear process with a clearly defined ending; the exact opposite of real life. I wonder what you'd think of me spending hours and hours on a sedentary activity like this, whether you'd find it endearing or pathetic. There's often a fine line between the two.

It's 9:13 p.m., I've been awake for a little over three hours, and I have no idea how I'm going to fill the next thirteen. The yawning of the temporal chasm is interrupted by a knock on the door.

For years no one has knocked on my front door, and now it's happened twice in two days. I am not at all pleased with this rate of increase. Nina Simone, although only quietly singing through the speakers, has given away the fact that I'm at home, so there's no use pretending otherwise. I stand up and assemble Sam's mannerisms and body language like I'm suiting up for battle and open the door. The dog greets me with an excited bark. It's a black Labrador, and through the lens of my narcotic haze, it appears redolent of the head of Anubis. It regards me with its curious canine face, indicating that the lines between this world and the next have become blurred, that death is not done with me yet, that the—

"This is Dante!" I only notice Nisha is there at all when she speaks.

"Oh, hey there, neighbourino-friend!" Dial it down a notch. This is Sam Clemens speaking, not Ned Flanders. "I mean good…morrow. Evening. Hi. Apologies, I'm on a lot of drugs because of, ah, well—"

"The back pain?"

I'd forgotten I'd already told her this lie. Good thing she remembered. "Yes. The back pain." Also the head pain and the leg pain and the knee pain and the stomach pain.

"Sam, you poor thing! Here, I made you a little something to help you through your recovery." She hands me a Tupperware container. "It's palak paneer. My father's recipe. You will love it. You don't have any allergies, do you?"

Not unless you count people. "No, but you really didn't have to—"

"It is also a thank-you in advance."

"A thank-you for what?" As soon as I ask the question, I realise I already know the answer. Dante steps forward and begins nuzzling my leg.

"See! He likes you. Dogs are excellent judges of character, you know."

"Yes. So I've heard." Mostly from people who are terrible judges of character.

"Sam, I hate to do this, but I have a family emergency. My father was in a car accident."

"In Brisbane?"

"In Jaipur."

"Jaipur…in India?"

"There is only one Jaipur. It's not like 'Portland' or 'Springfield.' I have a flight departing in a few hours, but Dante can't come with me. Sooooo, I was hoping…?" She leaves her sentence unfinished, both she and Dante regarding me with imploring brown eyes.

"Nisha, honey, ordinarily I would *looooove* to look after this gorgeous little guy! But with the state I'm in, it's just too much. Can't you take him to a pet motel or something?"

"Not at this time of night. Please, Sam. I have no one else who can help me. I am all alone in this city. And my father may only have a short while left. I have to see him." Her voice breaks as tears well in her eyes. I try and form words of protest, but I'm so tired that formulating a coherent argument feels like digging holes in clay. You always loved dogs; I can only imagine the ear-piercing shrieks of delight if you were here to meet Dante.

Nisha dabs at her eyes and implores, "Please, Sam? I am desperate. I can pay you?"

Unless it's a seven-figure fee, it's not going to do me much good. "No. Don't be silly. It's fine. I'll…figure it out."

"Thank you thank you thank you! You are a good man, Sam Clemens; you will not regret this."

Wrong on both counts. "It's fine."

She unslings her backpack and hands it to me. "Everything you need is in here there is his dog food and bowl and leash he needs to be walked twice a day or he goes crazy do not let him go near your shoes he will tear them to a million pieces he likes to be scratched behind the ears I will be back in a few days maybe a week thankyouthankyou thankyou!" She hugs me, but my hands are now occupied with the food and supplies she's given me so I just lean my body into hers.

She crouches down and holds Dante's face in her hands. "You behave yourself for our friend Sam. He's a good man. We are lucky to have him." She stands back up and kisses me on the cheek, then ducks into her apartment, slamming the door behind her. The sounds of furious last-minute packing emanate from inside.

Dante looks up at me, face radiant with expectation.

"So. You like Nina Simone?" I open the door and let him inside. He goes straight for my sneakers, reducing them to tatters in a matter of seconds.

Around midnight Dante falls asleep in my lap. I stroke his back gently with one hand as the floor carousels around us. I haven't taken any more pills in a couple of hours. It's not like the dog is any kind of canine panacea, but he appears to be an effective placebo. His weight on the outside of my body shifts the focus from the agony coursing through its interior. Everything is quiet and still. Even Edvard Munch appears to have taken the night off. My eyes drift to the kitchen table where I've left your photo. I run through a short list of potential explanations. Maybe one of my clients somehow found out about you and wants to taunt me? Perhaps Goldie is involved. I've never been able to tell if his deep disdain for me is potent enough to motivate him toward violence, be it physical or psychological. It could be one of your friends or family, or possibly Carlos, but that's drawing a long bow. I've covered my tracks well. My own family thinks I'm dead, no reason to think yours believe any different. None of these potential explanations survives more than a couple of shallow cuts from Occam's razor.

Reese's BMW roars into the driveway. The number plate of his BMW reads "BMW," an egregious offence which should make it not only legal but compulsory to scratch obscenities into the paintwork. The car stereo is blaring the kind of anodyne Eurotechno that appears to be the mating call of such vehicles. Reese shuts off the engine and stumbles up the stairs, slurring an incoherent monologue to himself. I add drunk driving to the list of things I hate about him. I'm already praying Emily isn't home. I only know Reese and Emily's names because I hear them frequently screamed at one another.

Tonight is clearly not going to break from tradition. Emily's voice begins as an urgent whisper that quickly crescendoes into screeching. He screams back, and the verbal volleying continues for a few minutes. Something smashes, probably a glass. Maybe the TV. I push Dante off me and stand up, reach for one of the cheap burner phones and dial 000. My finger hovers over the call button.

But calling would bring cops. And cops would bring questions. Checking of records. None of which is appealing to me, any of my aliases, or Saklas and the Demons. For the millionth time this year, I think about going up there and sorting it out myself. I could wrap a scarf around my face, run up the stairs, break a couple of limbs, and be back here with Dante in the time it would take to slightly overboil an egg. But the cruel irony is that Emily would then have to care for him. It's always the victims who have to clean up the shards after the hurly-burly's done. Meanwhile, people like Reese get to swing their sledgehammers and let everyone else deal with the damage left in their wake. I guess we have that in common.

Dante barks at the noise above us. He's been here only a few days, and he's already been brave enough to speak up while I've stayed silent. My thumb hits the call button. The ringtone is accompanied by the sound of a motorcycle thundering down the driveway and pulling up outside the front door.

"Operator, what is the nature of your emergenc—"

I hang up as Goldie hammers on the door yelling, "Leach! Oi! Leach! Open up."

I yank the door open, pull Goldie inside, and snarl, "Don't use my real name here, you fucking idiot!"

"Yeah, righto, don't get yer panties in a twist," he sniggers. I am convinced that the act of sniggering has evolved over millennia for the sole purpose of being employed in its hideous final form by the cretin in front of me.

Dante growls at him, baring his teeth.

"Ahhhhh, Leachy? What the *fuck* is this?"

"It's a dog, Goldie. Bit like a wolf, only friendlier. You might've seen one in a cartoon at some point, or a porno? I'm not entirely clear on your particular preferences." I crouch next to Dante and reassure him. The vibrations of his growling send shock waves into my body.

"You did not fucken' mention you had a dog."

"I didn't. I don't. I'm looking after him for a…friend. It's temporary."

"Well, I bloody hope he's not going to disturb our yoga classes. The boss is very keen on creating a calm, meditative environment. Hence why I have these." He unloads some of the contents of his backpack onto the table.

"You came all this way to deliver scented candles?"

"Yeah, nah." Goldie's Australianism sends me into a series of syntactic backflips until I realise that he is replying in the negative. "Gotta store some shit in yer fridge." He tramps into the kitchen, opens the fridge, and starts emptying its contents onto the floor. "What the fuck is hoisin sauce?"

"Quit chucking out my food!"

"Need room."

"What the hell for?"

"Blood and piss."

"Quit fucking around."

He opens up his backpack again and reveals medical packages filled with a selection of crimson and straw-yellow. "Blood's for when one of ours needs a patch-up; piss is for when someone we've posted in a legit job has gotta take a drug test. We'll pop round from time to time to collect."

"What if I'm not here?"

He flashes me his golden grin and jangles two sets of identical keys. He tosses one of them back to me. "Ta for the keys. I made copies."

"Are you saying that your crew is going to come waltzing in here, day and night, and you expect me to just put up with it?"

He throws the last of the blood into the fridge, considers this for a moment, and then says, "Yeah, that's about the long and short of it."

Dante noses at the food on the floor. I pull him away. He growls at Goldie again. Above us, Reese screams and smashes something, then slams the door, revs his car, and takes off.

"Fucken' inconsiderate, noise like that at this hour. Want me to pay 'em a visit, sort out a little serenity?"

"Stay the fuck away from my neighbours. They're civilians."

Goldie stands up and shoots me a knowing glance, cataloguing this information for future reference. He grabs your photo on the kitchen bench. "Faaaaaaark. I'd hit that! You stalking an ex or something?"

I snatch it from him, visions of violence kaleidoscoping in my brain.

He sniggers again and says, "Already got it locked in the old spank bank anyhow." He taps the side of his head, and I picture ramming it into the wall, watching blood blossom across brick, a Rorschach blot of red against—

Dante noses at Goldie, who punts the dog with his boot. Something inside me snaps, and I watch as my hands grab his shoulder and wrist and wrench them into a hold. I stop at the point of resistance. The sound of him growling in pain delivers an unholy degree of pleasure. One quick twist, and I could snap his wrist.

"Think real fucken' careful about what you do next. You hurt me, the boss is gonna take it personal."

I shove him away, and he grunts with satisfaction.

"Next time you come around, you knock quietly and wait. You hand me what you need to store, or request what you need to retrieve, but you do not set foot inside."

"Aw...not even for yoga class?" he mock pouts.

"If Saklas says I have to let the others in, so be it. But not you."

"He's not gonna like that."

"He's also not going to like hearing how you treated this poor defenceless animal. I've got a camera right there." I point to the smoke alarm.

He treats me to another signature snigger. "Yeah, righto. It's a shitty little apartment anyway. Catch ya later, Leachy. Don't forget yer first instalment's due in a couple of days." He waves at Dante. "Bye, pooch."

He exits, slamming the door behind him. Dante barks in his direction, turns in nine furious circles, then curls up to rest. If the Demons are going to start showing up here all the time, I really will have to get cameras installed. Not all of them are going to be stupid enough to buy my bluff. I throw the discarded food into the bin and then look at the picture of you, now crinkled and sullied by Goldie's hands. My head starts to spin, and I slump down on the couch. A ringing sound fills my ears. The stars outside come loose from their firmaments, slow stellar swirls of light in a sea of darkness. *I remember becoming nothing and everything. The thing I once thought of myself a mere raindrop in an endless ocean. Subsumed by light beyond light, sound beyond sound, holding—*

Dante's tongue on my face pulls me back into reality. He stares at me with eyes filled with a degree of affection wildly in excess of what is reasonable for a human he's known for mere days. I reach for the painkillers and swallow a few, chase them with water. Dante rests his head in my lap. I take a few more pills. Then a few more after that. My head slumps back into the soft embrace of the couch. The world collapses into oblivion.

6

Dante's barking brings my consciousness swimming back up to the surface. My eyes snap open, I push Dante aside, and rush to the bathroom, where a Japanese horror-moviesque stream of vomit deluges from my mouth. My reflection is barely recognisable; my face is wan and emaciated. My eyes look like they're retreating into my skull. I brush my teeth then walk into the kitchen and down a glass of water. Dante whines at my feet, water bowl in his mouth. Ah, now I see why he woke me up. I take the bowl from him and empty the rest of my glass into it. He dives his face in and starts lapping the water before I've finished pouring it.

I refill the glass with more water and pour that in too. Selfish of me to try and check out while another living creature was depending on me for its survival. I'm not used to having to think about anyone but myself. This temporary living arrangement is several orders of magnitude more complicated than what I would prefer. Then again, it looks like Dante might've just saved my life.

So there's that. My phone sits on the kitchen table. It's almost out of battery, unsurprising given that the calendar indicates I've been out for almost two days. Great. It's not like I have a deadline over my head or anything. Emphasis on dead. Luckily there aren't any missed calls or messages. I'd let all my other clients know that I'd be out of action for a few days for medical reasons (a.k.a. a temporary separation from the mortal coil). Saklas will definitely be checking up on me any minute though. My stomach rumbles like it's about to produce a Xenomorph. The fridge greets me with a cold blue light and a vast smorgasbord of blood and piss. The pantry offers up a few miscellaneous tins and some moth-infested flour. Dante whines at me again, this time carrying his food bowl.

I rip open the packet of dog food Nisha left me, take the bowl from him, and fill it. He ignores me while he tends to the void in his stomach. I'm about to do the same when the smell hits me. Shit. Yet another aspect of carrying for a living creature I'd blissfully forgotten. My appetite dispelled, I pull on some gloves and grab some paper towel to attend to the piles of excrement he's left around the apartment. I wrap the filthy mess in a plastic bag and dump it in the bin, then take the bag out and exit into the parking lot.

Reese greets me with a toothpaste-commercial grin, bags of Chinese takeaway clutched in his hands. "Evenin', pal!"

I hate the word "pal," almost as much as I hate the person uttering it.

"You alright? You look like my cousin the night after his bachelor party."

"'S just a touch of flu. 'M fine." My tongue feels like an unruly guest in my mouth.

His face sours. "Well, look after your health. It's your best asset. And, ah, coming from a real estate agent that should mean something huh?" He attempts a laugh, but it arrives stillborn.

"Are you okay?" I chastise Sam for asking. I've been spending too much time with him at the helm.

"Yeah. I, ah, no. I'm not. My mother is sick. Like, 'probably won't ever be well again' sick. Pancreatic cancer. Like Steve Jobs had." He brightens momentarily, as though this provides the malady with an elite prestige. "I've been trying to look after her the last few days; she doesn't have anyone else. It's…not looking good."

"I'm sorry to hear that, Reese."

"Yeah. It's, you know, pretty fucked up." He casts his eyes down, summons his real estate cheeriness back up to the surface. "Still, every day's a gift, that's why they call it the present, right? Later, pal."

He departs, and I slump with relief. Back inside the apartment, I light one of the sandalwood candles Goldie left behind and heat up a tin of baked beans. I take a leak while my food heats up, then close the toilet door, enter the bathroom to wash my hands, and glance at the bathtub. For a full minute my unwashed hands hover frozen in front of me. I extract myself from the stunned stupor and run them under the water, then step closer to the bath to let my fingers confirm the information my eyes are currently relaying to my brain. I poke the studded leather of his vest. Not a hallucination then. He's wearing a black T-shirt and jeans, massive beard spilling over his face and a gallery of tattoos adorning his arms. Clearly a bikie, but not one of the Demons. I grab Archibald Leach's phone and call Goldie.

"Leachy. Bit busy, mate. Can I call you back in—" he's interrupted by a muffled scream "—ah, reckon this'll take about ten minutes or so?"

"There's a fucking bikie in my bathtub!"

"Nah, yeah. Didn't Mazza leave a note? He was supposed ta leave a note."

"What?"

"He said when he got there you were passed out on the couch and he didn't wanna wake ya. He's got a newborn, so he's real sensitive when it comes to lettin' people get a bit of rest."

There's a crumpled sheet of paper stuck to the back of the door, hidden by the half-light. "Okay. Found it. It says–his handwriting's fucking inscrutable—ah, 'I put a bloke in yr bathtub. Maz.' Real helpful."

"Right. There you go then."

"Why is he there?"

"As per the conditions of your agreement with the boss, that falls under the category of nunya."

"What does that mea—"

"As in 'nunya fucken' business.'"

"What am I supposed to do with him?"

"Nothin'. You're storage, not disposal."

"He's dead?"

"Yeah." Goldie taps at computer keys. There's another muffled scream followed by someone talking to Goldie. He pulls away from the phone and calls out, "Yeah, just do the fingernails if he's still not talkin'. Remember the three Ns I taught you: nose, nails, then knees. Yeah, I fucken' know it's a silent *K*, smartarse! Sorry,

Leachy, just training up a new kid. Right, let's seeeee heeeeere. Fucken' Excel. Can't make heads nor tails of this shit. Okay. Here we go. That's KP. Ah, fuck. Nah, yeah. He's just resting after a bit of a punch-up. He'll be right in a bit. Give him some Gatorade and aspirin when he wakes up and send 'im on his way."

"*Gatorade?*"

"Yeah. Or, I dunno, Lucozade. Milo. Something with electrolytes. He—ohhhhh, hold up. That's Patrick. He's dead."

"..."

"You still there?"

"You're sure he's dead? You don't want to check you aren't looking at the 'waiting for a vasectomy' tab, just in case?"

"No need to be a prick, Leach. No more'n usual anyways. Besides, dead's dead. Someone'll come and pick him up in a day or two, nothing for you to worry about 'til then. Oh, and there's a note on the entry here: yoga class is going to be postponed. Boss said having a corpse in the place might create negative energy. Bad vibes 'n' that." Another muffled scream comes down the line. "Hang on. *Show me his hands? Yeah, nice one! You did that perfect. Boss'll be real impressed.* Sorry, Leachy, gotta go. Newbie here's just earned himself a celebratory steak. *Or, wait, you're vegan, right? I dunno then. We'll get you a baked potato or something.*"

He hangs up, and I throw the phone at the wall. Dante stares up at me with his leash in his mouth. His eyes communicate several Russian tomes of longing and despair.

"Yeah. Alright then."

⊖

After two more days of rest, I'm approaching a state of normalcy. The pain and dizziness have mostly subsided, but I'm still having visions of *heat light fire empyrean empires forming fractal planes,* but they're only fleeting, like a dream I'm starting to forget. Dante seems to like me for some reason, poor bastard. It's a cruel trick, taking a proud, powerful creature like a wolf and then gradually moulding it into a version of itself that will naively lavish love and affection on its own captor, so long as they're chucked a literal bone every now and then. No one on earth ever loved dogs as much as you do, and this guy would break your heart into a million shattered pieces. Or at least he would if I hadn't done that already. He stares at me with his big brown eyes, and for minutes at a time I feel peaceful. And then a wave of guilt crashes over me. I am not entitled to peace or happiness, not ever.

I take the milk from the fridge (very little room for anything else in there, on account of the blood and urine) and pour it over a bowl of cornflakes, eating as Dante watches me. It's quiet outside. Light drizzle gently taps on the windows. If it wasn't for the dead body in the bathroom, this would almost be a perfect evening. I've wrapped him in plastic and crop-dusted the bathroom with deodorisers, but I don't think anyone at Floral Scent Creations had 'masking the odour of a decomposing corpse' in mind when they wrote the product statement for Alpine Winter Ice Blast Sensation.

It's been three days since I showered. At least the toilet is in a separate room, have to be grateful for small mercies. I finish the cornflakes and dump the bowl in the sink, then open the drawer where I put your photo, glance at it, close it again. It's too big to think about, like trying to contemplate your own nonexistence, or what the world looks like through the eyes of an octopus. It simply shouldn't be here. Its very presence spits in the face of the rules of the universe I've constructed. I open the drawer. Close it. Stare at the handle. Will my hand not to move again.

Keys rattle in the front door. It shudders open, and two of the Demons stomp in, all but indistinguishable save for the difference in height. "Where's he at?"

"Good evening, I'm very well. Thank you for asking."

"It's not a social call, Leach."

"He's in the bathtub, through there. Can I get you anything while you're here, Jasmine tea? Scone?"

"You can fetch yourself a nice warm cup of shut-the-fuck-up, if it takes your fancy."

The banter is necessary. They know I'm not like them, but they don't respect anyone who doesn't take some kind of stand, even if it's just a little verbal sparring here and there. I look out through Archie Leach's eyes as he stares directly at them, shoulders straight, never breaking eye contact. He's always the last to look away; that was one of the first traits I built for him.

"Fuck. Why'd you have to wrap him in plastic?"

"Strange that I'd have to explain this to someone in your line of work, but corpses have a tendency to give off a rather pungent aroma."

"Yeah, well. Now we're gonna have to unwrap him before we feed him to the pigs. Can't have them getting all that plastic in their stomachs, they'd be sick for weeks."

"Sorry, I wasn't aware that murder pigs had such sensitive tummies. Just think of him as being 'packaged for transport.'"

The taller one grunts at me, and they move to pick up the body. Dante comes in to see what's going on and he pats him

with childlike enthusiasm, murmuring praise and commendation. It never ceases to puzzle me how people who treat human
beings like they're nothing but fleshy, bipedal knife-holders can
show so much affection toward animals. The shorter Demon
has his back to Dante and doesn't see him as he walks backwards
and steps on his tail. Dante howls and then clamps his mouth
around his leg. The Demon kicks him, hard. Dante lifts clean off
the floor and flies into the wall, then slides into a furry lump of
pitiful whimpering.

Before I've had a chance to form a conscious thought, my
hand grabs his wrist and snaps it back until it makes a hideous
crack that echoes across the tiles. The Demon's hand hangs
loose and limp, like it belongs to a dropped marionette. He
opens his mouth to scream, but the taller demon whips off his
bandanna, shoves it into his mouth, and says, "You had that
coming, dickhead!" He passes his partner a set of keys. "There's
some morphine in the glove box. But, between you and me? If
you ever hurt a dog like that again, I'll break plenty more than
just yer wrist."

The wounded Demon stumbles out of the room, his
eyes sending a Twitter troll's monthly quota of threats in a
single glance. The taller Demon turns to me and says, "You
shouldn't have done that. Boss'll be pissed. He tends to make
bad decisions when he's angry. Plus, I can't carry this fat
fuck on my own." He points at the body in the bathtub. "I'll
have to come back with one of the other boys tomorrow."
He takes out his phone, taps at the screen. My phone pings
with a message. "I just sent you the number for a guy we use
for the dogs. Off the books and that. He'll get your boy here
patched up."

"Thanks."

"It's not a favour to you, fuckwit. You just made my life a whole lot more complicated. I just don't want that gorgeous little guy to suffer any more than he has to. Go make the call now while I sort this mess out."

I dial the number and a reedy-voiced man asks me a few questions then gives me an address. I call a taxi and sit with Dante until it arrives. When I hear it pull into the driveway, I pick him up as gently as I can and walk outside. I hurry to the door and open it, ignoring whatever the driver is saying to me, then climb in and sit down. I'm so focused on placing Dante gently on my lap that it takes me a moment to realise that there's someone else on the seat next to me.

Nisha's face strobes back and forth between surprise and anger for a few seconds until she yells, "What the hell happened?"

"Nisha? Why are you in my taxi?"

"This is *my* taxi, I just came back from the airport. Why are you in it, and, more importantly, *what have you done to my dog?*"

Another taxi pulls up behind us, and I realise what's happened. Dante looks at Nisha with pained, pleading eyes. Sam Clemens does the same.

We stumbled back to your apartment, tripping over each other, laughing and howling at the moon. Making it up the stairs took a solid fifteen minutes. We opened a bottle of wine and toasted the full moon. It looked like someone had cut a perfect circle in the night sky, revealing some ethereal portal to unknown realms.

Outside there was the constant rollicking rhythm of beeping horns, drunken yelling, distant music. Havana's nightlife continuing its endless anarchic dance. You suggested we drink more, which I didn't think was a good idea, but you always had a knack for talking me into going against my better judgement. We sat on the balcony and toasted.

You said something in Spanish, too quick for me to follow, then made fun of my pathetic monolingualism. You stumbled off to the bathroom, knocking over a chair on the way.

Your phone buzzed, and I couldn't help but let my eyes be drawn to name on the screen: CARLOS. *I considered smashing the phone, throwing it into the street, but elected to simply hold it up to you as you came back. The smile on your face fell like a body from a balcony.*

7

"Nisha, sweetheart, you don't have to come with us. I can take care of this myself. You must be ex-*haus*-ted from the flight."

"You are taking my dog to what you claim is a vet *despite* the fact the sign outside very clearly states it is a twenty-four-hour laundromat and money change bureau. Sleep is not anywhere on my list of priorities right now. How did you even hear about this place?"

"A friend recommended it to me."

"A friend?"

"Yes. I know it seems strange, but at this hour the only places open will be way on the other side of the city and ludicrously expensive." I'm not sure if that's true, but she's new to town, so I'm hoping she doesn't know better. Nisha considers this, mutters something I assume is profanity in a language I assume is Hindi, and steps out of the cab, taking out her purse. "No, Nisha, let me pay."

She shrugs and moves to the trunk to take out her bags. I lift Dante out of the car, hand a fifty to the driver, and say, "Keep the change."

He grunts and replies "What change? You owe me $67.50." I take out a hundred instead and press it into his hand. He's delighted until he notices the flecks of blood in the upper corner. Bloodstained currency is one of many occupational hazards in my line of work.

"I had a nosebleed. Sorry." I tell him. He grimaces, holds the note gingerly between finger and thumb, and puts it away, then murmurs something vitriolic in what I guess to be Russian and drives off. It's quite the evening for linguistically diverse profanity. Nisha wheels her luggage behind her as we approach the alleged laundromat. I can feel the heat of her anger radiating out in waves.

"I'm really sorry." Sam Clemens's words limp out of my mouth.

"It's fine, Sam." She says "it's fine" in the exact same way you used to when you were on the edge of exploding, those two sharp syllables acting as the plume of smoke preceding a volcanic eruption. I think you'd like Nisha.

Inside the laundromat an elderly lady is reading a magazine next to her clothing tumbling in the machine next to her. I find this reassuring right up until the moment I realise that the magazine in question is hardcore porn. She murmurs libidinous approval as she drinks in the pages with her eyes.

"Sam!" hisses Nisha, distracting me from my study of the octogenarian porn enthusiast.

There's a tired middle-aged man sitting in a tiny change bureau booth in the corner. He calls out: "Change? Cambio?"

I walk over and say, "We need 3721 Peruvian Soles."

He perks up and replies, "No problem. Where in Peru will you be visiting?"

"Arequipa, then Lima, then Trujillo."

"Very good. Here is your currency. Enjoy your trip." He hands me an envelope and tilts his head towards the door behind him. I take the key card out of the envelope and swipe it against the lock. The door clicks open.

Nisha whispers, "This cloak-and-dagger shit is making me more and more concerned, just so you are aware."

"It'll be fine. Trust me."

"I have absolutely no reason to trust you."

I carry Dante through the door. We walk along a short corridor before entering what I can only assume is some sort of Narniaesque portal, because the room on the other side cannot possibly exist in the same reality as the one preceding it. The fixtures and operating area are a sea of steel and chrome, polished and resplendent. The floor is white marble, the lights the kind of high-end LED that have become popular amongst the environmentally conscientious and aesthetically pretentious (there's often overlap between the two). Several paintings hang around the room, awash with the kind of cold, abstract brushstrokes that suggest they've been painted by a rich kid who spent a summer in Morocco and went out of his way to get kidnapped just so he'd have some sort of inspirational well to draw from. The furniture in the corner clashes with gleeful incongruence; leather reclining chairs and a chaise longue backed by a well-stocked antique liquor cabinet. The air swells and swirls with soaring guitar chords colliding with glitching electronics pouring out of the six-point speaker system embedded in the ceiling.

All of this is strange, but it looks positively pedestrian compared to the gentleman who greets us. His bright blond hair is pulled back into a ludicrously tall quiff that sits above bright green eyes surrounded by ostentatious silver-framed glasses. He's wearing a lab coat accompanied with a fob watch and brilliant red cowboy boots. He looks like he's from the recent past and the distant future at the same time.

"Hel-lo! Go ahead and place this beautiful creature on the table there. Wow! What a shiny coat, just gorgeous! What's his name?"

"Dante," says Nisha.

The "vet" crouches down and looks Dante in the face. "I could get lost in those eyes!" He turns back to us. "I'm Cassius. You going on a trip?"

"What?" asks Nisha.

He points at her luggage.

"Oh, no. I've just returned from Jaipur. I was visiting my father."

Cassius replies quickly in a tongue I can't follow, and Nisha almost falls over with surprise.

"I have never met a single Australian who could speak Rajasthani!" She laughs and then replies in a similar series of sharply rising tones and phonemes. The effect is profound. She appears immediately relaxed and at ease, despite the strangeness of our surroundings. I make a mental note to acquire basic phrases in a greater catalogue of languages.

Cassius flips back to English and addresses us both. "I was just saying that Dante here is in very good hands. The best hands!" He holds them aloft for us to inspect. They are indeed very nice hands; moisturised and manicured. "We'll need around fifteen minutes together. Can I get you anything while you wait; cup of tea, mug of coffee, glass of wine, shot of tequila, eighth of weed? No extra charge!"

"I don't think—"

"Wine. Actually, whiskey," says Nisha. She clocks my expression and shrugs.

"Done and done. Help yourself, everything's in the cabinet there. I'm going to glove up and get started."

I follow Nisha to the liquor cabinet and whisper, "Are you sure you want to drink here?"

"Why? Is it not safe? Because you told me it was completely safe. You wouldn't lie to me, would you 'Sam'?"

I can't be sure, but it sounds like she's saying Sam's name with quotation marks around it. "No, honey, of *course* I wouldn't!" Sam splays our hand against our chest in an overly dramatic gesture of wounded sympathy.

"You folks wanna tell me what happened to this beautiful boy?" Cassius calls out from across the room.

Nisha shoots me an accusatory glare.

"I'm not going to call the cops, if that's what you're wondering. Secrecy is key to my operation. Although, I should mention that if you've hurt this precious creature on purpose, I'll peel your faces off with a scalpel and feed them to my own dogs." He flashes a congenial grin and stares at us—at me—with unblinking eyes.

"Someone kicked him into a wall."

"Was it one of S—"

"One of the crew that gave me your details, yes. And don't worry, they won't be going near him again."

Nisha glowers at me, but I avoid her gaze and pretend like I can't feel her eyes burning laser beams into my face.

"I see. Those guys send me a lot of patients, which is great. But on the other hand, those guys send me a lot of patients. You follow?" He strokes Dante's head and says, "His back leg is sprained, but I don't think he's broken anything. I'm going to prescribe a course of painkillers and plenty of rest. I'll also put the leg in a temporary splint. Might be overkill, but I prefer to err on the safe side. Go ahead and relax over there. I'll be done in two shakes of a basilisk's tail."

"Thank you, Cassius," says Nisha. She turns to me, and the anger on her face subsides for a moment. "Sure you won't have a drink with me?"

I flick my eyes over the liquor cabinet and make a quick assessment of her body language. "How could I possibly refuse the chance to drink at such a fine establishment? Take a seat; let me sort these out for us."

I turn my back to her as I pour myself tonic water and ice into a glass, garnish it with a slice of lemon. The question of why a twenty-four-hour illegal vet has such a well-stocked cabinet caroms around my skull, but I need to focus my mental energy on maintaining my facade. I pour her whiskey over ice and carry the drinks over. We clink glasses and sip. Look at the room. Each other. Our drinks.

"He's dead."

It takes me a minute to process what she's talking about. Given the cognitive load of switching personas and taking in the room and trying to read her gestures, there's not a lot of band-width left over. "Your father?"

She nods.

I take a risk and hold her hand in mine, look at her through the empathy-emanating portholes of Sam's eyes. "Nisha. I am so very, very sorry."

She nods again. "He died just a few hours after I arrived. My plane had been delayed an hour and a half. Any longer and I might not have been able to..." She drinks. "The funeral was the day before yesterday. I am devastated to no longer have him in this world. But I don't believe in death, not the same way most people do, especially here."

"You mean reincarnation?"

Her lips twitch into the preliminary sketch of a smile. "Something like that." Her tone tells me I'm way off the mark. I open my mouth to inquire further but she cuts me off asking "Have you ever been to an Indian funeral?"

I shake my head. I've never been to a funeral, period. One of the perks of cutting yourself off from anyone you might get close enough to care about, I guess.

"Every region is different, of course. In Rajasthan, we hire mourners. Professionals." She laughs at my reaction. "I know, it's strange. But perhaps no stranger than wanting your name on a building after death, or an elaborate mausoleum. Death makes fools of us all." She drinks again, the ice cubes rattling in the glass forming an odd accompaniment to Cassius's sterile electronica. "He lived a good long life; eighty-nine years old. He was riding in a tuk tuk. It's a kind of three-wheeled motorcycle t—"

"I'm familiar. I spent some time in Kolkata a few years back—"

She flashes her eyes at me, and I mentally chastise myself for interrupting. Sam Clemens never interrupts anyone, especially when they're emotionally venting. I run through a quick system check to make sure he's still in charge. Sam pulls Nisha into a hug for a few seconds. It's nice. I can't remember the last time I hugged someone.

"Thank you, Sam. You are the only friend I have here."

You poor bastard.

"What are you drinking?" she asks.

"Gin and tonic; it was my grandmother's favourite. She used to sit me on her knee and read me stories, interrupting herself mid-sentence to take a sip. We were very close; she was the first person I came out to. G & Ts always remind me of her."

"That's a nice way to remember her. Is it good gin?"

"I've had worse."

"May I?" she reaches out to take the glass, and I snatch it away from her.

Sam coughs, shifts in his seat. "My apologies, Nisha. I'm just getting over a cold, I'd hate to pass it on to you. Tell me more about your father. Or we can just talk about something else. Everyone grieves differently. I want to respect your process."

"You're very sweet."

That's true. Sam is very sweet. And kind. And thoughtful. That's probably why he's become my least favourite persona. I hate being reminded of what it's like to care about people. Then again, you would *hate* Sam. You always found anyone who was too emotionally candid to be exhausting. Your emotions were always enough to fill a room, a house, a city. Anyone else doing the same would just get in the way.

"You are also full of shit," Nisha adds.

My glass freezes halfway to my lips. "I saw the way you exchanged code phrases with the man in the change bureau. You were relaxed, calm, professional. Then the second you were done with him you slipped back into...this." She flicks a disdainful hand at us. "You keep company with violent criminals who harm dogs. You're a fucking liar, Sam. And do you know what is worse? You are *good* at it. You've had practise."

Fuck. I start running my heuristics, visualising a decision tree in my mind's eye, branches splitting and growing across diverging pathways.

"So which is the real you; the friendly, caring neighbour or the hardened criminal?"

Both.

Neither.

I flip through personas in my mind, mentally discarding them in rapid succession. Leach wouldn't be much help. Declan's a possibility, or Eric. Maybe even Maurice? Or, I could go for the nuclear option; tell her my real name. Just the thought of doing this sends waves of panic shuddering through my system. I don't know Nisha well enough yet to choose an optimal persona for her. Death has rattled my operating system. A month ago I could have done this in a heartbeat, switched personas faster than changing a pair of shoes.

Nisha stands up to leave and seethes, "Unfucking believable!"

I grab her hand. "Wait!" Sam's voice escapes my lips. Okay then, let's see if he can salvage this. He lets go of her hand. "Would you give me a chance to explain, please?"

She narrows her eyes at me.

"We have to wait for Dante anyway, right?"

She sighs and returns to her seat.

"Thank you." I take a beat, shuffle in my chair, make sure Sam is firmly back behind the wheel. "A few years ago, I was in Cuba…" I pause, emphasising the emotional weight of the story I'm about to tell.

Nisha leans closer.

"I was lost at the time, trying to 'find myself' in an exotic place that just happened to have a lot of great cheap rum. I know, I know *suuuuuch* a cliché! In any case, I went to a thousand bars, obviously, but one night I went to some tiny little hole-in-the-wall place and there was this jazz band playing. The singer had a voice that could've melted the heart of a serial killer. The way he moved was magnetic. He was beautiful; inconceivably, unbelievably beautiful. The moment he stepped onstage, my eyes locked onto him, and I couldn't look away."

I know, I know. Partially gender flipping our story and using it as the foundation for an elaborate deception isn't exactly the best way to honour you. I'm sorry. But in my defence, it is a beautiful story and it deserves to be told, even if I play a little fast and loose with the details. "He had these eyes that—"

"Okay. I get it. He was beautiful. Please explain how this caused you to become a two-faced liar."

"I talked to him after the show, which was unusual for me back then. I was a very shy soul. But he made all the first moves. We were back at his place an hour later. And he…moved in. A week after that."

Nisha raises a perfectly plucked eyebrow.

"I know, it was fast. Lightning fast. But it just seemed to make sense. At first, everything was great. He was sweet, generous, kind. He'd surprise me at work; he was an amazing cook. Our schedules were all over the place, I was working at a hotel, and he was either working at bars pouring drinks or performing onstage. For a while, everything was perfect." I pause and study Nisha's expression. I haven't quite won her over yet, but I can see she's at least hungry to hear the end of the story. "I saw a few shimmers of his true self early on, but it wasn't until about a month in that I realised that he'd been working very hard to keep himself hidden from me during our honeymoon period. One night, we had a bottle of wine. Each. I saw this change come over him, the way he moved, spoke, even his eyes seemed to be darker. He smashed a glass for no reason, then screamed at me to clean it up."

Remember that? Not your finest moment. Not that I have any right to be throwing stones, of course. I let the invented portion of the story take on a life of its own; much like an apple tree branch grafted to an oak, it is introduced and unnatural but nevertheless growing, bonding, bearing fruit. "Soon after that, he started hitting me, throwing things. Finally, I gathered the strength to break it off, move out. I left Cuba, went back to London. I thought I could just go back to my old life, that all it would take would be a plane ticket and a change of address."

I take a moment to assess how Sam is doing. Nisha's eyes are cast down, her breathing has slowed, she's chewing her bottom lip. We might just make it out of this intact after all. "But he found me. I came home to find my apartment trashed. He was sitting in an armchair, relaxed amongst the ruin with a glass of wine and a cigarette. He dropped them both to the floor when he saw me come in. He grabbed me and beat me half to death. I convinced him to let me take an ambulance to the hospital. I promised I'd tell them it was a random mugging, that I'd come home and we'd be together. He came with me in the ambulance, putting on a Daniel Day-Lewis–level show of caring and crying and pleading with the heavens.

"I spit up blood for days. He stayed with me at the hospital, talked to doctors and nurses, brought me coffee and flowers and chocolates. Eventually, he went back to 'our' place to sleep. I got up, walked out, and went straight to a friend's place. She worked in a club that was run by some people with a bunch of underworld connections. She organised for these guys to get me a fake ID, new passport, sort out a plane to Sydney. I gave them everything I had, but I was still short. They said that was fine, I could pay the rest in instalments. I'm not sure if you're aware of this, but gangsters who provide loan services tend to emphasise the 'pounding' in compounding interest. I'm still chipping away at it, but it just seems to keep growing. Earlier today, they sent a couple of guys to collect. I was short. Again. Thus, here we are."

"So your name isn't really Sam?"

"It is now."

"And this is why you're used to dealing with criminal types."

"Years of unwanted experience, yes. I'm just sorry you and Dante got caught up in it."

She finishes her drink. Says nothing for a moment. Takes my hand. "I have had plenty of experience being hurt by people who claimed to love me. It is always the ones closest to you who bury the knife the deepest, isn't it?"

Yes. It is. "Can you ever forgive me, Nisha?"

She considers this, then shakes her head. "Nothing to forgive. Fate, and love, dealt you a shitty hand. Those are forces too strong for mortals such as us to deny. That said, if you ever let anything happen to my dog again? I will rain hellfire on you."

"Thank you; that means a lot."

Cassius looks up from his work and calls out, "You two are looking very serious over there. Not to worry, almost done. We're looking good!"

Nisha's pupils pull to the left of her eyes. "How much do you owe?"

"A lot."

"Give me a ballpark. Four figures? Five?"

"Five." This week, anyway.

She nods, and I can almost hear the wheels whirring in her head. I would pay folding money to find out what's going on in her mind right now, but I feel like prying at this stage is only going to get me into trouble. Sam has only just earned her trust back, I need to quit while I'm ahead.

"Hooo-kay! We're all doneskies!" Cassius calls us over. Dante is passed out on the table, tongue lolling out the side of his mouth. "He is going to be just fine, but he'll need to take it easy for a while and have one of these per day, with food." He passes Nisha an unlabelled bottle of pills. "Also, he's not allowed to operate any aircraft or heavy machinery." He throws his head back in an enthusiastic laugh. "And here's what I require for payment." He hands me a folded piece of paper with a short list written in elegant, looping cursive:

Four litres of blood (human, type O)

Three litres of urine (clean, human)

Two thumbs (human, both from the same individual if possible)

Limited edition 2019 Detective Pikachu card

"I'll need everything there in the next seventy-two hours."

I scan his face to see if he's joking. He isn't.

"Just some supplies for some research I'm doing." Suddenly it's clear why he runs an operation like this. Someone with these particular "research" proclivities doesn't tend to thrive in a university environment. Luckily, Nisha is too preoccupied hugging Dante and collecting her luggage to have paid attention to the transaction. Cassius shakes my hand and bids us farewell. I try and not think about where that hand has been recently. I pick up Dante, and we exit out into the laundromat and then the parking lot.

Nisha orders a ride share, and we stand and wait. It's quiet save for the muted sound of washing machines thrumming inside. Dawn isn't far away.

"God, I am exhausted. I can never sleep on planes. I've been awake for almost forty hours now." A car pulls up in front of us.

"Let me get your luggage in the trunk for you. Go ahead and get some rest. I'll wake you up when we get there."

She closes the trunk and says, "Thank you, Sam. You are a good man. Except for the part of you that is a complete arsehole."

"Thanks."

We climb into the car, and she's asleep within minutes. The driver is silent; the only sound is the talkback radio host inviting callers to ring in and share their paranormal experiences. One lady calls up and tells a protracted story about her intense sexual encounter with the ghost of River Phoenix. The host neglects to ask her why a gorgeous young Hollywood actor would be spending his afterlife pleasuring middle-aged women in the Northern Beaches. When we arrive home, I try to wake Nisha, but she is completely comatose. The driver grunts with amusement and says, "My daughter's the same way, mate. Couldn't wake her with anything shy of a nuclear explosion."

I look in her handbag for her keys but can't find them. I ask the driver to wait while I step out and search under her welcome mat, in her potted plant, and above the doorframe for a spare key but come up empty. You would be laughing your ass off right now. You always found crisis hilariously entertaining.

I'm so tired I feel drunk. The tiredness seeps into my bones, my cells, my blood. I walk back to the car and apologise to the driver, then ferry first Dante, then Nisha, then her luggage inside my apartment. I put Nisha in my bed and Dante on the floor next to her. She looks so peaceful, calm. I can't remember the last time I saw someone sleep. It must have been you, I guess. You were the last person I saw do a lot of things. We're all so vulnerable in that state. Presidents, royalty, nurses, soldiers, judges. We all sleep, eventually; peaceful, still. Helpless.

I stumble out to the couch and stare at the pink-grey sky, minutes away from sunrise. I close my eyes and fall asleep to the sound of kookaburras cackling at the breaking dawn.

8

It's not until I hear the toilet flush that I remember Nisha spent the night in my apartment. My head is still a Lovecraftian fog of confusion. She greets me with a yawn and a wave as she points to the bathroom door and asks,

"This the bathroom?"

I rush to block her path. "Yes. But you can't go in there." My accent wavers a little but she appears to be still too half-awake to notice.

"I need to wash my hands."

Sam reassumes control of my consciousness and says; "Renovations. There's asbestos in there." Also a dead body. "You can wash your hands in the kitchen."

She yawns, stumbles into the kitchen. "Where have you been showering?"

"At the gym."

"Thanks for letting me stay. I feel like a human being again.

Or at least, some sort of human/vampire hybrid. You're clearly a night owl, like me. Ugh. I can't function until I've had a cup of coffee. Want one?"

"Yes. Thank you." Also if you could leave my apartment immediately, that would be fabulous. "But after a quick cup of caffeinated life juice, I'll have to get to work. Is that okay, sweetie?"

She glances at the clock and says, "At eight p.m.? What line of work did you say you were in?"

I hand Nisha the bag of coffee and a couple of mugs then turn on the stove as I reply, "PR." The perfect cover job, because no one really understands what it is. Especially people in PR.

Skepticism expels the last vestiges of tiredness from her expression. "You have to work. In PR. At eight p.m.?"

"Yes. I work as the Australian representative of a firm based in LA, so I often have to keep to their schedule. I prefer to be nocturnal in any case."

Dante wakes up and pads into the room, nuzzling Nisha. She cradles his face in her hands and murmurs a greeting, then places the coffee on to boil. Something about that sound induces panic. I've forgotten something important. "You take milk?" she asks, pulling the fridge door open. A mental image of its contents careens into my brain, and I kick the door closed. Nisha snaps around to look at me. We both stand frozen.

"I guess that's a 'no' to the milk then? Do you usually take it with blood, urine, or both?"

Fuck. "I can explain."

"I am beginning to realise that this is a signature phrase for you." She takes the coffee off the stove and pours it into the two mugs on the counter. "We'll just have it black." She carries them over to the table, sits. Sips. Dante takes his place at her feet. "Well? Are you going to join me?"

I sit down. Sip. Place the cup back on the table. Study her face.

She waves at the fridge. "Not exactly what I expected, granted. But I understand. You are obviously in the sub-legal arts. Your history with criminals? Forged identity? PR is a terrible choice for a cover story. You might as well have said you were an astronaut. Don't worry, I'm in the same boat. I work in 'specialised IT.'"

"Specialised, as in…?"

"As in the kind of IT the media typically presents as being performed by young men in hoodies working out of graffiti-adorned warehouses."

"You're a hacker?"

"Occasionally. Mostly I deal with generating online avatars. A sort of digital rent-a-crowd."

"Sounds interesting," I laugh and sip my coffee.

"Has anyone ever told you that you have a lovely smile?" she asks.

"Nooooo!" Sam replies, his voice lashed with false modesty.

"Good. Because they would be lying. That is a very goofy grin you have. What do you actually do then?"

Logistics collection security communications in-house medic accounts distribution… No. I think, for once, the truth might be the best option. "Delivery. I work as a specialty courier."

"Special, as in…?"

"Boxes are all sealed and anonymous. Contents unknown, designated for rapid delivery. No records."

"So, drugs and weapons then?"

"Like I said; contents unknown."

She snorts derisively.

"So. Yes. Mostly drugs and weapons." And occasionally eyeballs.

She drains the last of her coffee, bangs it on the table like a gavel. "This has been most illuminating, 'Sam Clemens.'" She accompanies my name with air quotes. "However, I should go. There's an election in Guatemala I'm working on. Polls close in a day or so."

"What do you mean 'working on'?"

"That's a long conversation we should have when we have both rested. Here, I got you something to say thank you for looking after Dante. I should probably keep it, given how that turned out. But I think you are deserving of a second chance." She unzips the top pocket on her luggage, tosses me a small brown bag. Then she unzips a slender pocket on the side and takes out her keys. "Guess I hid these a little too well. Thanks for letting me stay here."

I unwrap the bag. "Tea? Thank you, Nisha."

She waggles a finger as she slings on her handbag and then pulls up the telescoping handle of her luggage. "Not just tea. *Darjeeling* tea. As in tea that is actually from the Darjeeling region. Same as there is a difference between 'Champagne' from Champagne in France and everything else is just sparkling wine. It is magnificent."

"Thank you. You shouldn't have."

She shrugs. "I often do things that I should not. Like trust people." She stares at me, looking for a response. Sam stares back at her. My heart thrums like a hummingbird. "Can I take you somewhere tonight, Sam?"

"...where?"

"It will be a surprise. Do you like surprises?"

Not even a little bit. I would prefer to know that I am going to be stabbed at a specific time and place than be faced with an unspecified event at an unknown date and location. Sam, on the other hand... "I *live* for surprises!"

"Great! You're going to like this place. It's very, ah..." She mutters something in Hindi. "I can't find the English word for it. Have you ever taken mescaline?"

"No?"

"Ah. Well. I think it will be similar to that. Only more...layered. You will love it. Trust me."

I don't trust anyone, and I hate most places that aren't my apartment so I'd say that's unlikely.

She says goodbye and wheels her luggage out, Dante limping behind her. I close the door and revel in the silence and stillness for a few precious moments. Then I rummage around in the kitchen drawer, take out a meat cleaver, and head into the bathroom.

9

I'm in the process of loading up my bike with the various items Cassius requires for payment when Goldie shows up with a couple of Demons. I open the garage and they drive the van in. Goldie steps out onto the driveway and lights a cigarette while the other Demons enter the apartment via the garage side door.

"I told you I don't want you around here anymore."

He laughs and says, "You said you didn't want me inside yer front door. Garage don't count."

"A dog abuser and a pedant. Your mother must be so proud."

"My mother's six feet under, and the world's a much better place for it." He nods at the bike. "You headed out on a run?"

"Yes."

"Righto. Just make sure you don't lose the package this time, eh? First payment's due day after tomorrow."

"I'm aware." Between the rainy-day cash reserves I have hidden in the apartment and the jobs I have scheduled over the next day and a half, I'm still going to be a few thousand shy of what I owe. I'm going to need a Hail Mary, or else I'll have to expand my criminal repertoire with some burglary or a few muggings if I want to stay alive.

The Demons return with the plastic-wrapped body, and I close the garage door behind us just in case any insomniac neighbours catch a glimpse. They put the body in the van, and Goldie slams the doors shut but then pauses, narrows his eyes at me, and opens the doors again. He climbs into the back, turns the body over and takes a knife from his belt. He cuts the plastic as the other Demons stand either side of the van, arms crossed beneath their massive beards. They look like hipster gargoyles. Goldie slices the plastic apart and raises one of the bloody hands into the air. He regards me with a rancorous glare.

"Problem?" I ask.

"There is, yeah. But I just can't quite put my finger on it. Or thumb, as the case may be." He flaps the thumbless hand around to illustrate his point.

"He's dead anyway. You have to get rid of the body, I've just saved you a few grams of trouble. You should be thanking me if anything."

"You messed with our property."

"Your *rubbish*. That you want disposed."

"Not the point." He lets the arm flop back to the floor of the van with a sick, wet thud.

"Isn't it?"

"What'd you need a pair of bloody thumbs for anyway?"

"Art project."

He aims the knife at me. "Quit fucken' around!"

"It's payment for Cassius. I had to take the dog to him because one of yours attacked him. I can pass the bill straight on to you, if you prefer."

Goldie chews his lip, murmuring. "Fucken' Cass. What a bloody creep." Coming from Goldie—a man who is rumoured to harbor a predilection for dinosaur erotica—that is certainly saying something. "Boss isn't going to like this."

"He's not going to care. He's a rational businessman. Usually."

"Fine. Then *I* don't like it."

"You can not like it all you want, Goldie."

"First eyes, now thumbs. You're one sick puppy, Leach."

"That's what it says on my LinkedIn profile. You boys have yourself a pleasant evening now."

Goldie grunts his disapproval, then closes the doors and yells at the driver to start the car.

Cassius greets me with an undertaker's grin and checks off the contents of the box against his list. "Hoo-kay, let's see what goodies you've brought me. Two human thumbs, four litres of type O blood, the limited-edition Pikachu detective card, aaaaaand three litres of clean urine! That's for my son." He winks at me. "The Pokémon card, not the urine."

"I figured." I'm not sure what's worse; the fact that he had to clarify or the fact he has a son.

"I am veeeery impressed you managed to put this all together so quickly!"

"It was mostly just stuff I had lying around the house."

He throws his head back with laughter and attempts to punch me in the arm in a display of bonhomie, but I grab his fist and apply just enough pressure to let him know he'll regret ever trying it again. He pulls his hand away and says, "Gosh. You're a lot grumpier than you were when you visited with your wonderful dog! Right-o then. Fuck off into the sunset." He carries the box over to a fridge in the corner and starts unloading.

I turn on my heel and reach for the door handle then pause and turn back. "Cass?"

His head pops back out from behind the fridge door. "Yes?"

I draw myself up to my full height, step close enough that our noses are almost touching.

"Oh, dear. I do hope you're not trying to intimidate me. I don't respond well to threats. Also…" Cassius glances down at my waist. I follow his eyes and see that he's unclipped the knife from my belt and has it a hair's breadth from my crotch. He leers at me, flips the knife into the air, catches it with alarming adroitness and bops me on the nose with the handle. He presses it into my chest. "Nice blade. I like a leather-bound handle myself, but each to their own. As for your question? Yes. A little birdie did pop around here with a photo of a fellow who looks just like you."

I take the knife back and return it to its holster. "What did this 'little birdie' look like?"

"Ohhhh, come now. Confidentiality is the cornerstone of my business! That said, you're a former customer, and the little birdie wasn't. Soooo maybe if you ask nicely?" He treats me to another gleaming grin, and I resist the temptation to grab the pliers from his operating table and yank out his teeth.

"Cassius, could you please describe the person who was asking about me?"

He almost shudders with pleasure. "Tall, athletic, big

brown eyes, quite pretty, if you're into that. She was Latina, or are you supposed to say 'Latinx' these days? I swear I just can't keep track anymore! Her accent was Guatemalan, I think. Or maybe Cuban?"

He keeps talking, but his words become distorted like they're playing off a warped record. I grab the side of the door to steady myself and heave great gulps of air. It can't be you. It's not possible. You can't be here. You can't be *anywhere*. Not anymore.

"You alright there? Want a little something to settle you down? I've got valium, Xanax, ketamine, Mary Jane?"

"What did you tell her?"

"Nothing! Like I said, client confidentiality. Plus she was looking for some guy from Chicago, and you're English, right?"

"..."

"Well, there you go then! Nothing to worry about. Cheerio!" He pushes me out the door and slams it behind me.

I walk outside in a daze. The moon is bright and full. You always loved a full moon. You loved a lot of things. You loved with a fire and intensity I'd never seen in any living soul.

And you hated the same way.

Your phone buzzed, and I couldn't help but let my eyes be drawn to the name on the screen: CARLOS. *I considered smashing the phone, throwing it over the balcony, but elected to simply hold it up to you as you came back. The smile on your face fell like a body from a bridge.*

You snatched it from my hand and hurled a rapid-fire barrage of verbal artillery, words as bullets from a Gatling gun, ricocheting off the walls.

You drew your hand back and slapped me. You careened from

accusations about invasions of privacy to lengthy tangents about my multitudinous shortcomings to the faintest shimmering outline of an apology. You slumped against the wall, head hung low, and dropped the phone to the ground. The screen cracked and splintered, dividing the words on the screen into a fragmented array of indecipherable glyphs; destruction as encryption.

I waited until I was sure you were done, then said: "You told me you were finished."

You looked up at me, eyes filled with tears, regret, anger, confusion, contempt. "Yes. I did." You swept hair back from your eyes, reached your hand out to my cheek. "But we both knew I was lying."

10

I knock on Nisha's door a little after midnight and wait for her to answer. Dante pants and shuffles around on the other side of the door, but there's no sign of Nisha. Edvard Munch descends behind me, announcing his approach with a series of syncopated grunts. He has a nicotine-yellow beard, eyes like two dead black beetles, and he's wearing far too many layers of ragged brown and grey clothing for the warm spring weather. He looks like Santa Claus after three divorces, a meth binge, and a kidney failure. Edvard turns the corner in the stairwell and freezes when he sees me. In all the years I've been here, we've never encountered each other in the flesh like this, just listened to the sound of each other shuffling and scraping and screaming in our respective cocoons.

He locks eyes with me and takes a series of deep asthmatic breaths that make his beard rise and fall like waves of yellow follicular froth. He raises a gnarled, accusatory finger in my direction.

"Are you alri—"

He screams, the sound piercing the night like a scythe executing the silence. It is wild, pure, stentorian. Seconds pass, and all I can focus on is the furious trembling of his all-too-visible tonsils and the unbridled force issuing out from between his teeth. I want to speak, run, escape, but I am frozen as though his scream is some infernal inversion of the siren's song, rooting me to the ground.

A young man dressed in khakis and a polo shirt dashes out onto the stairs. He shoots me an apologetic glance as he finishes fastening his belt and yells, "Sorry! He got out while I was in the bathroom." He places his (presumably as yet unwashed) hand on Edvard's shoulder and whispers, "Mason? Mason? It's okay. Count back with me, like we've been practising. Ten. Nine. Eight..."

The scream continues unabated, now approaching operatic length. How has he gone this long without taking a breath? The heat and force of the scream wash over me, my heart thrumming at amphetaminesque speeds. Nisha opens the door, and I feel her eyes on me, but I'm completely immobilised. The carer's quiet pleas appear to be completely ineffective at first, but when he reaches three Edvard—Mason—closes his mouth and grunts in time with the countdown.

"Three..."

Grunt.

"Two..."

Grunt.

"One!"

Grunt.

The carer guides Mason back inside, turns back to me when he reaches the door. "Thank you for looking after him. I know it can't be easy being his neighbour, but he doesn't have any family left. He can only afford this place, and care, because his brother left him a bunch of money when he passed away a few years back. But that'll run out soon enough."

"What happens then?"

He frowns, lowers his voice. "Nothing good. Certainly won't be able to afford to live on his own. Sorry again for the disturbance. Have a good evening."

A door opens behind me. Nisha peers out, her face painted with confusion.

"I was, ah, he just…you know what? I am just com-*plete*-ly spun out! Could I trouble you for a cup of tea before we head off, sweetheart?"

"Sorry! I'd love to, but my place is a bit of a mess, I'm afraid…" Through the narrow opening I can just barely catch a glimpse of the interior; a cavalcade of screens, wires, and blinking lights. It looks like she's running the Matrix from her lounge room. "I am actually remodelling my bathroom as well." I try to parse this; wondering if she's seeking confirmation that we're acknowledging each other's' falsehoods or simply hoping I'll believe hers. "Let's head straight out to the place I mentioned."

"Okay. Sounds terrific!" Terrifically awful, that is. Why did I let Sam get us into this? I have less than twenty-four hours to meet my deadline. Maybe I can swipe a few wallets at whatever bar we're going to; drunk rich folks tend to be easy prey. "What's this place called?"

"The Orrery. I will just need a minute to get ready. I'll knock on your door shortly." She closes the door. Opens it again. "Oh! I almost forgot. You don't have epilepsy or any kind of heart condition, do you?"

"…no? Why would—"

"Perfect! See you in a minute." She slams the door closed.

Upstairs, Mason resumes screaming.

◉

Nisha grips my waist and yells into my ear, "I haven't ridden a motorcycle in years!"

"Why not?" I yell back. Motorcycles are not conducive to polite conversation.

"My cousin was in a serious crash when I was in high school, and my dad made me promise that so long as he drew breath, I would never be within spitting distance of one of these 'death machines.' I kept my promise, technically speaking."

I say nothing. It's difficult to figure out what Sam should say when he can't read her facial cues. We swim through a neon sea of billboards and bright lights, until at last Nisha taps me on the shoulder and says, "Here! Pull in here!"

She points to a narrow opening in a circular brick fence so long that I can't see the end of it in either direction. It looks like the outskirts of a prison, or a gated community gone to hell. I suppose there's some parallels between the two. For a moment I'm sure she must be mistaken. The gate has broken off its hinges, and metal scraps and debris litter the ground on either side of the overgrown trail we ride down. But once we pass the first derelict building in the complex, I gain a view of an abandoned basketball court that appears to have been transformed into an impromptu parking lot. I scan the odd array of vehicles; limousines and Lamborghinis parked alongside ancient Corollas and rust-encrusted Barinas. We park and take in our surroundings.

There's nine buildings in all, eight smaller ones orbiting a nine-storey tower in the center. All of them are covered in complex, interweaving tattoos of vines and graffiti.

Nisha takes off her helmet and takes long, eager strides towards the central building.

I quicken my pace to catch up to her. "Have you been here before?"

"No."

"How did you hear about it?"

"I moderate a forum for people who are interested in topics related to altered states of consciousness, whole-brain emulation, simulation theory, and artificial intelligence."

"Soooooo, like, weird brain stuff?"

She snorts. "Sure. If you wish to be reductive. One of the subgroups documents establishments frequented by individuals who exert an atypically pronounced level of cultural and societal influence, whether it be via ideology, methodology—"

"Nisha, sweetheart, could you perhaps dumb this down for me? The last time I was in a freshmen sociology class was never."

She increases the pace of both her step and her speech. "You know how *Time* magazine makes a list of the most influential people? They make a show of choosing people with 'revolutionary thinking,' but their metric mostly analyses the amount of media influence a person exerts, not whether they have anything useful or transformative to say. It's more about retweets than revolution, hence why a lot of vapid actors and models make the list."

"And mentally unstable world leaders."

"Also those. Our metric focuses on people who produce ideas that contribute to the disruption and dismantling of oppressive hierarchies. So, Jeff Bezos appears on all sorts of *Forbes* and *Time* lists, but he would not be a blip on our radar. 'Capitalism, but bigger and faster!' isn't the kind of thinking we are interested in." We reach the entrance of the building, a rusted-out revolving door. The glass is dirty and opaque. Amorphous silhouettes float in front of hazy ethereal lights inside. Nisha stops to face me. "We track people who create, synthesise, or articulate potentially revolutionary ideas. We want to find people who are developing tool kits that can be used to dismantle and disrupt the status quo. Think of it like an underground antiestablishment who's who. Part of our work is to search for places where they congregate."

"...why?"

"Think about Montmartre, in Paris, in the 1920s. At the time, no one would ever have guessed that the collection of broke, drunk, chain-smoking comrades who loitered around in bars and cafes knocking back coffee then whiskey then coffee again would ever be of any importance. But Gertrude Stein, Hemingway, and the Fitzgeralds all shared that space and time. Breathed the same air, walked the same streets. Imagine discovering that in real time, while it is happening!"

"Okay. Consider my interest level a few notches above zero. What brought this place onto your radar?"

A group of women walk up to the entrance ahead of us. They stand at the doors, take a deep breath, reassure each other, and then push the door in unison. It moves slowly, metal scraping against metal in a demonic yowl as it turns. "The founders of three of the top ten most popular cryptocurrencies, the author of a world-shattering post-post-capitalist manifesto, a scientist who is currently conducting human trials on a psychedelic compound that allows users to dissolve trauma in a single use, a musician who has composed a seventy-nine-hour symphony rumoured to lift IQ by several points with each listen, a choreographer who has created a performance that explains the nature of dark matter *and* a linguist who has developed a language that allows the user to articulate the emotional intensity of one's entire childhood in just a few short phonemes. All of them have spent time here," she gestures grandly to the building in front of us. "In the Orrery."

"Isn't an orrery one of those little clockwork models of the solar system?"

"Exactly! This, the central building, the only one currently in use, is nine storeys; the sun. The centre. Each of the others orbits around it; the first building has one storey, the second has two, and so forth."

I study each of the buildings she points to, wondering how I missed this odd detail when we arrived.

"It was originally envisaged as an exclusive gated community; a luxury complex that would house the ultra-wealthy. Apartments, shops, cafes, gyms, etc. But a few weeks before construction was complete, one of the contractors fell from the sixth building over there, and there was a lot of bad press. At first they tried to keep going; accidents happen, after all. Then they found out that the developer's daughter had been using his keys to sneak in at night. Apparently, she and her friends were lighting candles, trying to summon spirits, that sort of thing. It'd been going on for months without anyone knowing, but a week before the site opened, they were messing around with vodka and candles, and there was some sort of accident and the developer's daughter caught on fire right outside the seventh building. She had third-degree burns all over her arms."

"Jesus. The poor girl."

"I know. It must have been horrible. The developer's wife blamed him, moved out, took the daughter with her to England. A day before they were set to open up and start moving people in, he climbed to the top of the eighth building, right near the wall over there, and jumped. After he died they discovered he'd been failing to pay contractors, embezzling money, partnering with organised crime. The company was dissolved, and this whole area was tied up in never-ending lawsuits and insurance claims.

"Eventually someone—no one knows who—decided to just break down the front gate and take up residence in this central building here. Over time it became a meeting point, then a kind of psychedelic-favouring speakeasy. Now? It's nine storeys, each independently owned and operated and with a unique...focus. There's some sort of overarching esoteric philosophy that I am not quite clear on. I've heard that they sweep you for devices at the door, and there's a signal jammer inside so there's no photos online, just sketches, and even those seem to disappear very quickly."

"Nisha, honey, we aren't walking into some kind of *Eyes Wide Shut* scenario, are we?"

"I hope not. I really do not feel like participating in an orgy again any time soon." She pushes her shoulder against the revolving door, struggling to force the scraping metal to budge enough for her to enter. Not the warmest of welcomes.

"Did you say 'again'?" I ask, pushing it wide enough for us to squeeze through.

She ignores my question and steps through into the lobby.

11

The interior is a lavish cavalcade of chandeliers, chesterfield couches, and art deco ceilings. It's all very luxurious, but with a faint hint of the surreal and subversive; upon closer inspection the art deco designs reveal a twisted array of mythic figures fighting and fornicating. The carpet is executed in a classic Persian style, but there's a modern fractal pattern woven into it. The oneiric interior is so at odds with the outside of the building that I have to reassess the angles of the walls to check if I haven't entered a new dimension rather than the lobby.

A burly security guard in a three-piece suit clears his throat and interrupts my awed study of the room. "Welcome to the Orrery. Is this your first time?"

We both nod.

He intones what is clearly an oft-recited spiel in a bored monotone, "Welcome to Level 1: Veneer. On this floor you are invited to remove the masks you wear in the outside world and expose your true self, free from the fear of records and recrimination. What goes on behind these doors stays here. Everything is permitted, save recording and documentation. If you are found to be making or subsequently distributing recordings, there will be dire consequences which may include termination." I get the distinct feeling that the *termination* he's referring to doesn't pertain to any kind of membership card. Strange to hear a mortal threat recited in the same tone as a corporate health and safety briefing. "Arms up."

"Ah, I should mention that I have—"

He ignores my protest, lifts my arms and proceeds to search me. He removes my phone, knuckle dusters from my pants pockets, the dagger from my belt sheath, the polycarbonate pen-shaped tactical blade from my jacket pocket, the pepper spray from my key chain, and the fiberglass push blade from the lining in my jacket. Impressive. I've made it through airport security more than a few times without them finding the last one. He examines them carefully and then hands everything back except my phone, which he places neatly on a wooden bookshelf behind him. "You're good to go."

"You don't want to hold on to them for me while we're inside?"

He shakes his head. "It's only recording devices that are forbidden. Weapons are permitted." He leans in and whispers, "And if you make it up to Level 7, they're recommended."

He moves on to Nisha as I put my gear back where it belongs. He takes her phone, places it next to all the others and says, "You're good."

She scratches her neck and asks, "Do we get…a receipt or something for those?"

"No. I'll give them back to you when you're ready to leave."

"How will you know which ones belong to us?"

"I'll remember."

"Are you sure?" There's a distinct tremor in her usually confident voice. Interesting.

"I'm sure you should stop asking me." The security guard sweeps his arm across the room and pronounces, "Welcome to the Orrery! As above, so below. As within, so without. As the universe, so the soul."

Nisha turns to me and says, "I need to go to the bathroom." Her voice is terse and strained. I take a seat at the bar and study the crowd. My usual process of threat analysis and identification of exit and entry points somewhat complicated by the heinously heterogenous nature of the clientele. There are people reclining in gimp suits, guffawing in dog costumes, pontificating in ball gowns, popping and locking in burqas, and snorting powder in police uniforms. It's like if a sex club, a cosplay group, a religious conference, and an anarcho-capitalist think tank had quadruple-booked the same venue.

I turn my attention away from the punters for a moment and flip open the leather-bound menu in front of me. It's roughly the size of a small-town phone directory. The bartender, an androgynous-looking woman with a shaved head showcasing a tattoo of vines spilling over her skull, approaches and says, "You're new."

"You remember all your clients?"

She taps her skull. "Nootropic memory enhancers. I never forget a face."

"Isn't the science on those things pretty murky?"

She shrugs. "You here to discuss peer review efficacy or order a drink?"

"I can't do both?"

"Sure, but you gotta figure out what to order first. Let me walk you through the selection. Our menu is organised according to potency. You'll find sodas, mocktails, and milkshakes at the start; then beer, wine, whiskey, vodka, etcetera aaaaaall the way to the end where you'll find Viagra-laced tequila—a disturbingly popular item—and black-market absinthe that will make you see through space and time. If you're chasing some really transcendent stuff, head on up to Voyage, that's Level 6. They've got gear up there that'll help you lick the face of God."

I close the menu. "This is all a little bewildering. Could you be a star and grab me a tonic water with lime and a whiskey over ice? Glenfiddich, if you have it."

"You got it." She reaches for a couple of bottles and begins flipping and pouring with the easy, fluid grace of a rhythmic gymnast.

"This seat taken?"

"All yours," I reply, gesturing towards it. As I turn I catch the speaker in my peripheral vision. I'm more than a little thrown by the fact that such a feminine voice belongs to a gigantic, hirsute man in a black suit and sunglasses.

"My eyes are down here!" The voice says, which is strange, given that the man's lips are completely still. It takes me a second to register the fact that his leather-gloved hands are holding a tablet displaying an image of a striking blond woman wearing a cocktail dress and pearls sitting on a blue velour couch. She sips a martini and points through the camera at me. "You're new."

"So people keep telling me."

"And handsome."

"I am told that…less frequently."

"More's the pity." She leans forward, pouts her thick red lips. "Buy a girl a drink?"

"You...already have one?"

"Yes. I have a drink. But what I want is a 'drink,' by which I mean the two of us consuming beverages over a short period of time as a preamble to running through a few pages of the Kama Sutra."

I look up at the suited man holding the tablet to get his read on this, but he is utterly impassive. "Ignore him!" She snaps. "Think of him as my chauffeur. Long story short: I'm deathly allergic to almost everything, housebound, and horny. So what's the word, want to throw down?"

"But you're...there?"

She throws back her head and laughs. "Oh saints be praised! He's handsome *and* thick, just the way I like 'em! I didn't mean fooling around in meatspace. Yuck! Don't make me puke, literally. Human contact would make me violently ill. I meant you and I head into the nearest bathroom and help each other out remotely."

"You want to have cybersex?"

"It's just called 'sex' these days, darling. The 'cyber' part is redundant."

"I'm sorry. I'm not into women." Sam saves me yet again.

She clucks her tongue. "That's a pity, for me anyway. Have yourself a pleasant evening. Might see you up on Level 2 later. Sergei, take me over to the tall guy over there. The one with the lip piercing." Sergei and his employer march off towards fresh quarry.

The bartender places the glasses in front of me. "She's here a couple nights a week. The cleaners hate her."

"Why do they—oh. Right. Gross. Also weird."

"Newblood, if you think that's strange? You might want to

keep away from the upper levels until you've adequately moved the goalposts of 'normal.'"

I thank her for the advice and pay for the drinks. Nisha returns and sits down next to me. "I know, I know! I was gone forever. But I started thinking about my father, and then I cried and had to redo my mascara, and *then* I got caught up with some woman who's in the middle of a divorce and had to tell me all about how it was supposedly connected to her recently acquired gluten intolerance. Something about my face seems to scream 'confess all your problems to me!' to white women. Perhaps I should start a business where I counsel wealthy white people. 'First-world problems? We've got first-class solutions!' In any case, I assume it gave you sufficient time to think of an explanation for the arsenal of pointy objects you are carrying?"

"…"

"Really? You've just been sitting here assuming I wouldn't want any kind of explanation for the fact that you're carrying more weapons than a police evidence locker?"

Sam scrambles for an answer. "I'm still worried about my ex. He found me once, I know it's a long shot that he could ever find me again (although someone seems to have managed it), but I have to be ready, just in case."

Nisha keeps her eyes locked on me as she drains her glass in a slow, single hit. She slams it on the counter and motions for another. She points at my drink. "How is the gin around here? Would your grandmother approve?"

"It's—"

She snatches the glass from my hand and downs it, slams the glass on the counter. "That. Is. *Tonic water.*"

"Actually, it's an empty glass."

"Stop being cute! By which I mean annoying."

"What's wrong with not drinking?"

"There is nothing wrong with not drinking, but there *is* something wrong with pretending to drink." She grabs my hand, draws her face close to mine. "Sam. Look at where we are. The whole point of this place is for people to drop their facades."

"..."

"How about we make a deal? I'll share something with you, if you do the same?"

"Nisha, honey, I'm a private person. Why should I have to divulge all the skeletons in my overcrowded closet?"

The bartender refills Nisha's glass. Nisha thanks her and holds her gaze for a few beats. She turns back to me. "Two reasons; the first is selfish. I am lonely, and I want to get to know someone. The second is altruistic. Right now, you are a pressure cooker. You have crammed so many secrets and deceptions inside of you that if you do not release a pressure valve soon, you are going to have a complete breakdown."

She's wrong, isn't she? You were the only person I was ever really able to open up to, my emotional vault has been vacuum-sealed since I left Havana. What would you tell me to do?

"Perhaps we should let that idea marinate while I go first?" Nisha suggests.

I signal the bartender. "Honey, could I get a beer, whatever lager you've got on the taps there?" What the hell is Sam doing? He knows we can't drink. Drinking reduces inhibitions impairs cognitive function and gross motor ability allows secrets to slip from liquor-lubricated lips—

She slaps the glass down, and I throw some cash on the table. Sam raises the glass to his lips while I cower at the back of our collective consciousness yelling *nononono*! But then finally whispering; *yes*. I slide the frothy liquid down my throat, and it feels like coming home from a nine-year prison stint.

"Ready now?" Nisha asks.

I nod.

"To begin with; my job. I have not given you the whole story. I work as a digital narrative editor."

"Like an influencer?"

She scowls. "No. Influencers are models with delusions of grandeur. What I do is a lot more complex, and requires a much higher level of technical ability. I craft and utilise a range of online personas; at any one time I'm running a few dozen personality profiles ranging from teenage pansexual nonbinary ultra-left drug-running anarchist through to octogenarian anti-immigration pro-choice hardline religious uber-conservative."

"That sounds exhausting." And uncomfortably familiar.

"People often use the term 'avatars,' but what I do goes deeper than just a photo, name, and listing a handful of hobbies. I like to call them my homunculi. I don't just jump on Twitter and use a stolen profile picture. These are complete people with credit histories, dating profiles, bank accounts, phone numbers. They have entire lives."

"Soooo, you're basically a professional liar?"

"Only in the same sense as a novelist or politician. I prefer the term 'fabulist.'"

"What do you do with these digital Frankensteins?"

"I hire them out to people. Could be simple things—writing reviews, retweeting promotional campaigns, power levelling in MMORPGS, botnest harvesting, white noise campaigns, amplifying conspiracy theories, digital mystery shopping, vetting potential partners on dating apps, buying dark web goods on someone else's behalf—"

"I think I understand you better when you speak in Rajasthani."

Nisha laughs. "Not very tech savvy?"

"I don't even own a computer."

She looks at me like I've just told her I've never eaten bread. "How are you even alive? Not having a computer in the twenty-first century is like not having *plumbing*!"

"I can do email and whatnot on my phone. I don't really see the point."

Nisha groans, buries her head in her hands, finishes her drink. She recovers and orders another round for us, then grabs my arm. Her eyes are wide with sudden realisation. "Sam, you aren't an alcoholic, are you?"

"What?"

"I've been scolding you for pretending to drink, and I didn't even stop to think it might be because you have a problem with alcohol!"

I do; it's the same problem I have with sodium pentothal. It tends to make me tell the truth. "No no no, sweetie! I just, ah… it's complicated. But, no, I'm not an alcoholic."

She heaves a sigh of relief and gives my arm a friendly squeeze. You'd like Nisha. Did I tell you that already? I might have told you that already. I take another drink (Sam takes another drink) even though I very definitely shouldn't, but on the other hand it's delicious and has the highly desirable effect of shutting down the part of my brain that usually feels like it's being pulled apart by horses.

"Do you like the work you do, with the hummus guys—ah, homunculi?"

"If I had been born a few generations ago, I would have been married to a middle-aged man when I was fourteen and forced to keep house, pop out babies, and tend goats. This is a much better situation."

"Not a particularly strong commendation."

She drinks. Pauses. Drinks again. "Sometimes I have to work with—and often pretend to be—people who are unfathomably foul. It is difficult to come away from that unscathed. But it's all an illusion anyway."

"But it clearly has real-world consequences?"

Nisha laughs. "That's cute, calling meatspace the 'real world' But, yes, the outcomes are significant. I mean all of this isn't real." She throws her arm in a wide arc around us, the alcohol loosening her movements.

I wait for her to elaborate. She doesn't. "Are you talking about the Hindu concept of maya?"

"I am not. But I'm impressed you are familiar with the term."

"What then?"

She rests her chin in her hand, levels her eyes at me. "I do not think we are ready for that. In any case, it's your turn!"

I drain the rest of my beer. Say nothing. Sam is eager to run his mouth, but I think he's done enough damage this evening. I force his—our—lips closed.

"Would you like me to start you off, 'Sam'?" My heart races at double-kick drum speed. "For starters, you are definitely not gay."

I pull back in confused, horrified shock, hand splayed against my chest.

She rolls her eyes. "You see? *That* is exactly what I'm talking about. Also, you are a little trigger happy with the 'sweethearts' and 'honeys.' Although you carry yourself convincingly, for the most part. I am sure you have all the breeders fooled."

"But you're—"

"Not one of them. I've noticed your eyes drawn to the same women as me. You don't have the slack-jawed gawk that many straight men exhibit, but it is definitely discernible to someone who's paying attention."

I say nothing. Sam says nothing. I can feel him dissolving inside me like an ice sculpture.

"You pulled me in with that story about your ex though. That felt as real as something I'd invent for my homunculi, and the best lies are always built on a foundation of truth, are they not?"

"That part about how we met was true, except for the gender flipping." I'm sorry forgive me I've been keeping it all in for so long I've been a wall a vault a safe a black hole.

"I thought so. Second; your accent. It's good, very convincing. But you aren't English."

"..."

"You spent too much time perfecting the accent and not enough working on your lexicon. You say 'trunk' instead of 'boot,' 'freshmen' instead of 'first-year,' and the Brits say 'spat' as the past tense of spit. Where are you actually from, America?"

I say nothing, as good a confirmation as any.

She raises her hands heavenward in celebration. "I knew I could get inside that angsty little brain of yours! One question; why didn't you just pretend to be Australian, if you're living here?"

"Are you fucking kidding me? The accent is *impossible*!" I slap my hand over my mouth, shocked at hearing my natural voice.

Nisha raises her glass. We toast. "Hello, stranger. It is nice to meet you."

"Fuck." I concede, my real voice now well and truly exposed. "I tried. Watched a slew of Bruce Beresford and Peter Weir films, but it always ended up sounding like a mangled blend of English, Kiwi, and South African." Why am I so drunk already? I can hear the words of my unleashed Chicago accent beginning to slur. I brush my hand against the packet of pills in my pocket. The ones that are not supposed to be mixed with alcohol under any circumstances. I guess I can blame Sam for this mess, considering that he's more or less dead now.

"So you are from... I'm hearing Chicago?"

I nod, defeated.

Nisha opens the drinks menu, flips through the pages. "I looked you up online. 'Sam Clemens?' Interesting choice for an alias."

"Yes, I know. Using Mark Twain's birth name is a pretentious choice. But look; my real name—" Don't tell her don't tell her don't trust her she'll burn it all down choose a new persona or adapt one do it quickly before she tears it all apart tell her your name is "Archie Leach, which is Cary Grant's birth name. My parents had no idea they'd inadvertently named me after a Hollywood icon until a high school buddy of mine unearthed that little gem of information. I thought it would be...funny's not the right word, maybe fitting, to use an alias that was also the real name of a person better known by their pseudonym."

She tilts her head, soaking in the new information. "I name all of my characters using IMDb and obituaries. I take the first name of an actor and splice it with the last name of a recent death, or sometimes it's the other way around."

I snort a laugh.

"What is so funny?"

"I just can't believe I'm trading tips on constructing fake identities. We're quite the pair of professional liars, aren't we?"

"Fabulists," she corrects. "*Fabulous* fabulists."

My head is swimming swam swum in a warm, hazy glow. The bar beneath my hand suddenly feels malleable, like I could pick it up and turn it into a balloon animal.

"Are you alright?" asks Nisha.

I slap my face and say, "Yeah. Just. The beer. 'S been, y'know. A while."

She plucks it out of my hand. "I had no idea you were such a lightweight."

I really want to pay attention to what she's saying, but it's quite difficult given that the floor is undulating.

"Archie? Do you mind if I ask you one last question?" It feels odd, having her address me by the name I only use with my clients. "What are you running from?"

No. No. Nononono that's too big can't look at it looks like, ah, like looking at the sun too much and it'll burn burn burn and— "About nine years ago, in Cuba..." *Who is moving the hole in my face? It can't be Sam. Sam's gone. But it can't be me because I could never would never tell anyone that "...*I met—" You. I met you. The ground ebbs away from me. "Feel. Bit. Woozy."

Your face fills my mind. The sound of your singing rings in my ears. I heave a few more breaths.

"Archie, are you alright? Do you want to go home?"

"..."

"Perhaps this was a mistake. You are still recovering."

She's right. Who knows what sort of postmortem aftershocks

are shuddering through my psyche? I stand up in order to assess my sobriety. "I think I'm too drunk to drive."

"After one beer?"

"Mixed with pain meds that do not play nice with alcohol."

"Ah, of course. We could get a taxi?"

"I'd have to come back for the bike, and I need to have it with me so I can be on call at short notice. I think I need to clear my head anyway." The photo of you in still in the kitchen drawer, waiting to taunt me. Best to stay away as long as I can. "Should we try another level?"

She raises an eyebrow. "You sure?"

"No. Which is why we'd better go before I change my mind."

Nisha stands up and holds out her hand. I let her pull me up and we head upstairs.

12

Veneer

Venus

Voracity

Venture

Vengeance

Voyage

Violence

Vision

My finger traces over the buttons on the elevator, pausing at the ninth-floor label, which has been left curiously and conspicuously blank. "Do you think they're ordered in terms of intensity, or expense? Would you need to be a high roller with thousands of dollars to spend to visit the higher levels?"

"Money seems like it would be too crude a hierarchical mechanism for this place. Perhaps it's more like levelling in a MMORPG."

"…?"

"In some games, you can freely visit any area on a map, but until your character has acquired the requisite experience, you'll be quickly demolished by the creatures in that area. You gain access through experience rather than some sort of gate being unlocked. It's your skills, wisdom, and abilities that allow you to move through new parts of the world."

"Level 2 then? Venus was the god of love, I suppose that bodes well?"

"Depends on what you love. If it is a dendro-necrophiliac's romantic fantasy, we are going to gather a few memories we will need to violently repress."

"Dendron-what?"

"I will tell you some other time. Just don't do a google image search."

I hit the second-floor button, and the elevator glides upwards. The doors "ping" and slide open to reveal a long, red-carpeted corridor that would look perfectly at home in a luxury hotel, save for the odd glyphs in lieu of numbers on the doors. We approach the first door and examine it. "Any idea what this means?"

Nisha furrows her brow, traces her fingertips over the circles. "I have…seen these before…in an ancient Sanskrit manuscript my father kept on the shelf in his library…"

"Really?"

"Yes. I believe this one translates as…" she closes her eyes, murmurs quietly to herself, "'you are very gullible.'"

"Very funny. Should we just take our chances, see what's behind door number…three circles that look a bit like a Venn diagram?"

"What if we're forced into a game of Russian roulette?"

"You should ask to play first."

"Fuck you!"

"In a standard revolver the weight of the bullet makes the cartridge spin to the bottom, your odds are best on the first turn."

"How did you learn—"

The hard way. The smell of blood and brain staining your hair is not something you easily forget. "It doesn't matter." I push the door open and immediately back out and slam it behind me.

"Did you see—"

"The bearded man in a suit holding a tablet with a video of a woman pleasuring herself on a velour couch next to a bed with a rotund gentleman covered in talcum powder? No, I didn't really get a good look."

Looks like my allergy-encumbered acquaintance managed to find a dance partner for the evening then. We laugh the kind of laughter that makes your cheeks hurt. I place my hand against my face, surprised those muscles haven't atrophied from lack of use. I'd completely forgotten that alcohol can give the world a soft gloss of hilarity. What a curious quality in a depressant.

Nisha wipes her eyes, steadies herself. "Shall we see what's behind door number…two concentric circles redolent of lopsided breasts?" She turns the handle, throwing the door open with theatrical flourish. This room is much larger; roughly the size of a studio apartment. It is utterly bereft of furniture, which would be odd if not for the activity taking place. The waves of groaning form a carnal chorale, an orgiastic "om." The floor is covered in a carpet of skin; thrusting, grinding, grasping. Nisha slams the door shut. "To quote my father, 'I do not think I fit the demographic for this particular establishment.'"

"That makes two of us. Perhaps we should try another floor?"
"One last door," she suggests. "Your turn."

We pass a few more doors, inspecting the inscrutable glyphs
on each of them. I pause outside a large double door embla-
zoned with a single dot in the middle of a lone circle. I place my
hand on the doorknob, turn it, and enter.

Again we are met with a sea of bodies; but these are thank-
fully both clothed and vertical. We are engulfed in flailing limbs
and shouts of adulation. I drink in the vision of writhing bodies,
a forest of fingers raised to the ceiling, the phalanx of feet crushing carpet. The music is wild and wordless; the rhythm is the
beating heart of a great forgotten god; the vocals are the adulation of delirious angels. A rhapsodic, rubbery bass line rumbles
through the floor, the walls, our chests. The effect is euphoric
and epiphanic, febrile and frenetic.

It seems impossible that music of such tremendous volume
would be inaudible behind a closed door. Soundproofing that
effective doesn't exist. And yet.

Nisha grabs my hand, pulls me through the door and closes
it behind us. The room is almost entirely dark, the only light
coming from a few pusillanimous rays from the street-lamps
outside. The crowd moves with a sense of unified rapture, hands
thrust heavenward, whoops and cries of delight subsumed into
the soundscape. Nisha drags me into the thick of the crowd.
She lets loose an exultant cry. I am somewhat more reticent.
You always made fun of my dancing, and for good reason. A few
months in Cuba gradually transformed my two left feet into a
competently opposing pair that could adequately manoeuvre
me through a few salsa songs, but salsa is built on a set pattern.
This is dance as meditation, elevation, and reincarnation. The

revelers are bathed in gleeful chaos, but my attempts at pattern recognition and replication fail miserably. There's no system here to learn and imitate.

I close my eyes and let the music consume me, drowning out my internal voice. It feels tribal, primal, unbridled. Why haven't I spent every moment of every day pursuing this feeling?

Because you don't deserve joy. You deserve penance and suffering. You owe her that much, and more.

Amongst the heaving crowd I glimpse the faces of the kids from Kolkata; gaping voids where their eyes should be, bellies swollen with famine, teeth grinding in time with the beat.

Nisha leans towards me and the faces disappear. She leans in to my ear and yells: "I AM GLAD I MET YOU, ARCHIE! YOU'RE A LOT MORE FUN THAN YOU LET ON!"

"You too! The first bit, anyway!"

She plants a kiss on my cheek, surrenders to the music again.

I don't deserve this. I don't deserve companionship, music, happiness.

Shut up. Shut up. Penance can wait until you get home. I gaze around at the throng of revellers and wonder if this is normal; this kind of joy, this freedom. Is this what ordinary people do? Is this what we'd be doing together if I'd been able to pretend I'd never seen that message on your phone?

I turn my focus back to the bacchanalian bass line, let my ego dissolve into the ether. After minutes or hours or days or aeons, Nisha yells into my ear: "I am exhausted! Let's get some air."

I follow her outside. The doors close behind us, swallowing the music with implausible silence. I crack the door open and the bass erupts like a low-frequency volcano. I close it again and the hallway becomes a library.

"I assume you are aware that you resemble a toddler investigating a jack-in-the-box?" I follow her to the elevator. "I enjoyed your dancing. It reminded me of one of those movies where they bring a puppet to life."

I roll my eyes and press the elevator call button. The doors slide open and we're greeted by an unpleasantly familiar golden grin.

13

"G'day, Leachy!" Goldie is the only person I know who actually uses the iconic Australian greeting, as though the "ood" in "good" is an insufferable linguistic burden.

Behind him, Saklas leans against the wall flanked by two of his Demons. "The fine and honourable Mr. Leach! Why don't you and your..." he pauses, sniffs the air, "lady friend join us?" He holds out his hand.

Nisha places a tentative hand in his. He raises it to his lips, kisses it gently, inhales her scent. "Fascinating. I'm getting...Chanel's Coco Noir...sweat, aaaaand...don't tell me... Glenfiddich?"

She withdraws her hand with a slow and deliberate motion. "You have a keen nose, Mr....?"

"Sammy Saklas, entrepreneur." He takes a low bow.

"Nisha Mukherjee, lowly IT grunt."

Saklas chortles and motions for Goldie to close the doors behind us.

"Mr. Saklas, it's such a pleasure to run into you, but I'm afraid we were just on our way out."

"I'm not a big believer in chance, me. I'd call this fate. Kismet. Goldie here tells me that the item you were storing for us was returned in a somewhat dissatisfactory condition, is that correct?"

I run a mental scan of the weapons I'm carrying, calculating which would be most effective at this range, but in close quarters like this there'd be no way to ensure Nisha emerged unscathed. I put a hand in my pocket, slip on my knuckle dusters as a last resort. "Mr. Saklas, I can explain—"

He raises his hand and says, "Level 7." Goldie hits the button marked 'Violence.' "Goldie, remind me when Mr. Leach's next instalment is due?"

Goldie makes a show of checking his watch. "Just so happens that it's a touch past four in the morning, day of."

The elevator begins its climb. "I wasn't expecting you until the morning—"

"It *is* the morning," says Goldie with the kind of pedantic interjection typically employed by trust fund children correcting the pronunciation of a word like "oeuvre" or "accoutrement."

"I wasn't expecting you until after sunrise. But the money's all there. I could ride home and get it, be back in thirty minutes." A quick stop at a convenience store to empty the cash register should bring me into the black.

Saklas strokes his beard. The doors open and he motions for us to exit.

"Mr. Saklas, I'm happy to accompany you, but Nisha really does have to be going, she—"

He raises his hand for silence, turns to face Nisha. "Ms. Mukherjee, might I be allowed to feel the contours of your face?

I'm blind as a bat, and I'd love to get an image of the face that matches your incredible scent."

"Of course." Her words are as taut as a lynching rope. She closes her eyes.

Saklas cradles her face with slow and delicate movements. She watches her own anxious face reflected in his mirrored sunglasses. He pulls his hands away, shaking his head in disbelief. "Bloody hell! Apologies if it's inappropriate to say so, but your skin is miraculously soft! What moisturiser do you use?"

"Maaemo revitalise mist," she answers.

"Goldie, order me a metric ton of that shit. I am done with those pricks at Nivea. Fucken' overpriced German snake oil."

"Will do, boss."

Saklas crooks his elbow and points it at Nisha. She takes it with a stricken look that I am grateful he cannot see. "This way, ladies and gents! I am inviting you to be my esteemed guests tonight! What a thrill it is to have the fates see fit to deliver you to my establishment."

"You own the Orrery?" asks Nisha, curiosity momentarily trumping her fear.

"This floor, I do. Each level's under a separate jurisdiction. Violence—the seventh, and might I say most exciting, floor—is under my humble command."

I knew Saklas had a diverse portfolio, but I've never heard him mention Violence or the Orrery. Then again, I doubt he's in the habit of giving out any kind of information for free. He walks down the hall in long, proud strides, his voice booming. "Owning a venue like this provides a number of perks—" A muffled scream echoes down the hall, followed by an ecstatic cheer. "—not least of 'em, the ability to vertically integrate a little conflict resolution into my general operations. Goldie! What's chapter twelve tell us?"

"'Vertical Integration creates voluminous innovation.'"

Saklas slaps him firmly on the back. "Too right. Glad to see that's finally sinking in!"

"I switched to the audiobook boss, listenin' to it while I'm doin' weights an' that."

Saklas clucks his tongue. "Well, I guess that's better than nothing. See, I've been teachin' Goldie here lessons from *Nineteen and a Half Secrets of Great Leaders and Innovators*. He's been learnin' about the art of business management. In particular, that violence isn't always the solution. Although, granted, in our line of work it is the solution *quite* a lot more often than in other industries. And in this particular case, it's definitely the solution. Which is why…"

He pauses for dramatic effect, then motions for Goldie to open the door. He pulls it back to reveal a screaming crowd, money and betting tickets clutched between sweaty fingers, gathered in a circle around two shirtless men covered in sweat and blood. I watch in horror as the taller of the two lands a brutal uppercut. He opens his mouth wide, exposing twin rows of meth-addled teeth, and proceeds to sink them deep into his opponent's shoulder. The crowd applauds.

"We're going to employ a valued technique from chapter nine, which is, Goldie?"

"Ahhhh, don't tell me… 'Using effective reward techniques to motivate productivity.' Givin' people raises and bonuses an' that.'"

"No, that's chapter eight. Points for trying. Chapter nine is about employing mediated conflict resolution in order to facilitate a collegial work environment, thus ensuring a dramatic reduction in workplace dissatisfaction and staff turnover. Sounds good, don't it lads?"

The Demons murmur sycophantic assent, although they've clearly no idea what he's just said.

"Or, to put it another way, we want to keep things Sardinian, ain't that right, Leachy?"

"That's correct, Mr. Saklas."

"So. Seein' as how you've fortuitously stumbled into my little neck of the woods, let's put this lesson into practise, shall we?"

The meth-toothed combatant releases his jaws at last, following up with a two-fingered attack on his opponent's eyeballs. It looks almost slapstick, right until the moment it lands and sends the smaller man reeling in agony. Meth-teeth seizes the opportunity to land a devastating blow to the back of the head, earning rapturous appreciation from the crowd. His opponent falls to the crowd, and the match dissolves into a brutal flurry of kicks rained on the fallen combatant. Someone blows a whistle, and the crowd releases twin cries of joy and dismay, contingent on how they've placed their bets. Two of Saklas's Demons appear on the mat, carrying a stretcher. They roll the fallen fighter onto it. His face looks like a Francis Bacon painting.

"Mr. Leach, in lieu of this fortnight's payment, I'm gonna announce you as our surprise contender for the evening."

Goldie sniggers quietly, winks at me.

"Along with Goldie."

The smirk falls from his face. "Boss! Why do—"

"Because this fucken' mess is your fault too. You're always ribbing him, one of our best workers. You let shit get too personal. You decide you don't like someone, and you constantly harass and harangue them. It's fucken' unprofessional, is what it is. You think I like half the scumbags we do business with? You gotta learn how to take yer feelings out of the equation."

"Sure thing, boss. Good talk, will do. But do I really have—"

"You're a kinaesthetic learner, Goldie, not an aural one."

"…?"

"You learn shit by doin' shit. Hence, you're doing this. No backchat. Time to rip the Band-Aid off this little problem. Although, when you're done you'll probably both need quite a few Band-Aids. Maybe a few stitches. Possibly a quick trip to the ER."

Nisha whispers in my ear, "We should run."

"No, my dear, you most certainly should not." Saklas flicks his ear with his index finger. "Hearing of a wax moth." He brings his hands together in a decisive clap. "Righto then! A few ground rules for this round. No shoes. No shirts. No weapons."

I wait expectantly for the rest of the rules, but this appears to be the end of the list. Goldie removes his shirt, revealing a large chest-piece of a young, mustachioed man in profile with a Golden era of Hollywood look to him. Above his head, written in flowing calligraphy, are the words: *Jamieson Boondoggle. Beloved father. 1958–1988. Rest in peace.* Goldie must have only been a child when his father died. A flicker of sympathy slithers through me, but Goldie vanquishes it by saying: "The fuck you lookin' at? Suit up already! I promise I'll make this quick." He spits at my feet for emphasis.

I kick off my shoes, momentarily amused by the realisation that Goldie's last name is "Boondoggle."

The younger, scrawnier of the Demons stands on a table and announces the impending new round. The crowd cheers and begins placing bets. Hundreds of pairs of eyes study us. I remove my knuckle dusters, dagger, pen-shaped tactical blade, pepper spray, and fibreglass push blade and place them on the table.

A few dozen punters adjust their bets. The crowd forms back into a circle, an eager chant of "Gold-ie! Gold-ie! Gold-ie!" echoes throughout the hall. To be fair, it's a very chantable name.

Saklas climbs into an armchair on a riser in the corner, allowing him an ideal vantage point that in his case is purely symbolic.

Nisha pulls me close. "Are you sure there's no way out of this?"

"Doesn't look like it." I remove my shirt.

Nisha's eyes scan the various scars and burns adorning my chest and shoulders. "In that case, make sure you win."

"Once the match starts, you'll be able to slip out—"

"Nonsense, I will be here. We're in this together, Archie neé Sam."

There's a few more 'neé's in there than she knows, but this probably isn't the time. A Demon taps me on the shoulder, points to the ring. Goldie steps into the circle, hands raised, soaking up the chanting and applause. I follow him. A handful of punters raise the competing chant of: "New guy! New guy!" If not for the fear that I might be about to die for the second time this month, I'd probably find this quite amusing.

Saklas stands up, raises a hand high in the air. The effect is swift and startling. The room is transformed into a monastery at midnight; silent and reverent. "I trust we're all enjoying ourselves this evening?" A roar of approval gushes from the crowd and is then truncated when he again raises his hand. "Glad to hear it. Got a special match for you all next. Been a bit of tension between my right-hand man and one of our contractors, so I thought we'd resolve it the fun way."

Goldie glowers at me, rolls his shoulders, takes a fighting stance. I assess his form; the mass of muscle rippling beneath his skin is certainly intimidating, but his stance is all wrong. I've seen him in action once or twice when I've made a delivery at an inopportune time. Goldie is a thug, he knows how to throw a punch—and take one—but it's all brutal, primal chaos. The good news is he doesn't have much in the way of formal training. A few deftly placed pressure point strikes and I should be able to manoeuvre him into a finishing hold. The bad news is that he's unpredictable, and that will make those hits hard to land. Goldie is a blunt instrument, I need to be a surgeon's scalpel.

"Bets are now closed!" yells Saklas. "Gentlemen, are you ready?"

I take my stance, feigning nervousness and making sure to effectively distribute my weight but hold my hands inexpertly in front of my face. Goldie takes the bait and doesn't bother hiding his smirk. He thinks this will be easy, which should hopefully make it easy for me to prove him wrong.

"On my count! Three! Two—"

Goldie's fist launches towards my face, the crowd roars in approval of his insolence. I manage to sidestep the blow—just—but it's not a good start. Technically, he hasn't broken any of the three Spartan rules; he's just used my foolhardy adherence to etiquette to his advantage. I step back, regaining my stance and squaring my shoulders. When I met you, I'd never thrown a single punch. I wonder what you'd think of me now that—

Goldie flings his fist again, and I try to dodge it, but his knuckle grazes my ear. A high-pitched ringing fills my head. I was distracted, thinking of you. Can't make that mistake again.

Goldie laughs giddily, revelling in the moment. Violence is

his mother tongue, but his vocabulary is limited to a handful of kicks and punches. He rushes at me again with yet another right hook. This time I sidestep and slam my elbow into the back of his head as he rushes past. His screaming is inaudible over that of the crowd. He turns back to face me, enraged. He's not badly hurt, just embarrassed. Goldie is a schoolyard bully who's simply expanded his territory from the playground to the whole city. He's not used to anyone fighting back. He runs at me with a shoulder charge, hoping to use his significant mass to overpower any defensive strikes I might employ. Adrenaline slows the passage of time, and Goldie advances towards me at what appears to be a lazy afternoon stroll.

I line myself up and allow him to see the confident smile creeping across my face. His expression clouds with confusion and a delicious trace of fear. When he finally reaches me, I pivot my body away from his charge and kick his feet away from him. As he hurtles into the air I grab his wrist with one hand and shoulder with the other. Using his momentum rather than my own strength, I flip him over, grinning at his exasperated expression as he comes to grips with the fact that the ceiling and the ground have been inverted. The crowd is ecstatic. I try and not take too much pleasure from this, but honestly, I'm only human.

Goldie scrambles back to his feet, inflamed with pugilistic rage. "I'm gonna fucken' *rip you ta shreds!*" He lunges at me, hands raised high above his head, telegraphing the fact that he's going to attempt to grab either my shoulders or my throat.

I feel almost sorry for him as I plan my response: shoving his arms aside and outward, manoeuvring his right wrist into a pressure point hold behind his back. It's the kind of technique they teach in a basic self-defense course. I watch it all play out in my mind's eye, then take a step back to execute the manoeuvre. Unfortunately, the pool of blood on the floor has other ideas. My foot slips in the red-black liquid that had until recently resided inside a (presumably) human body. I fall backward, and Goldie lands his shoulder grab.

He draws his head back, lips peeled wide to allow full view of his grill glinting in the harsh fluorescent lights. The moment before our faces collide I glimpse something in the crowd, but before my brain can properly process the optical input, the crack of Goldie's head against mine creates new cosmologies of pain inside my skull.

I think I'm screaming, but it's impossible to tell over the nightmarish howling of the crowd. Goldie shoves me back onto the mat, allowing me a moment to wallow. He takes a lap; arms raised exultantly, soaking up the attention like a second-rate wrestler.

My vision doubles, then refocuses, then doubles again. The ringing in my ears returns. I don't even notice Goldie approach until his foot slams into my chest. The breath leaves my body. I gasp in angry, heaving bursts. He follows this with a stomp on the back of my head. The pain becomes fractal, each node of agony giving birth to new and never-ending spirals.

He draws his foot back and I watch it approach my face with a kind of abstract curiosity, studying flaked and scarred skin growing closer at what appears to be glacial speed. He strikes me firm in the face, and stars of pain supernova inside my skull.

I turn my head and spit a pool of blood onto the mat next to me. The siren song of oblivion sings somewhere in the depths of my consciousness. It would be so easy to just slip down there, where it's warm and dark and silent. The crowd chants: "Kill him! Kill him! Kill him!" Their voices are distant and washed out, like I'm at the bottom of a swimming pool listening to sounds on the surface. I can't even remember why I've been holding on all these years; not living, just surviving. Too cowardly to exit my own empty existence. A foolish notion of penance and repentance the only thread connecting me to the world. Perhaps it's time to surrender.

To let go.

To die.

(Permanently, this time.)

Goldie takes another showboating lap of the audience, a preemptive victory dance.

The roaring chant of "Kill him! Kill him!" fills my ears. It takes me a second to realise that one of the voices chanting is my own. I study the faces in the crowd, the Greek chorus bearing witness to my defeat.

And there you are.

This time I'm certain. Even through the haze of blood and pain and *eeeeeeeeeeeee* in my ears I'm sure it's you. You look like you haven't aged at all. Which makes sense, given that I watched you die. Your piercing eyes are perched just above the shoulders of the frenzied spectator in front of you. You push him aside, step to the front line of the ring, revealing that unforgettable dress in all its sanguine glory. You're really here. A cacophony of questions cascades through my brain: *howareyoualive howdidyoufindme howisthisreal?*

And most importantly: *doyouforgiveme?*

You look at me. Right at me, the way you always did when you were angry, like you could mentally strip away the layers of skin and muscle and bone and see directly into my raw and tender soul. Your lips start to move, and I study them as they mouth: *"des-troy him."* Then you turn and disappear into the crowd. I leap to my feet, suppressing the pain and dizziness and nausea as I scream: "SOPHIA!"

Goldie finishes playing to the crowd at the sound of my scream. He turns to face me, preparing to land the killing blow. His hands turn in slow circles as he murmurs, "C'mon, Leachy! Let's see whatcha got!" He's cocky now, which is good because it'll make what I'm about to do all the more satisfying.

I feint a right jab and he takes the bait eagerly, ducking aside, directly into the left hook I send soaring into his face. Blood erupts from his lips. Before he's hit the ground, I follow up with a sharp jab to the gut. He doubles over and I greet his descending face with my rising knee. His head flies upwards, painting a red arc of blood through the air as he falls. The crowd is ecstatic. I'm not sure who I'm more disgusted with, them or me. I scan their ranks but you're well and truly gone.

Again.

Goldie hits the floor with a wet thud. He turns onto his hands and knees, trying to clamber back to his feet. I deliver a sharp kick to his stomach. The crowd loves this. Goldie, obviously, has other feelings on the matter. I take my time lining up another kick, like a soccer player taking a penalty. I can feel the anticipation buzzing in the air. *Des-troy him.*

I pull my foot back and scream as I drive it into his face. He sputters again, and, this time, along with the blood, a shiny metal gewgaw clutters out of his mouth. The crowd falls silent. I pick it up, wipe it off on my pants, and hold the golden grill aloft. "Might be time for a new nickname." I toss the grill insouciantly into the crowd as they scream in adoration. I pull my fist back, assessing my strike. If I land it at the right point on his spine, I could likely cripple him. A few inches higher and I could put him into a coma. Or kill him.

Breathe in. Then out. Then strike.

In.

Out...

Two soft hands close around my fist. I spin around and say, "Sophia?"

Nisha's eyes are lit with fear as she says. "No. It's me. You've won. Leave him. You're better than this."

I look away, spit blood onto the mat. "You don't know what I am."

"Yes, I do. You are the guy who looked after my dog."

The crowd is chanting *kill him kill him kill him!* I look around at the ring of faces, wonder how many of them have partners to whom they whisper, "I love you"; children they cradle in their laps as they read them fairy tales; friends whom they console in times of crisis; and how many of them manage to conceal this bloodlust beneath the veneer of civility in the world outside. Everyone here is just like me—a liar.

"You're also my ride home," Nisha adds.

This is so absurd I can't help but laugh. I look up at Saklas and call out, "We good here?"

One of the Demons whispers in his ear, presumably describing the scene that's just played out. Saklas responds, "We're all Sardinian, as far as I'm concerned." The crowd—clearly hoping for further bloodshed—groans with disappointment. Spoiled children denied their dessert. "Ladies and gents, tonight's victor; Archibald Leach!" They applaud politely, a few of them rushing to claim their winnings. One of the Demons hoists Goldie over his shoulder and carries him away. The younger one tosses me my weapons bundled up in my shirt and jacket. I dress and return them to their hiding places. We sneak around the outside of the crowd, who're distracted by the announcement of the next round; two women this time. Good to see that blood sport is an equal opportunity industry.

Nisha and I are silent all the way to the elevator.

The doors open.

We step inside.

Nisha hits the button for the ground floor.

The elevator descends.

She turns to me and says, "I think it's about time you told me about Sophia."

I waited until I was sure you were done. Then I asked: "You told me you were finished."

You looked up at me, eyes filled with tears, regret, anger, confusion, contempt. "Yes. I did," you said, sweeping hair back from your eyes, reaching your hand out to my cheek. "But we both knew I was lying."

We screamed at each other. You broke the window, then smashed the wine bottle against the wall. The splintered glass carved a red stripe across my chin. We flung curses and accusations and recriminations, and tears cascaded from your eyes as you climbed up onto the ledge.

14

Dawn is breaking as I pull my motorcycle into the driveway. Nisha climbs off and we stare at each other and say nothing. Then she lifts my arm around her neck and helps me stagger to the door. "I really think we should get you to a doctor."

"It's fine. I've taken worse damage before."

"Is that supposed to be encouraging?"

I unlock the door, step inside. She tries to follow me in but I slide my shoulder into the doorframe to block her way. "I just need to sleep. And take several labs' worth of high-grade pharmaceuticals. Give me a day or two to rest, then we can talk about..."

"Sophia."

Your name sounds like an incantation on her lips. "Yes. About Sophia."

"Very well. Thank you for an unforgettable evening, Archie. You certainly know how to show a girl a good time, immediately followed by a very traumatic time."

"That's what my Tinder bio says."

She squeezes my hand, I yelp and retract it. "Oh god oh god I am so sorry! I wasn't thinking."

"I'll see you soon, Nisha. I'll even cook, if you like. Say hi to Dante for me."

I slam the door closed, stumble into the kitchen and slide open the drawer with the painkillers. And there you are again, smiling at me. I turn the photo facedown, close the drawer, down the meds, stumble to the bedroom, and surrender to sleep.

Two days later I'm healed up enough to work again, and with the clock ticking on my next instalment to Saklas, I don't really have the luxury of taking time off. I pull up outside the lavish glass-enshrined mini mansion of one Gordon Wallace, who likes to use the street name of "G-fitz," despite the fact that the kinds of "streets" he's most likely to spend time on are "Wall" and "Easy." I ring the doorbell and he answers dressed in pink slippers, Calvin Klein boxers, and a silk robe which swings wide enough to expose the mass of tattoos spilling across his pasty white chest. Notorious BIG carouses with Mario next to Batman fornicating with Marilyn Monroe in a hideous pop culture tableau that is such an affront to good taste I can only assume the tattoo artist responsible committed seppuku immediately afterwards.

To make matters worse, he's vaping. "Whattup, Leachy." He expels a cloud of toffee-scented smoke.

I hand him the package and say, "Two hundred fifty dollars."

He raises an eyebrow, makes a show of checking his oversized

Cartier watch. "Don't think so, homeslice. I was told if you delivered late, it would be free. Like with pizza."

I take out my phone and show him the time and then the message, time-stamped twenty-eight minutes earlier. "I'm two minutes early."

He holds out his watch, taps it. "Nooooo, your piece of shit phone is wrong. According to this, you are two minutes *late*."

"Your watch is fast."

"That's a fucken' forty-dollar burner phone you prolly bought from a petrol station. This watch cost five grand!"

"This forty-*five* dollar burner is connected to an international satellite network that adjusts for special relativity. Your ostentatious hunk of metal operates via a battery and a bunch of gears. It's wrong. Or you set it wrong. The time is the time, the price is the price."

"I ain't fucken' paying, bro." He prods me in the chest. After having had a wealth of experience dealing with criminals of varying levels of success, I can attest that the more money people have, the stingier they get. Wallace is a rich white trust fund kid cosplaying as a gangster because he couldn't be bothered to pretend to be a banker.

I grab his wrist with one hand and the offending finger with the other, then bend it slowly back.

"Hey wha-oh what the *fuck stop*!"

I pause, holding his index finger a couple of degrees past the point of pain.

"I'll pay, I'll fucking pay!"

I drop his hand and hold my palm out.

"Jesus Christ, no need to get fucking *Reservoir Dogs* on my arse. *Fuck*." He reaches into the pocket of his robe and removes a money clip, peels off a few fifties, and hands them to me. I snatch the clip and peel off a few more, toss it back to him.

"What the *fuck*, dude?"

"I have a firm no-touching policy. First infringement is two hundred dollars. Next is double that plus I break a couple of fingers. And just so you know? That 'Cartier' is a fake."

I walk back to the bike, ignoring his protests. The no-touching policy is an obvious and unspoken rule in my line of work. But for entitled newbies like this, unspoken rules sometimes have to be spoken, and then spelled out s-l-o-w-l-y.

⊖

In my previous, diurnal existence I used to loathe grocery shopping. These days it's an almost meditative practice. Over the last few years I've established that on Tuesday nights the manager flagrantly defies the store policy of playing the corporate radio that intersperses in-store advertisements amongst songs about *being in love forever! And dancing all night! And being free!* Instead, she tunes into the local community radio station which favours a selection of sprawling, esoteric post-rock songs occasionally interrupted by DJs muttering drug-fuelled diatribes about the effects of single-origin fair-trade coffee consumption on late stage capitalism.

Then there's the people. Along with the expected cast of truck drivers, doctors, musicians, coders, drug addicts, and garden-variety insomniacs are the people who come to the grocery store to use it as a confessional. Lonely souls who purchase a single tin of baked beans and then spend twenty minutes unloading to the person behind the counter about their diabetic cats or their estranged father's mistress or their struggle to find the perfect nasal spray. I long ago gave up on television, but as a regular late-night customer at the twenty-four-hour grocery store, I can understand people who become addicted to soap operas.

The automatic doors slide open with a hiss, and I'm greeted by a squalling sonic haze of distortion and erratic drumbeats. I wander the aisles with my basket, inspecting vegetables. Nisha has a salt allergy, which has removed a key weapon from my culinary arsenal, so I've elected to cook a stir-fry, which is going to suffer a little but should still be edible.

I move onto the pasta and sauces aisle, assessing products based on a complex moral rubric of lowest carbon footprint, fewest food miles, minimal labor exploitation, least plastic packaging, and the corporate responsibility of the producer. You'd no doubt find this hysterical, given how I've been earning my income since I left Cuba. It's the karmic equivalent of someone who orders pancakes, bacon, maple syrup, and ice-cream but then asks for their coffee on skim milk to save on calories. Like these people, I acknowledge the ridiculousness of my convoluted karmic calculus. Also like them, I persist regardless.

I'm in the process of choosing a packet of noodles, attempting to recall which company's CEO is infamously homophobic so I can steer clear of their produce, when the agonised mewling of a young baby pulls me from my computation of ethical algorithms. I look up to see a young mother dressed in a terry-toweling dressing gown, black bags blossoming underneath her eyes, cradling a baby and whispering, "Shhh, it's okay, sweetheart. I know, I know. Mummy's going to find something to make you feel better."

She catches me looking at her. "Sorry, I don't mean to disturb you."

"No need to apologise."

"I'm so embarrassed, leaving the house like this. Two years ago I wouldn't set foot outside without concealer and lipstick, at a minimum." She sighs wistfully. "Clara here has a terrible fever, I had to drive across town to find somewhere that sells baby Panadol at this hour. There's no all-night pharmacies in our neighbourhood. There's a fucking *strip club* a few blocks away that doesn't close its doors until dawn, so if I need a lap dance, I'm covered. But medical supplies for my baby? Not so much. Do you know what aisle they keep the drugs in?"

"Second from the end."

She touches me gently on the shoulder. "Thank you, you're a saint." She turns and walks away murmuring reassurances to her daughter.

I throw a packet of noodles in my basket. A stream of quiet cursing emanates from the next aisle over. I peer around the corner to find the mother muttering to herself,

"You stupid fucking idiot. Dumb dumb dumb fucking—"

"Are you alright?"

She spins around, wipes her eyes and says, "Hrm, what?"

"You seem upset. Is everything alright?"

"Yes, of course!" The smile on her face is strained. Her daughter erupts in another wail. "Fuck. No, that's not true. I haven't had a decent night's sleep in months and my maternity leave is up in two weeks and I haven't found a daycare centre yet and I have baby brain and I left my phone and purse at home so now I have to drive all the way back and all the way here again and that'll take an hour and my tank is almost empty so I'll probably have to stop for petrol and I was really hoping to wait until I get paid tomorrow bec—"

"How much is baby Panadol?"

"Huh?"

"Five bucks, something like that?"

"I…ah, I think so?"

I take out a tenner and hand it to her.

She looks at it like I've just presented her with a mystical sword plucked from a lake. "I…I couldn't!"

"It's just a few dollars. Don't worry about it."

She takes the note and effuses, "Oh, God. You've—thank you so much. It's so nice to know some people are, you know, good! You must give me your bank details, let me send it back to you."

"It's fine. Forget about it."

She wipes tears from her eyes. "Well, thank you. I should—" The sentence collapses in her mouth as she stares spellbound at the note in her hand. I follow her gaze and realise it's speckled with blood. Her eyes widen and she turns to me, mouth gaping. I mentally scroll through a list of possible reassuring explanations (it isn't long). By the time I've selected the wildly implausible "my nephew was playing with red marker," she's plucked a pacifier from her pocket and popped it in her baby's mouth, rendering her immediately silent. She squeezes my arm admiringly and scans me from head to foot. "It's you…"

"I'm sorry, I don't think we've met."

Her face, lit by the sterile glow of the halogen lights, is waxy and tired, but her eyes now exude an unbounded enthusiasm. "Oh, yes we have." Her voice is low and breathy. "I only get out once a week, when my husband, ah, ex-husband.

Soon-to-be-ex-husband—we haven't signed the paperwork yet, but you know what I mean—takes care of Clara. So I have to make the most of that one evening of freedom..." she leans in close, her lips almost brushing against my ear as she whispers, "...and I always, always go to the Orrery. Normally, I'm more of a Level 2 girl, if you know what I mean, but I've also spent a few nights on Level 6. The other night, when I saw you, was my first time on 7. And I was. Not. Disappointed." She punctuates each word by walking her fingers up my chest, then runs her hand along my cheek.

"I'm afraid you have me mistaken for someone else."

"Don't be so coy!" she whispers conspiratorially as she reaches into the deep pockets of her dressing gown and produces a purse. She opens it and reveals a fat wad of bills. She catches my reaction and winks at me. "Apologies. Just a little scam I like to pull now and then. Girl's gotta get her kicks somehow, right?" She takes out a business card and hands it to me, along with the blood-besmirched note. "Call me sometime; maybe we can visit Level 2 together," she purrs. "And I know what you're thinking, new mum and all that. But I can promise you everything downstairs is in perfect shape. Just like all. Of. This." She waves her finger up and down my torso.

"I'm very flattered, but I'm quite sure you've confused me with—"

"Heard you call out after that girl, what was her name; Susie, Sophia? I bet I can make you forget all about her. Or, you know, become her for a little while. If that's what you'd prefer."

I sigh with resignation. "Sure. I'll think about it."

"Good. I know I'll be thinking about it. Over and over and over." She dashes out the exit, conspicuously bereft of baby Panadol.

Her card reads:

Carol Whitestone
Editor
Good Parenting Guide

You are a complex woman, Carol Whitestone. I pocket the card and finish collecting the items from my grocery list. I'm about to head to the counter when the lyrics of the song playing from the tinny, rattling speakers in the ceiling capture my ear. Over hypnagogic loops of synths and swirling guitars the androgynous voice half-whispers, half-sings:
The form of the formless
The body of the bodiless
The face of the invisible
The word of the unutterable
The clerk greets me with tired eyes and starts scanning items. "Hey there, how are you?"
"Good thanks."
I can almost feel the relief radiating off her when she realises I'm not going to launch into a lengthy monologue about feline health issues. "Do you have a customer rewards account it's so bright it's so bright it's sobrightthepleroma…"
"I'm sorry I don't quite understand what—"
Her eyes roll back into her head and she slumps forward, her head glancing against the counter as she collapses. I run around the other side of the counter, a red wound has opened in her forehead, and she's in the throes of a full-blown seizure. I take out my phone and log the time to record the seizure's duration, then start to dial 911 before realising my error and changing the

call to 000. The operator picks up, and I attempt to explain the situation over the droning music in my head and the clerk's flailing limbs in front of me.

The store is callously empty, leaving me unaided. Where is Carol Whitestone when you need her? The clerk stills and falls into silence, her head resting in a halo of blood. The operator asks me to find something to stop the bleeding. I run over to aisle ten and hurl lozenges and sunscreen and Q-tips to the ground until I locate the bandages, right next to the baby Panadol. I run back to the clerk, tearing the packaging open. The operator's soothing voice on the speakerphone talks me through checking the clerk's airway and pulse, both of which appear regular, and then gently lifting her head to wrap the bandage.

She starts to murmur, "Pleroma pleroma pleroma…"

Hearing the clerk's voice over the speaker the operator says, "Dizziness and disorientation are common before and after a grand mal seizure. It's good that she's talking. You're doing great. Paramedics are two minutes away."

"Thank you for your help," the voice coming out of my mouth is my natural Chicago accent. Now that I've let it slip a couple of times, it seems to be creeping out more and more. I wonder if I've been talking like this the entire time.

"No problem. It's my job."

"How many lives do you think you've saved tonight?"

"…"

"I'm sorry, that was a strange question. I'm feeling a little—"

"It's fine. I understand. You're probably flooded with adrenaline. You're doing a great job. It always makes our work easier when we have someone on the scene who's willing to help. Paramedics are a few blocks away. Stay on the line just a little longer."

"Do you think it's possible to atone for a heinous transgression with acts of kindness?"

"Ah, I'm not really in a position to give professional life advice..."

"I'm asking you as a human being. Is it possible to even a karmic ledger, or should guilt and suffering be the eternal burden of someone who's performed an egregious act?"

"I'm sorry, I really don't think I can answer that. Paramedics are right around the corner."

"Please. I don't want to just sit here in silence, worrying what might happen to her."

"..."

"Please?"

"..."

"If I have to listen to the sound of nothing but her murmuring incoherent nonsense any longer I swear I'll go insane."

The operator's sigh crackles through the speaker. "In junior high I was friends with this girl, Lisa. She was a little overweight. Not fat, just not thin. We'd all tease her about her 'love handles,' hint that maybe she should pretend to have her period so she could avoid the 'embarrassment' of being seen in togs at the swimming carnival.

"I don't know why I did it. It didn't make me feel good. It wasn't like it was funny. Over time she started dropping weight, and we kind of all just forgot to mention it. She got thinner and thinner, until she looked like a marionette. One day, she stopped showing up to school. Wouldn't answer her messages. No one knew where she'd gone. Two weeks later our homeroom teacher told us that she'd been committed to a health clinic with chronic anorexia. She moved to a new school, never contacted any of us again. It wasn't until years later I heard she passed away senior year."

"Is that why you do this work now, to atone?"

She says nothing for a while. Both of us are still and silent, me in the halogen glow of the supermarket, her in an office I imagine populated with headset-clad operators issuing commands and reassurances. A siren screams into the parking lot. Doors open and close. Her voice resumes its confident, professional tone as she says, "Paramedics are arriving now. They'll take care of her. Good night, Anthony." She hangs up.

She used my real name.

My real, actual, haven't-told-it-to-anyone-since-Cuba name. She must've asked me to introduce myself at the start of the call. I'd almost forgotten what my real name was underneath all the layers of deceit I've built on top of it.

Are emergency calls recorded in Australia, are they publicly accessible? What if someone—

"Sir, step aside please." The paramedics move me gently out of the way and load the clerk onto a medical stretcher. I walk out to the parking lot, ignoring the voices trailing after me. The cool evening air brushes against the thick beads of perspiration on my skin. I don the my helmet and start the bike.

I'm halfway home when I realise I've forgotten my groceries.

15

Nisha knocks on the door just after eight p.m. My apartment is thick with the smell of sandalwood candles, which I'm hoping will drown out the lingering aroma of bleach and the residual *eau de cadavér* in the bathroom. I open the door and find her dressed in a resplendent red and orange sari. She greets me with a kiss on the cheek and pushes a bottle of wine into my hand. Dante follows her into the apartment, covering my face in a flurry of licks before choosing a spot next to the couch to turn in a circle and then yawn and sit. "I realise I might be somewhat overdressed, but this is my first dinner invitation in my new city. Jaipur reminded how much I missed seeing people in Indian clothing."

"The colour is magnificent," I open the wine, pour us each a glass.

She studies the tumbler I give her with suspicion.

"Sorry, I don't have any wineglasses. This is actually the first time I've drunk wine in years."

"Is it as good as you remember?"

I swirl the wine in the glass, sip. "Oh, *God*. Better. So much better."

"I hope you don't mind me bringing Dante; I thought you might appreciate the opportunity to see him."

"I do. How is he holding up?"

"He is somewhat slower than usual, but he is recuperating." She takes a seat on the couch and strokes him gently. "You don't have a single screen in here. What do you do with all those hours when you aren't tearing around on that motorcycle of yours?"

I lift the hinged surface of the coffee table open wide enough for her to see the puzzle underneath, close it again.

Nisha laughs. "I should have known."

"I realise it's not the most fashionable pastime, but I find it meditative, creating order from chaos."

Nisha crosses her legs and her sari lifts up an inch or so, revealing a bright flash of intricately sculpted metal. She catches my gaze but doesn't comment. I sit down in the armchair opposite. "I am very intrigued to find out what a drug courier cooks for his neighbour and new best friend."

"I told you, it's not just drugs. In fact, I was recently tasked with delivering some cutting-edge medical equipment."

"'Tasked with'?"

"I didn't actually complete the delivery."

"What stopped you?"

"Death."

Her glass pauses halfway to her mouth.

"It was just a fleeting case. Didn't take."

"Ah. Does this have anything to do with the debt you owe Saklas?"

"…"

"I see. Well, I am glad you did not die, during the delivery or at the Orrery. If you could continue to avoid death, I would be most appreciative. I have no other friends in this city. I am quite fortunate to have you as my neighbour. The last man I lived next to used to watch pornography at stadium rock volumes."

"Disgusting. I always use headphones."

"You see? Chivalry is not dead."

She takes another sip of wine. "Are you going to ask me about my leg?"

"That's quite a non sequitur."

"That's quite a nonanswer."

"I was a little surprised. You never mentioned it."

Her face contorts, freezes, breaks into a laugh. "'Mention it'? I was not aware that people are expected to list their various ailments and oddities as introductory banter. I also have a deep fear of commitment and mild claustrophobia, if any of that is directly important to you."

"And a salt allergy."

"Also that, hopefully that did not cause too much trouble with the cooking?"

"About that…"

"Did a 'fleeting case' of death get in your way?"

"Not quite. The clerk at the grocery store had an epileptic fit. I had to call an ambulance, and then I completely forgot about the groceries."

"Was she alright?"

"Yes. I think so."

She shakes her head in disbelief. "She was lucky you were there."

"Maybe."

She peers at me like she's examining a crooked painting in need of adjustment. "Aaaaand there it is again."

"There what is again?"

"Your whole 'I bring misery upon all who dare to cross my path' attitude. As though the fates have turned all their attention to bringing misfortune to anyone around you." I say nothing, and she sits back, again revealing the glint of her ankle. She notices my gaze again and taps at the metal leg. The intricate latticework pattern looks like it would be at home on a yoga instructor's back tattoo. "I had this made for me by a designer in Melbourne. I love this patterning, it's so elegant, futuristic but classic all at once. She is a master."

"It is beautiful." I make a few runs to the kitchen and arrange everything on the table, thinking how odd it is to see it set for two. I pull out a chair for Nisha and she laughs and says, "I think I finally have it figured out; no TV, no internet, nineteenth-century manners, your anachronistic name. You're a time traveller, aren't you?"

I hold up my hands in surrender, "Madam, I confess you have unmasked me. But I implore you, tell no one else, for if the duchess discovers I have been remiss in my temporal-adjustment duties she will be *most* upset."

"You are quite good at that, the accents. Were you an actor in your previous life?"

"In a manner of speaking." Cover stories populate my mind's eye, but when she fixes me with that measured gaze they fall away and the only thing that tumbles from my mouth is the truth, atrophic from lack of use. "My parents owned a small hotel in London—"

She narrows her eyes at me.

"Sorry, Chicago. Force of habit. We had a reasonably happy existence. Then one day, I think I was around five, a woman shows up dragging a boy a few years older than me, demanding to see someone named 'James Penderghast.' Mom told her she had no idea who that was, but then Dad came back from the storeroom and dropped the box of glasses he was carrying."

Nisha crunches a spring roll, swallows. "Secret lover?"

"Former wife. He'd been living in Arizona, racked up a ton of debt, then just picked up and left town. Changed his name, started a new family. He and Mom split up not too long after that. He moved on to Philadelphia. Then Florida. Eventually he just stopped sending postcards and child-support payments. Last I heard he was in St. Louis, caught up in some pyramid scheme and starting his third family."

Nisha drains her glass. "I am sorry. No one can damage you quite like family."

"Exactly. But I remember, even as a kid, even through the haze of confusion and betrayal, the thought of being intrigued at the fact that you can just choose to become someone else. Choosing a new name, a new identity? It seemed like something a superhero would do."

"I am fairly certain Superman did not invent Clark Kent to escape gambling debts and alimony payments back on Krypton."

"No. There certainly wasn't anything heroic about it." I refill my glass. When I told you this story, you talked of revenge, violence, retribution. Nisha displays only a reserved and contemplative calm. "Mom and I lived at the hotel, and once I was old enough I started working at the desk. We had this one regular guest, Adrian Tempest, who always fascinated me. He'd hang out with a cup of coffee in the morning, wine in the afternoon, whisky in the evening. Usually he'd write notes in a little leather-bound book, or make phone calls, but sometimes he would simply sit in the corner and watch people coming and going.

"Occasionally, he'd invite me to sit with him. He had these incredible stories of all the places he'd travelled: Kenya, Australia, Afghanistan. Places that seemed impossibly exotic to a teenager who'd never left Chicago. He said he worked as a consultant in corporate restructuring, and his work had taken him all over the globe. Working with so many different cultures and languages, he needed to be able to read people and interact with them in a way that would optimally benefit negotiations. He talked about analysing body language, inflection, personality. There was a sort of artistry to it, he called it 'interpersonal alchemy.'

"He taught me how to look for what gamblers call 'tells,' to study the way someone touches their face or brushes their hair away. I started using these little tips and tricks with guests, and the effect was immediate, almost magical. They'd tip better and leave glowing reviews. It felt like a subtle form of hypnosis."

"People are disappointingly easy to manipulate," Nisha sighs.

"That's what I discovered. He became a mentor of sorts. He'd watch each of my interactions, and give me notes and tips afterwards. It felt like mastering a new language. When Mr. Tempest was away, he'd send me postcards from Tokyo, Nairobi, Havana, Sydney—"

Nisha swallows and says, "Did you say Havana? He was consulting on corporate restructuring in...Cuba?"

"Yes. That should've been a red flag. But I was a teenager; it didn't quite click at the time. Mr. Tempest told me about how he was preparing for retirement in Sydney. He was going to buy a beachfront property in Bondi, learn to surf, sip coffee by the beach. He said Sydney was the perfect mix of skyscrapers, sun, and sand."

Nisha scoffs. "He forgot to mention all the charming traffic, homelessness, and systemic racism."

"He was looking through rose-colored glasses, no question. But in any case, I didn't hear from him for a few years. I figured he was kicking back, enjoying his retirement. My plans to go to college got derailed when the hotel hit a slump. I had to work there full-time to keep us afloat. Eventually I more or less resigned myself to the fact that I'd never do anything else with my life. Then one day a letter turns up for me from 'the estate of Hans Geldenstaff.' I was sure I'd never met him, and yet he's included me in his will. Then I notice that there's something else in the envelope, a postcard from Havana. All it says is: 'Thank you.' Signed by—"

"Let me guess, Tempest."

"Got it in one."

"Who was he really?"

"Some sort of white-collar criminal, I'm guessing. Ponzi schemes, drug distribution, corporate con man. Something high up on the food chain. The fact that I never found out, and he died a very rich man indicates he was good at his job."

"How much did he leave you?"

"Enough."

"Enough for what?"

"Enough for me to decide to take a few years to travel before coming back, doing my degree, and then settling into a quiet life running the family business. My first stop was Cancún—"

Nisha groans. "Typical American."

"—so that I could board a charter boat to Havana. It was still tricky for Americans to travel there at the time. I wanted to put some of my interpersonal alchemy to the test. I paid my first bribes, sorted out a fake passport. It was a rush."

Nisha moans with borderline erotic enthusiasm. "Nothing quite like the first time, is there?"

"It was thrilling, and so was Havana. The whole city hummed with life and music."

Nisha snorts. "This is where you met Sophia?"

I nod.

"And she really was a singer, like in Sam's story?"

Another nod.

Nisha slurps at her noodles, leans back and stabs in my direction with her chopsticks. "Tell me about her."

"When we met she was wearing this incredible red—"

She shakes her head. "That is not what I asked. I do not want to hear about what she was wearing, about where you met. I want to hear about *her*."

You always told me I knew you better than anyone else, but Nisha's demand throws me. I've spent so long in the corridors of my memory, chasing your ghost, I've forgotten how to describe the person you actually were.

"She was…mercurial."

Nisha's lips curl into a smile. "Is that a polite way of saying she was prone to fits of rage and delirium?"

"I suppose so. She was a singer, though; being tempestuous goes with the territory."

I stand up and open the kitchen drawer. Close it again. Open it once more. Close it. Nisha looks at me quizzically, but it's not too late to pretend I was simply searching for some miscellaneous kitchen implement.

She gets up, opens the drawer, takes out your photo. "She is devastatingly beautiful. Not my type, personally, but without question a face that would launch a thousand ships. And then sink them." She hands the photo back to me. "Why is it in your kitchen drawer?"

I return it to its resting place, and we sit back down. "I wish I knew. Someone dropped it off in an envelope not long ago. I don't know who it was, or how they found me."

"Curious," Nisha runs her finger around the rim of the wineglass. "Had you been in love before?"

"Not before. And not since."

Her mouth drops open. "That is a long time to be alone. Everyone deserves—"

"Not everyone."

She rolls her eyes, "You really need to stop with the self-flagellation."

"You wouldn't say that if you knew what I'd done. How it ended."

Nisha replenishes our glasses, "I just tipped the scales of an election in Guatemala. I am not in a position to be making any kind of moral judgements."

"You don't feel guilty?"

"No, because this is the playing field now. It is no different from being paid to put up posters or give airtime on a radio show. Also, none of this is real in any case."

"You mentioned that once before. I don't quite understand."

"All of this," she waves her hand in a circle, "is a simulation."

"You're talking about Simulation Theory? Wasn't that disproven recently?"

She draws herself up straight and begins to speak in a manner that suggests she's given this speech before. "There has been some preliminary experimentation which suggests that a full-scale simulation would not be possible within the parameters of the physical laws of this universe. However, this just means that the administrators have a different playing field and more advanced tools than the players, like with any video game."

I take in the parts I can understand. Years serving behind the hotel bar taught me that the more ridiculous the philosophy being expounded is, the more passionately the believer will defend it. Zealots tend to tip well if you nod politely.

"I can see you are sceptical, which is fine. I do not expect everyone to agree with me, just people who've done the work."

"The work as in homework?"

"No. You mentioned 'interpersonal alchemy' before. In the actual mystical process of alchemy, 'the work' was the term for the techniques you would employ to transmute metal and create eternal life. The instructions were always written in esoteric language. The idea was that it should not be easy to understand because dedication to the craft was proof that you were worthy."

"You're suggested that understanding the simulation is modern-day alchemical enlightenment?"

"I am saying that each era translates the concept of transcendence into language appropriate to its cultural context."

My head stings with the blinding ethereal light I close my eyes cover my face with my hands try and block it out but it's inside of me and outside of me and part of me and all of me and—

"—you alright?" Nisha's hand on my shoulder snaps me back to reality.

"Yeah. S'all good. Just…a little migraine." I squeeze my eyes closed and open them again, steady myself, then walk slowly back to the table. "So, if Christ was around today, he wouldn't rise from the dead, he'd respawn?"

"If Christ is your cup of tea, perhaps you could phrase it that way. But here, let me help you with that migraine. Look at this." She taps her phone, passes it to me. The screen is filled with pink.

"What am I supposed to be seeing?"

"Baker-Miller Pink, it makes people temporarily calmer and weaker. A chromatic hack."

"That's ridiculous." I say, although I have to admit my headache is gone. I pass the phone back to her.

"Ever heard of the Konami code?"

"Take a wild guess."

"The Konami code was a cheat code that the video game developer built into many of their games, a sequence of buttons that would grant various powers and abilities. Chromatic hacks are visual cheat codes. Like some types of drug use and transcendental meditation, they allow the user to elevate themselves beyond the normal parameters of reality." She laughs, drains the rest of her wine. "I apologise. I hijacked the conversation. What happened next with Sophia?"

"We were happy, for a while. She'd been in a car accident when she was younger; it gave her this long, straight scar that ran along her belly. She told me that her early brush with death had given her an unrelenting desire to drink deep from the cup of life. She took me to restaurants that were basically a couple of tables set up in people's living rooms and jazz clubs at the top of abandoned shopping malls.

"Unfortunately, my tourist visa was all too temporary. Sophia took me to a guy who helped me bribe the right people to keep extending it; he said it would be a lot easier if we lived together."

Nisha's eyebrow ascends her forehead.

"She'd only just broken up with someone else, a low-level drug dealer named Carlos. There may have been some…overlap."

"I am so shocked I am nearly falling out of my seat." She deadpans.

"They had to gradually divide up their possessions. It dragged on and on. Then on her birthday, he showed up. She said they had all the same friends; it would be strange not to invite him."

"You must have been thrilled by her magnanimity."

"It gets worse. She loaned him money, which made me furious because she only contributed her half of the rent every few lunar cycles. There were other signs. She'd have these wild mood swings—"

"Typical bloody sheila, amirite?"

"Your Australian accent is *terrible*, Nisha. Anyway, I'd occasionally find men's clothes in our apartment, and she'd tell me it was his stuff that somehow got mixed up in hers when she moved out. Obviously, I feel like an idiot saying this out loud now. Every time I suggested that there might be something going on we'd have a huge argument, so I stopped bringing it up. Hoped that the problem would just go away."

"A famously effective method of problem-solving."

"Indeed." I finish another glass. The edges of everything are beginning to feel soft and malleable. Drinking is the laziest reality "cheat code" around. "This dragged on for a few more months. Then one night we both got deliriously drunk, and we had a slurred conversation about the big questions: should she move back to Chicago with me, get married, have kids…"

"All of the standard discussions you have when you've been dating someone for six months."

"Don't even start. So we're talking about the future, we're in love, we're drunk, the city is alive with music, and everything is perfect. She goes to the bathroom, and her phone pings with a message. I looked at the preview on the screen."

"Why do people leave that function on? You might as well connect your phone to a projector. I have an extensive diatribe about how everyone should use Signal, an encrypted open-source messaging app, but I will save it for another time. I presume you saw something less than pleasing?"

"Yes." I can't bring myself to go into detail.

"She broke your heart."

"And the window. With a chair. We went out onto the balcony, yelling at each other. She smashed a wine bottle into the wall, and the glass fractured. A piece of it cut into my skin, gave me this." I point to the blank space on my chin where my stubble refuses to grow. "Then she showered me with a barrage of apologies, tells me she loves me, all the stuff I've heard a hundred times before. I pushed her away from me. She climbed onto the balcony railing and said she'd jump if I didn't forgive her. It wasn't the first time she'd done this. She used it as a way to win arguments. One time she climbed up there because we couldn't agree on a fucking movie to watch. I looked up at her and said…"

Don't tell her.

If you tell her, then it's real.

"…'you can't even commit to love. I doubt you can commit to death.' She looked at me with those deep brown eyes, then closed them, crossed her arms beatifically across her chest and began to tip her body backwards. I lunged out to grab her, but I only managed to brush her flailing hair with my fingers. She landed spread-eagled on the top of a van below, like some kind of macabre art piece. Someone was already calling an ambulance on the street below. If they could've seen her from my vantage point, they wouldn't have bothered."

Nisha takes my hand in hers. Says nothing.

"I looked over to my right, and our neighbour was staring at me, eyes wide with horror. I could see the thought forming in his head, I knew what this would look like to the authorities. I was there on a fake passport, funded by money from a suspicious source, and I had just found out about her other lover. A jury would have to be crazy not to convict me. I grabbed my bag, threw in a couple of changes of clothes, my wallet, and passports and ran out to the street to hail a cab. I was halfway to the airport before I realised I had blood on my shirt."

Nisha squeezes my hand in hers. "I can sense you are waiting for a condemnation. I should inform you that none will be forthcoming. It was not your fault."

"I should've stayed."

"And gone to prison, would that have brought her back? I can see you have written quite a script for yourself as the condemned man. But you cannot save someone who is intent on destroying themselves." She releases my hand. "Tell me, where did you go?"

"Singapore first; it was the next available flight. I walked out of the airport, got on a bus. Fell into a sort of fugue state. Somehow made my way through Malaysia. Particularly the bars. Woke up in Thailand at some point, drank putrid alcoholic concoctions from buckets. Fell asleep on a train, woke up in Vietnam. I can confirm they also have bars. At some point I ended up in Kolkata, briefly entertained the idea that I could do some charity work to balance my karmic ledger. It did not go as planned. I'd kept the postcard Mr. Tempest had given me with my passport. One night in yet another bar, I pulled it out, looked at it, then went back to the hotel, got my stuff, and headed to the airport. It made a strange kind of sense, ending up here in a stolen country that idolises tin-can-wearing fugitives."

Nisha tips the wine bottle towards her glass, frowns when only a few meagre drops spill into it. Drinks them anyway. "Tell me something; the other night—at the Orrery—you saw her?"

"Yes."

"But she is dead."

"Yes." I consider whether or not to say "I still talk to her. In my head. Even though I know she's gone." I didn't mean to say that out loud. "I didn't mean to say that out loud."

"I understand. I have been doing the same thing, with my father."

"Oh, God, Nisha. I've been sitting here talking about this tragedy that happened all these years ago, and you've only just lost—"

She waves her hand. "I am not ready yet. I need to give the grief time to distill before I pour it into glasses to share. But tell me this, if she is dead, then who did you see the other night?"

"The logical solution is that I'm going mad."

"Or..."

"Or what?"

"There are the obvious explanations; ghost, revenant, zombie, evil twin..."

"I think you and I have different definitions of 'obvious.'"

"Perhaps she—" Nisha is interrupted by the sound of something shattering upstairs, followed by Reese unleashing a tirade of viral abuse. Dante jumps up and barks at the ceiling. "We should call the police. He sounds violent."

She catches my expression when she mentions the word 'police.' "Alternatively, we could contact one of your friends from the motorcycle club?"

"We shouldn't meddle."

Something thuds against the floor. Emily unleashes a stream of profanity. Nisha fixes me with a commanding gaze. "You either need to let me call the cops, or figure out something on your own. I cannot tell you how many times I wished someone would have 'meddled' in my childhood."

I look at Nisha. Dante. The ceiling. Emily screams. There is another thud.

And then silence.

16

It takes a few minutes of knocking and threatening to call the police, but eventually Reese opens the door. He's dressed in silk pyjamas. Their apartment is immaculate, no sign of the destruction I heard moments earlier. I assume that somewhere behind the African redwood entertainment unit or underneath the tufted mirror sofa that looks like it's been stolen from the Sun Palace, I'll find shards of glass and china, maybe a few drops of blood.

The wall is adorned with framed prints of cliched cursive non-art: *Shoot for the Moon—If You Miss You'll Reach The Stars!* and *Be Yourself, Everyone Else Is Already Taken!* A picture of Reese and Emily hangs on the wall; they are pearly-toothed, rosy-cheeked, and airbrushed to perfection. They look like humans created by a corporation as display models to sell our species to potential intergalactic investors.

"Heyyyyy, pal. Sorry about the noise. I lost my keys, such a dingus. We got a little carried away looking for them. Might've knocked a couple of things over, and then let a few curse words fly. Emily found them though, bless her. They were right there in my jacket pocket the whole time!" He guffaws and slaps me on the shoulder.

It takes every ounce of will not to grab his hand and slam it in the door. Instead I slip inside, close and bolt the door behind me. Before he can protest, I pin him against the wall and raise my left forearm to his throat, applying enough pressure to lightly choke him as I call out to Emily. "Emily, are you alright?"

Silence.

"Emily?"

The bedroom door cracks open and she peeks her head out, "Sam, is that you?"

It's not until she says this that I remember that's the persona I should be using. I slip Sam's voice into my throat and reply, "Hey, gorgeous. Would you be a doll and come out here for just one teeny tiny mo?"

"Oh, I can't, I'm in a nightie. But it's like Reese said, we were just looking for his keys. Silly old Reese had them in his pants pocket the whole time!"

I snap my eyes back to Reese, increase the pressure on his windpipe. "Be a gem and slip into a dressing gown or something so we can have a quick chat, would you?"

She shuffles around for a minute and then steps out into the hallway, hands in her dressing gown pockets. She looks fine, if a little tired. "Sam, I know you mean well, but it's late. Reese and I have work in the morning."

"Could I get a quick look at those hands, Em?"

She shakes her head.

"I know you're scared. I promise I'm just trying to help. I'll let Reese go, okay?" I pull back slowly and turn to face her. Reese snarls and throws his arms around my neck. I grab onto them and fling him over my shoulders onto his back, then plant my boot on his throat.

"Stop! I'm fine, see?" She raises her left hand, throws me a wave and a scared little giggle.

"Other hand, Em."

She shakes her head. Her terrified eyes dart down to Reese, back to me.

"He's not going to hurt you. I won't let him."

She hesitates, then removes a trembling mess of blood and broken skin. Red drops paint the ground at her feet. Tiny shards of glass embedded in her skin glint in the light.

"It's going to be alright. I want you to go down to my apartment, downstairs. My friend Nisha is going to look after you. Tell her my first aid kit is in the bathroom cupboard, underneath the sink. Got that?"

Emily places her hand gingerly back in her pocket, making it bloom with red. She edges past us and exits the apartment.

I look down at Reese. "We are going to talk. You are not going to scream. You are going to sit calmly on the couch. Clear?"

He nods with as much mobility as he can muster with a boot on his neck.

I let him go, and he does as instructed. "By the time Emily comes back, I want you gone. Grab whatever you can pack in the next fifteen minutes, shove it into the physical manifestation of a swollen ego you drive around, and leave town. If I see you again, I will kill you. Understood?"

He makes a series of painful whimpering noises. "Please.

I'll stop, I promise. But don't make me leave. I'm nothing without her."

"In that case? As of now, you are nothing."

"I love her, I do! I just let my temper get the better of me sometimes!"

"If you loved her, you wouldn't hurt her."

"No no no, I lose control. I'm a good person, really! I give to charity and I'm sponsoring a kid in Africa; Masika. There's a photo of her there on the fridge."

I land a right hook dead in his nose. Twin streams of blood gush from his nostrils. His moral justifications are loathsome, irrational, and—worst of all—familiar.

"Please, Sam. What about my mother? She's got no one else. If I don't look after her..."

I'd forgotten about her (like the rest of the world). Looks like this time I've managed to ruin the life of someone I haven't even met.

Reese senses me wavering and kicks into real estate agent negotiation mode, trying to crowbar the opening into an escape route. "I could pay you? Think of it as reparations for what I've done and *definitely* won't do again. Or I could donate to a women's charity or something? There's got to be a way to fix—"

"Emily will be back here in fifteen minutes. Be gone when that happens."

I slam the door behind me and run downstairs to my apartment to find Nisha removing shards of glass from Emily's hand. They both look up as I enter, and Nisha says, "It's bad, but I can take care of it. I'll get the shards out and clean and dress the wound. Also, you have a militia's worth of painkillers. So that will help."

Emily winces as Nisha removes another shard, drops it with a *ting* into her empty wineglass. "Emily, Reese is leaving. You won't have to worry about him anymore."

She gasps and grips me with her undamaged hand. "No, please. He loves me! He'll stop, I know he will. It's only when I do something wrong and he gets mad—"

Nisha clamps Emily's face between her palms, draws her close enough that their noses are almost touching. "Listen to me, you pathetic, snivelling little *wretch*. If you go back to him? He will kill you. It may be next week, or next month, or five years from now, but it will happen. And *when* it happens I will find your grave and carve curses into your tombstone."

"Nisha! She's—"

"I know you think he loves you. But someone can tell you they love you and still find it in their heart to bring you to the brink of death. They can beat you and tell you it is love, hide you from the world and tell you it is compassion, control your every movement and tell you it is kindness. And worst of all? They will believe emphatically that this is true. This is an illness for which there is no remedy, only amputation. You cut him from your life, or you die."

Emily breaks into tears, and Nisha pulls her close to her chest, rocks her back and forth. There is no trace of empathy, just steely determination. Footsteps tramp on the stairs outside. A garage door opens. Reese's car starts up, backs out. Emily peers up, looks like she's about to say something. Nisha places her hand on Emily's mouth. Reese's car disappears into the night and Emily buries her head in Nisha's shoulder, sobbing.

Nisha looks up at me, her eyes lit with grim satisfaction.

⚥

After Emily leaves, we sit in silence for a while. Dante sits between us, luxuriating in the attention of two pairs of eyes, two sets of hands. "Nisha, I have to say, you scared me a little back there."

She scoffs. "Really? You, the man I recently watched pummel a bikie thug into a bloody mess?"

"What you said to her. You were speaking from experience, weren't you?"

Nisha lowers her nose to look at Dante. "Our friend is so cute when he's asking stupid questions, isn't he?" The sound of possums brawling outside interrupts us. She frowns. "Only in Australia could adorable marsupials sound like warring demon samurai."

"The first time I heard that noise I thought a cat had been caught in an in-sink-erator."

She laughs and then catches herself, "That is awful. My father would never forgive me for laughing about animal violence, he adored cats." She looks up at me. "You did the right thing."

"I'm not so sure about that."

"Good. Doubt is a sign of a functioning moral compass. A Venn diagram of those who are always sure they are doing the right thing and history's most violent dictators would be a perfect circle."

"Also, I have a problem."

"Only one?"

"One to add to the pile. Even if Reese is smart enough to never come back, he's going to call the police and spin them a story. He's a wealthy, respectable member of society. They're going to believe him, at least enough to bring me in for questioning. If Saklas finds out I've been talking to the police, there's a good chance he'll think I'm snitching. To be honest, it's an option I've seriously considered. This place is burned. I can't stay here. But I also can't move out, Saklas has set this apartment up as an operational location. If I abandon it he'll come after me for that, too."

Nisha beams at me.

"That is not exactly the reaction I was expecting."

"Come and stay with me."

"What?"

"Just until the situation calms down. That way you can keep your eye on the not-drugs and not-weapons and blood and urine and whatever else you're storing here, but if the police bust in your door they will find the place unoccupied."

"No, that's crazy. I'll get a hotel room or something."

"I make excellent coffee. Actually, I make terrible coffee. But the conversation that accompanies it is world class."

"I don't know, Nisha. I'm not used to sharing space with people."

"You are *such* an only child!"

"Aren't you also an only child?"

"Yes, but I am one of the more pleasant ones." She says this brightly, but there's a glint of something in her eyes; fear maybe. Or desperation.

"You talked about how the ones who claim to love you hurt you the most. The person who hurt you, are they still around?"

Her eyes fall to the floor. "Not close. But I am worried that I cannot remain hidden for long."

It's a terrible idea, obviously. I haven't shared an apartment with anyone since our place in Havana, and look how that turned out. I swig the last of the wine from the bottle.

"And look, Dante misses you! He wants you to stay with us!"

Dante looks at me with imploring brown eyes. There should be a law against canine-assisted emotional blackmail.

17

I pull a backpack onto my back and throw a duffel bag over my shoulder. When I open the door I'm greeted by a regrettably familiar face. "G'day, Leachy!" Goldie's lips are peeled into a thin, toothless smile. I have to admit, I am curious to see what his actual teeth look like. Mom always used to say you could tell a lot about a person from their smile. I pointed out to her a few times that she was creating a false equivalency between quality of dental hygiene and quality of character, a sort of orally fixated phrenology. "Going somewhere?" His lips peel back to reveal twin rows of perfect pearly whites. If only Mom was here.

"Not far. Just making a little more room for Saklas to use as storage. No need to thank me, all part of the service."

"Yeah, well. Top marks. Anyway, I'm here to collect." Goldie holds out his hand.

"I'm all paid up for the next two weeks, Goldie." I think about reminding him why, but the black eye and bruises adorning his face seem like they're probably doing the job. Not a good idea to go looking for trouble right now.

"Yeah, nah. New arrangement. Interest rates have gone up. Nasdaq and Chow Jones an' all that. Price has doubled, as has frequency. Now it's fifty K per week."

"That means the price has quadrupled."

He closes the distance between us. His breath is minty and fresh, contrasting sharply with the ruined mess of his face. I guess spending a lot of time around meth heads serves as a potent reminder of the importance of flossing. "Yeah. Righto, if you want to be pedestrian about it."

The urge to tell him that he means to say "pedantic" is so overwhelming that it takes the sum total of my will to restrain myself. "Saklas knows what I make. He knows I can't afford repayments at that rate. He wouldn't increase them that much for the same reason banks don't suddenly quadruple their interest rates: it's bad business. Let me give him a call, sort this out."

Goldie draws himself up to his full height, prods me in the chest. He's doing that thing that standover men do—same technique as a frill-neck lizard or a puffer fish—trying to appear bigger than they are. Trying to make you flinch, feel intimidated. If Goldie was a book, its title would be 'Whaddya Fucken' Gonna Do About it?' written in size-fifty font in bright red letters. "You're hearing it from me, which means you're hearing it from the boss, got it?" Great. Another problem. Clearly Goldie is a sore loser in both the literal and metaphorical sense. "And if I find out you're bothering him unnecessarily, I'm going to have to take it up with that friendly neighbour of yours."

I make a quick assessment of his vulnerabilities: eyes, ears, the reliably devastating design flaw of the external scrotum, but violence isn't going to get me out of this. Or rather, it's only going to make things worse for the people around me. Nisha was wrong when she said I didn't bring damage into other people's lives.

"Goldie, there's no way I can make that kind of money. You know that."

"Yeah, well. You're always walking around like you're smarter an' better than everyone else. Design a fucken' app or something. Or take up driving for Uber."

I need to either take Goldie off the board, or convince Saklas to do it for me. But right now I need to focus on keeping Nisha safe, at least until I can get her to leave town. "Okay, fine. Obviously, I don't have that with me right now. Let me get it to you first thing in the morning."

"You got twenty-four hours." The words leap out of his mouth in a manner suggesting he's been hungry to issue the threat since this conversation started. He realises his error and pushes past me. "Gotta grab a few supplies before I go."

He's also choosing to flout our agreement about not entering my apartment. Best to let it slide. "Oi!" He calls out, emerging with a shopping bag he's taken from my kitchen filled with bags of blood. "You're one short! There's a missing half litre of A plus, and a bag of piss."

I want so badly to tell him it's A positive, not A plus, but I bite my tongue in the interests of preserving its residence inside my face. In all the chaos, I've forgotten to replace the blood and urine I had to give to Cassius. "Are you sure there wasn't some kind of clerical error?"

"Yes, I'm fucken' sure!"

"Because—I don't mean to be rude—but you don't exactly

have a perfect track record. What's more likely, one of your boys made a completely understandable mistake with the inventory, or I decided to take up vampirism?"

I watch the gears grinding inside Goldie's head. He snorts and says, "Fifty large. First thing tomorrow." He shoves the blood into his backpack and climbs onto his bike. I wait until he's well and truly gone and then knock on Nisha's door.

She opens it dressed in a food-stained hoodie. Her eyes are red-rimmed, underscored by thick black bags. "Hi. I know, I am a mess. I am in the middle of creating a white noise campaign for a politician who was accused of sexually assaulting his head of staff."

"Is he guilty?"

"How should I know? I'm not a judge." She picks up my bag and carries it inside. "But yes, he definitely is."

Nisha's apartment has an identical layout to mine, but the contents couldn't be more different. I follow her into what appears to be more of a control room than a living room. The whole apartment is bathed in the soft blue-green algae glow of monitors. They are hunkered on the desk, mounted on the wall, perched on bookshelves. There's a bizarre collection of dissonant images dancing on the screens—social media feeds, news sites, strings of code, video games, and one screen that's showing an endless three-second loop of clowns laughing and cutting off each other's limbs. One of the screens is divided into four quadrants displaying security camera feeds. From a distance it looks like she's monitoring the outside of the building and the interior of her apartment, but there's something strange about the quadrant showing the kitchen. I step closer to the digital mosaic.

Nisha taps a keyboard and the screens all fade to black. "Sorry! I know it can be visually overwhelming. I will try and remember to keep the screens off when I am not working."

"It's fine. What's a white noise campaign?"

"If a client has a story that is impossible to bury, you create a distraction instead. Get enough people talking about something unrelated and it takes the heat off them long enough for people to forget. The middle Kardashian just adopted a white band-faced lemur. Twitter is going crazy. It is ideal fodder."

"What's a Kardashian?"

Nisha laughs, slaps my chest. "You are too much."

I stare for a few beats at the slender black object adorning her bookshelf before asking, "Why do you have a katana?"

"It was a gift from a Japanese pop star. I helped clear his reputation after he was caught snorting cocaine in a confessional booth. Here, this is your room." I follow her into a small room furnished with a steel-framed single bed and several boxes of energy drink powder piled against the wall. She notices me staring at them and says, "It is cheaper to buy it in bulk. I throw some of the powder in with some SodaStream, it's cheaper, less waste, a lot less sugar."

I drop my bags onto the bed. "Right. Are you familiar with a popular local beverage called 'coffee'?"

"Coffee is the white wine spritzer of caffeinated beverages. Fine for social occasions, but for real work, it does not cut it. In any case"—she sweeps her hand expansively around the not-very-expansive space—"please think of this as your home for the next…however long you need. And do not think me rude if I seem to be ignoring you most of the time. I sometimes become distracted when I am deep into a project. My ex called it my 'trance time,' but Dante will be here to keep you company."

"Thanks for this. I appreciate it. Really." I should probably tell her I'm sorry for placing her life in danger, but I'm hoping I can just sort the situation out before that conversation becomes necessary.

She places her hand on my shoulder. "I heard your conversation with that thug outside."

Fuck. "Nisha, I am so sorry. I won't let anything happen to you, I promise."

She squeezes my shoulder and drops her hand, ducks into her bedroom. "It is kind of you to always want to play the white knight. But you know in chess? The Queen is far more agile." She reemerges, tosses me an envelope. "Fifty thousand."

"Dollars?"

"No, Baskin-Robbins coupons. Yes, dollars!"

I ease the envelope open, stare at the bills inside. "I really can't…"

"It is not a gift. It's a down payment. I need you to help me with something."

"A delivery?"

"A retrieval. Of something very valuable."

"When you say 'retrieve,' I assume you mean steal?"

She considers this. "Perhaps 'repatriate' would be a more accurate term."

A valve releases somewhere inside my psyche. A part of me is relieved to discover that she's been working me this whole time. Friendships have complex parameters, protocols that are difficult to define and harder to follow. Transactional relationships are efficient, clean, comprehensible.

"I am asking you as a friend, Anthony."

The sound of my real name acts like an incantation, dissolving the strength in my body. In mythology, a person's true name grants the speaker power over its owner. I imagine arcane tendrils of power flooding from Nisha's lips, consuming me under their influence. I slump into the rickety wicker chair next to her dining table and drop the envelope onto the floor. The room lurches and sways. My bags are sitting on the bed mere feet away. I'm already packed and it's only an hour to the airport. This time I'll have to go somewhere more remote. Tibet maybe. Or Polynesia.

Nisha sits down opposite, her eyes are fixed and unblinking. "I know who you are, Anthony Voynich. I research everyone I meet. It is something of a compulsion. You were by far one of the most challenging cases I've ever encountered, and one of the most interesting."

I stand up, head still spinning, and walk into the spare room, grab my bags.

She blocks the door and says, "Please. I was not lying, I do need your help. But I also think we can help each other. Someone has been looking for you. One of the first things I found when I ran a facial recognition search on you was a post asking for your whereabouts. I know that you want to stay hidden. I can help with that. You are great with the acting, the charm, what we call 'social engineering' in my field. But this is the twenty-first century. If you work with me? I can make sure no one ever finds you again. Please, would you sit, hear me out? The money is yours either way." She picks it up and presses it into my hands. The money is a sandbag preventing me from drifting off into a waiting storm.

I sit down.

She takes the seat opposite. "I know we have been keeping a lot of secrets from each other. But I promise you; ask me anything, and I will answer honestly." She is calm, impassive, a little scared.

"Tell me about the message."

"There was a posting on a dark web message board where I get some of my clients. Do you know what the dark web is?"

"I'm an atavist, not a fucking moron."

She opens her mouth to continue.

"But I might need a quick refresher." Great to see my pride gets in the way of everything, including information imperative to my own survival.

"The dark web is like the underground of the internet. You need a Tor browser to access it. It is a hub of illegal activity; you can buy fake identities, hire mercenaries, sell stolen and illegal goods. To be honest, if you wanted to increase your client base you really should let me put up an ad for—"

"My services aren't scaleable. Stick to the story."

"Of course. My apologies. I get most of my work from word-of-mouth referrals, but once in a while I pick up a client from a job posting. And given that I am a naturally curious person, I often end up falling down a research k-hole. I stumbled across an ad that had your picture, and your name. Your *real* name: Anthony Voynich."

I've gone from hearing my true name zero times in the last nine years to twice in the last ten minutes. It feels like she's talking about someone else. In a way, she is. Most of my cells have changed over. My bones have all been replaced. Anthony Voynich was declared officially dead years ago, and was actually dead just a couple of weeks ago. If there's anything left of the person I once was, I'm not sure I want to examine the corpse for the purposes of identification.

"Why were they looking for him?"

She raises an eyebrow.

"For me. Why were they looking for me?"

"They said you were involved in the death of a young Cuban woman, Sophia Valis."

"You already knew my story."

"I knew *their* side of your story. That is not the same thing. It said that he—you—had been declared dead in a car crash in Thailand."

"It's not just beer that's cheap in Thailand. Police are also available at bargain-basement prices. Wasn't hard to get a death certificate issued."

"That is a quite a length to go to in order to stop people looking for you."

"It wasn't about that. I just didn't want my mom to keep looking. Hope can be a slow and insidious cancer."

She leans back. "Interesting phrasing. But, yes, I think you did your mother a kindness. However, these people? They have not given up. I assume they think you killed her, which you did not."

"I drove her to death. Same thing."

"A judge would likely disagree with you."

"It's not a judge who's offering a bounty on the dark web. How much was it?"

She shakes her head. "Perhaps it is better you don't know."

"You said you'd answer me honestly."

She lowers her voice, leans in close. "Three Bitcoin."

I laugh with relief.

Nisha furrows her brow, opens her mouth. Closes it. "Ahhh...I guess you do not deal with cryptocurrency very often?"

"I don't do crypto. I prefer cash."

She looks like she's been clipped in the head by a wrecking ball. "You don't 'do' crypto, in your industry? That's rather like a volcanologist saying they prefer to avoid warm climates."

"Is three Bitcoin a lot?"

She snorts a derisive laugh. "It is a notoriously volatile currency, but as of right now..." She taps at her phone, pulls up a trading website.

It's my turn to catch a hit from the wrecking ball. "That's impossible. I assumed it was her ex, Carlos, but he wouldn't be able to scrape that kind of cash together."

"You left Cuba a long time ago, maybe his drug business has really taken off? If he has managed to make it to the top of the food chain then his means and resources could be dramatically improved."

I've been thinking of Havana as a snow globe, frozen in time. But she's right, nine years is a long time, and Carlos definitely had it in him to become a kingpin. "But if it's Carlos who's looking for me, why do I keep seeing Sophia?"

"Or *thinking* you see her? You have thus far only seen her in the dark, at a distance or in a crowd. You said police can be easily bought? The same is true of actors. This city is crawling with aspiring movie stars. Perhaps Carlos managed to find one who looked like Sophia."

No one looks like you, Sophia.

"I can see from the look in your eyes that you are sceptical. But love clouds vision as well as judgement. If you do not believe me, browse one of those celebrity lookalike agencies. You can hire a Marilyn Monroe, Tom Hanks, Morgan Freeman, whatever you like. That said, nine years is a long time to continue dreaming of revenge."

If someone else had done this to you? I would still be dreaming for ninety years. Nine hundred.

Nisha takes my hand, squeezes it. "I am sorry to cause you suffering. We have met in strange circumstances, Anthony. But then again, we are both strange people. And I have grown very fond of you."

I study her face and can't detect anything but sincerity. She's a liar, like me, but I think I know her well enough to tell when she's being honest. "Thanks. You too, Nisha. You are by far my favourite person who's ever hunted me."

"A rare and treasured compliment." She releases my hand, walks into the kitchen. "We need wine."

She rummages in the cupboards and produces a bottle of Malbec and wineglasses. Dante pads over and nestles at my feet. Nisha places a glass in front of me and says, "I am going to send you home with wineglasses so when I visit I can drink red wine in the proper manner."

"You're very confident of being invited back, given what's happened thus far."

She raises her glass. "Not confident. Optimistic."

We clink our glasses together.

I study her as she drinks, ruminating on the inherent strangeness of sharing a living space. The last person I shared a dwelling with was you. The image of your red dress flailing like a flag as you descend fills my mind. I am suddenly grateful that Nisha's apartment is on the ground floor.

"Anthony? Yes or no?"

"Sorry, I missed that."

"I said leftover pizza, yes or no?"

"Yes."

She removes the carton from the fridge, dumps it on the table next to the envelope of cash. "I fear I may have overloaded your system. Let's forget the retrieval job for now. I do not think either of us have the energy for it at present."

I shovel the cold mass of dough and cheese into my mouth. Did cold chain store pizza always taste this good, or have they started infusing it with some euphoria-inducing chemical in the years since I've last eaten it? "Suits me."

"However…"

"Strong start, Nisha, best to quit while you're batting ahead."

"Perhaps. But I think you will like this suggestion." She pauses. "We should go back to the Orrery."

"I think you left out the word 'never.'"

"I am serious!"

"…"

"I know, you did not have the best experience there last time."

I choke back a laugh.

"*But* each floor is its own kingdom, and I have been reading some very interesting things about Level 6."

"I'm focused on survival right now. I don't have time to go exploring the dangers and delights of cursed kingdoms built on burial grounds."

She bites her lip. "What if I told you I was not asking?"

I drop the pizza back into the box. "I'm impressed with how quickly you've graduated from bounty hunting to blackmail."

"Not blackmail. Just an invitation which precludes the option of refusal. After all, I could really use three Bitcoin…"

I study her face. She's not lying.

Nisha holds up her hands in defense. "I am sorry to hold this over your head. Please believe I have both of our best interests at heart. There is something I want to show you. Something which I think will help with your healing."

"Odd terminology for a blackmailer."

"Please, Anthony. I am proposing we go on this journey together. I help you out with this money, keep the wolves from your door. And then you help me with this retrieval job, for which I will pay handsomely."

"In bitcoin?"

"In whatever currency you wish. Not only that, I will offer you my services and make sure your digital identity is buried so deep that no one will ever find you again, craft you a new one that will allow you to live as an ordinary citizen here. You are still young, you can start over. Stop looking over your shoulder. Work in a job where you do not have to deal with criminals."

"Criminals like you."

"Criminals like *us*."

I chew another mouthful of pizza. Chase it with wine.

Nisha leans across the table, clasps my hand between hers. "Come back to the Orrery with me. Please."

I pull away from her, swig the last of the wine. "I'll cancel my plans and wear my prettiest frock."

We screamed at each other. You broke the window, then smashed the wine bottle against the wall. The splintered glass carved a red stripe across my chin. We flung curses and accusations and recriminations and tears cascaded from your eyes as you climbed up onto the ledge.

"Sophia, for fuck's sake. I can't do this again. We both know you're not going to jump."

"You don't know anything, let alone what I might do. I will jump! I will jump if you don't forgive me."

"You can't even commit to love, I doubt you can commit to death." As soon as the words left my mouth I wanted to grab them and shove them back down my throat, but it was too late. You climbed higher. Closed your eyes. Folded your arms across your chest. Leaned back.

And fell.

You landed with your legs twisted at a grotesque angle, forming a deep impression on the black van you plummeted into. People were screaming and running in the street. My reptilian brain took over, thinking of nothing but survival. The klaxons of my conscience blared at the back of my head as I grabbed my passport and wallet. I picked up my keys and phone by instinct and then realised I no longer had need of them, tossed them into the bin. Slammed the door behind me as I hurried out into the street.

My head hammered with guilt and shame and desperate cries of "do something do something do something!" but I reasoned that I could already hear someone on their phone, calling an ambulance, what more could I do? A bystander pointed their phone at you. I had the audacity to feel disgusted that they would film something like this, as well as the obscene sense of self-preservation to throw my arm in front of my face as I passed them.

I ran out towards Avenida 23. The timbre of the screaming shifted dramatically; cries of "Gracias a Dios!" jettisoned into the night air. I turned around and there, on top of the black van, I saw—

18

The nine-story tower of steel and glass stands before us like a sacrificial knife carving the night, spilling its innards of stars and satellites in the service of unnamable infernal forces. If I'm being honest with myself, it wasn't Nisha's threat that brought me here. It was you. If there's even a chance I'll see you here again, then I have to take it. I'll scour every storeroom, bathroom, and bedroom until I find you. Or what's left of you.

"You are thinking about her again, aren't you?" asks Nisha.

"Who?"

She throws her head back with laughter. "I thought we were past lying to each other."

That's the problem; lying comes so easily. It's hard to remember how to do anything else.

"You get a distant look in your eyes. I can see you disappear into yourself. It looks like love. Or concussion." She walks towards the entrance ahead of me. Even though her gait is uneven, she manages an arrhythmic, hypnotic elegance. We cross the carpark. The moon hangs low and heavy in the sky, like it has grown weary of its orbit and is preparing to plummet towards eternal nowhere.

"The forum has been lighting up about activity here in the last few days. There have been stories of strange lights hovering in the sky above it, anomalous and highly localised weather events—"

"Forgive me for being sceptical of reports written by people with a professed fondness for hallucinogens."

"Don't be so dismissive. The DNA double helix was discovered during an acid trip. And also from stealing from the work of an under-credited female colleague."

"Good to know the system works."

"There is more; I have read reports of people speaking in long-dead languages, indigenous Australian tongues which have been lost for over a century. Apparently some of the graffiti in the men's bathroom on Level 8 is written in an ancient protolanguage precursor to Sanskrit that no one has seen for thousands of years."

"I assume you're aware it's not generally a good idea to use bathroom graffiti to add legitimacy to an argument?"

She laughs, a bright sound that bubbles through the darkness. "Depends on the graffiti. And the bathroom."

We enter and go through the rigmarole of being searched and surrendering our phones, then walk into the elevator. Nisha scratches her neck. Fidgets. Mumbles something to herself.

"Everything alright?"

She nods irritably in a manner that indicates it most certainly is not.

"Are you su—"

"I don't like being without my phone."

"Are you waiting on an important call?"

She snaps her neck to face me, her eyes lit with irritation. Then she relaxes and leans against me and laughs. "A *call*? You are such a relic. An adorable, charming relic." She pulls back, pats my chest somewhat patronisingly, and says, "I have a minor internet addiction."

I hold her gaze. I've heard of this condition, but the concept seems so ludicrous. I've been so tirelessly working to completely disconnect and isolate myself that I find it impossible to relate to someone investing so much time into doing the opposite. I feel like an anorexic talking to a sumo wrestler. The doors ping open.

"Perhaps minor is an understatement." She eyes the elevator buttons.

"We can go, if you like?"

She shakes her head. "No. My addiction is something I need to work on. Besides, I should be fine once I get some drugs into my system."

I open my mouth to make a snide remark but she interrupts me.

"*Yes*, I know how that sounds."

We step out into the hallway, and a hostess greets us with a halogen smile. She glows with the kind of beauty that is the result of devout dedication to exercise, abstinence, and makeup so expertly applied that she appears to be somehow airbrushed in real time. Her hard-won beauty demonstrates a single-mindedness that suggests she'd be an ideal candidate for recruitment into a terrorist organisation.

She draws her manicured hands out and open in a welcoming

gesture and says, "Welcome seekers! My name is Charisma—" (of course it is) "—and it is my dis-*tinct* pleasure to welcome you to Level 6 this evening!"

This feels a lot more like an upmarket health retreat than a crack den. Behind Charisma is a long corridor of white doors and red plush carpet. We are blanketed in soft synth that is sonically proximal to music, music's stoner cousin.

"Is this your first time here?"

"It is," replies Nisha, approaching her eagerly.

Charisma illuminates with a practiced enthusiasm and claps her hands together in celebration. "Oh how *mar*-vellous! It is always an ab-*so*-lute pleasure to welcome new seekers. It is my honour to be your escort through the realms of the fantastic today!"

She hands us each binders with a design aesthetic commensurate with that of the hall. We flip them open to find a narcotic cornucopia of hallucinogens, psychotropics, tranquillisers, amphetamines, synthetics, organics, nootropics, and a dizzying list of other options that makes me want to lie down just from glancing at it.

Charisma produces a burst of charm school laughter and touches me gently on the shoulder. She smells incredible. "You have just the most ad-*or*-able face right now! I know, it can be a little overwhelming. Why don't you start by telling me what kind of experience you're searching for, and I'll guide you towards it. Sound good?"

Nisha snaps the menu closed and declares, "We are looking for some top-shelf transcendence. Something warm and transportive, with an edge of the ethereal, soft overtones of the astral plane and a light sephirothic aftertaste."

Charisma grins, impressed. "Are you *sure* this is your first time? I *looove* a girl who knows what she wants. I have *just* the thing for you! One of our chemical chefs has just developed an artisanal psychotropic blend of salvia, MDMA, LSD, and ayahuasca, with just a *hint* of cinnamon for flavour. Objective trip time is about half an hour but subjective experience can feel like anything between hours and days, depending on the neurological calibration of the user. It is a worldwide exclusive; you cannot get this anywhere else on earth! We're calling it Abraxas.'"

"Sounds perfect, sign us up," says Nisha.

"Splendid! Will you be paying in cash, crypto, services, stock, information, or organic materials?"

"Cash is fine," Nisha removes her purse from her handbag and unclips it.

"Super! So it's two thousand dollars for the two of you—"

I baulk, and Charisma looks at me like I've just coughed up blood at Christmas dinner.

"This includes our top-of-the-line proprietary bespoke psychotropic, your own private voyaging room, snacks and refreshments from our in-house chef, and a concierge who will be with you the entire time."

"Nisha, I don't know about this. I was imagining mushrooms and beanbag chairs. This seems like a lot, I really don't know if I want to spend—"

She slaps me in the chest and says, "Hush. This one is on me."

"I don't feel comfortable taking more money from you. Perhaps we should—"

She apologises to our hostess and pulls me a few feet away from her, leans in, and whispers, "I have something to confess to you."

"Great. More confessions."

"I know. I have several transgressions to atone for. Not least among them…" She drops her gaze to her feet.

"Spit it out or I'm leaving and you can do this 'retrieval' gig on your own."

"The other night, when we came here for the first time…"

"And I was forced into blood sport against a professional thug?"

"Yes." She exhales. Meets my gaze. Looks away again. "I placed a bet."

"…"

"Which I won."

"How much?"

"N-nine." The word writhes recalcitrantly out of her mouth.

"Nine hundred?"

"Nine…thousand."

My vision floods with red and for a moment I can't bear to look at her, but then my curiosity gets the better of me. "Him or me?"

"What?"

"Did you bet on Goldie, or me?"

"You. You were the long shot."

I stare at her, saying nothing.

She continues gazing at the ground and says, "We are here because I think it will genuinely help you, but it is also my way of saying sorry. I spend a lot of time in the virtual world, and sometimes I find interaction with flesh-and-blood people difficult. I make mistakes. But I do really care about you and value you. Even if I have hurt you." Her eyes meet mine. "Can you forgive me?"

What would you do in this situation, Sophia? Your forgiveness was always violently capricious. You deleted people from your life for what I thought were minor infractions (forgetting your birthday, cancelling coffee dates), and completely absolved heinous transgressions (spiking your drink as a prank, emotional blackmail). It was as though you were spinning a gameshow wheel in your head to decide whether or not someone should be granted mercy.

Nisha stares at me, her eyes lit with penitence. "Please?"

I look over her shoulder at our hostess. "We're ready. Lead the way."

19

The room is cocaine white. Two single beds sit parallel in its immediate center, surrounded by an orbit of cushions. In the corner is a small buffet table laden with pastries, juice, fruit, and something called "hydrogen-infused water," which in many ways sounds like a far stranger substance than the hallucinogen we are about to imbibe. A sleek, tablet-operated stereo system is built into the wall. Currently it is lathering the room with the same music-adjacent sounds as the foyer. The whole facility resembles a celebrity rehab joint. Charisma informs us that our concierge will be with us shortly and departs with a knowing grin.

"You had a very specific idea of what kind of experience you wanted to chase," I say to Nisha as I nibble an unreasonably delicious almond croissant.

"People put plenty of time into researching what brand of television to buy, where to go on holiday, why should narcotics be any different? One thing that a lot of people underrate is the importance of set and setting; you need the right environment and mindset to optimise your experience. In the same way that a date with a wonderful person would be soured by attending a terrible restaurant with mould-encrusted walls and obnoxious waiters, you need the right circumstances as well as the right substances for an optimal trip." Nisha lies back on her bed, takes in the room. "This place reminds me of a hotel I stayed at in Kolkata a few years ago. I had a brief holiday romance with a TV reporter. I was there in monsoon season. I used to stay out on the balcony and watch the sky transform from blue to black in minutes. You would see people on the ground below begin to run and scamper like ants and then…"

She makes a *phwoash*! sound and opens her hands and eyes wide, grinning. "The heavens would unleash a deluge. Spectacular. But also very dangerous at times."

"I wish I'd been there during monsoon season. Kolkata mostly makes me think of…" The sentence collapses under its own weight before I can complete it.

"Are you okay? You seem agitated. I know it has been a while since you've had any kind of psychedelic, but there is a concierge here to look after us. We will be—"

"That's not it."

She sits on the bed next to me, takes my hand. "What then?"

"You mentioned Kolkata. I told you that I'd stopped to do some charity work there, try and redeem myself. That wasn't the whole story."

"I did not think it was. But you don't have to tell if you don't want to."

"After I'd spent a few months trying to drink myself to death,

I decided that maybe I could even my karmic ledger. I planned to renounce joy and pleasure and devote my life to charity. Live like a godless monk. I found a room in a cheap, rat-ridden hotel. It had one tiny window that only let in the smallest slant of light. I volunteered at Mother Teresa's orphanage. The people I volunteered with were impossibly kind and charitable. They seemed to get an endorphin rush from the work, whereas I was there to earn my penance. I didn't *want* to enjoy it. They were mostly students, doctors, and teachers and scientists-in-training. They truly loved the work. It made them *glow*."

"And you?"

I glance at the door, wondering how much longer it will be before our concierge arrives. "Some of the children were congenitally blind. They kept their eyelids half-open, little slots revealing…nothing. A void. I was repelled. I know that's awful. But I felt what I felt, and I wasn't able to ever look at them without feeling a deep-seated sense of dread and unease. And then there was the sound."

"What sound?"

Scraping of tooth against tooth grinding crunching over and over the noise echoing throughout the halls repeating and restarting and cascading like some chthonic choir—

"Their teeth. They were always grinding their teeth. I don't know why but that noise affected me on a primal level. I couldn't look at them. Couldn't be near them. After about half an hour, I was in the middle of helping this kid with some kind of muscular dystrophy eat his food, and I just couldn't take that noise anymore. I said I was going to the bathroom, stood up, walked out the front door, hailed a tuk tuk and went back to my hotel. I still see those kids sometimes, hiding in shadows, around corners, sometimes when I'm asleep. And I hear that sound of scraping teeth. After Kolkata I gave up on redemption, decided to stick with the original plan."

"Flagellation."

"You really enjoy that word, don't you?"

She grins. "Normally there are precious few opportunities to use it in everyday conversation. With you it is as natural as talking about the weather."

I bury my head in my hands. "I felt so revolted with myself. To be repulsed by disabled, orphaned, impoverished children. Kids who have drawn the worst possible lot in life, whose suffering astronomically eclipsed my own. Sophia would have been disgusted."

I look up at Nisha, and she returns my gaze, saying nothing. Her eyes have a depth and intensity that is mesmerising. I study the flecks of color in the iris, tiny constellations of light against a bed of soft brown. She pulls my head onto her shoulder. We sit there like this for a few minutes. The noise in my head falls quiet. My vision blurs with tears. I open my mouth to say something just as the door springs open.

"Hello, voyagers! My name is"—the diminutive, dark-haired facilitator stops mid-introduction as she looks at us—"ah, perhaps I should...come back in a minute?"

I pull away from Nisha. "It's fine. We were just talking."

She perks back up, crossing the room pushing a small silver cart in front of her to sit on the bed opposite us. "Okay! My name is Ojal, and it's my pleasure to be your facilitator for your journey this evening!" She sweeps her hand with a game show hostess flourish across the selection of vials, pills, flasks, and powders on the tray in front of her. "A few formalities to begin;

with a drug like this, set and setting are extremely important."
She's clearly been reading the same literature as Nisha. "You
should rest assured that you are extremely safe, that myself and
our professional team are here to assist you. I'm a qualified psy-
chologist, and we have on-call access to doctors in the extremely
unlikely event of a medical emergency. They're usually kept
pretty busy on Level 7..." A momentary cloud of disdain passes
over her face. She clears her throat and continues. "Many people
who take a powerful drug like this in a more, shall we say, 'urban'
setting, find they have a negative experience that is primarily
induced by the environment. This space has been tailor-made
to induce calm and relaxation. We have cameras here, here, and
here." She points to the corners of the room. "I'll be monitoring
you from the next room over." She takes out a small tablet computer and passes it to us. "If you want the cameras and microphones turned off for a little privacy, just hit this button." She
winks at Nisha, who rolls her eyes and wiggles her finger.

"He wishes."

Ojal looks confused for a second, then continues, "Well,
that option is there if you want it. However, generally it is best
to turn off the microphones but leave the cameras on so I can
make sure you're having your optimal voyaging experience. If
you want me for any reason at all—whether it's for reassurances
or refreshments—just press this green button and I'll be right
in, quick as a flash!" She passes me the tablet, and I lay it on the
bed next to me. "Any questions, queries, qualms?" Her cheeriness is infectious, in much the same way as cholera.

"Does Sammy Saklas have any role in managing this level?"
Nisha asks.

Ojal grimaces like a Victorian matriarch who's just been

asked directions to the shitter. "Absolutely not! Each level of the Orrery is independently operated. Mr. Saklas runs Level 7, but he and his associates have no affiliation with this level or the work we do. In fact, ever since an incident a couple of years ago, they aren't even allowed to set foot here. But you didn't hear that from me." She taps her nose knowingly, then straightens up again and says, "Now for the fun part! We have a range of delivery options available. Abraxas is extremely versatile. You can take it as a liquid, in pill form, or intravenous injection."

I choose the pill, Nisha opts for the liquid. Ojal hands us each our requested forms. "You may experience some slight numbness in your extremities and a teeeeeeensy bit of an upset stomach for a few minutes after consumption. But this will quickly pass, and you should start to feel the desired effects within five to ten minutes. Ready?"

We both nod, and she clasps her hands with schoolgirlish excitement. I wonder how much of her behaviour is artifice. If she goes home, dons a sour expression, and binge-drinks scotch whilst watching horror movies. I've always found this level of jubilance exhausting to be around. I find it difficult to fathom how a human can maintain it for a prolonged period.

I take the pill and swallow it with the small paper cup of water provided. It takes like soap and rockmelon.

Nisha downs her glass and returns it to the tray.

Ojal stands and says, "Happy travels! I'll be right next door if you need me." She departs and the door slides gently closed behind her.

"I can't believe you talked me into this."

Nisha shoves my shoulder. "Oh, please, you were a pushover! You should see what I can do when I really want to manipulate someone. I once convinced the head of a far-right anti-LGBT religious group to publicly endorse a gay mayoral candidate based on his obscure interpretation of church zoning rules. He was oafish only. I mean, ah, he was *officially* erected, no! Not erected, elected… I think I might be feeling the effects already. This drug does not mess around. Please excuse me for a moment."

She runs to the bathroom, slamming the door behind her. The room is bathed in silence. My toes feel like they're being nibbled by tiny invisible fish. Sophia, do you remember the way I used to massage your feet? You always looked at me with such gratitude afterwards, like the act of gently rubbing them while we watched TV was a kindness on par with kidney donation. You would hate this decor. You'd call it sterile and lifeless and bland. You always preferred mayhem over mediocrity. I lie back on the bed and stare at the pearl-white snow-white star-white ceiling as it begins to gently undulate, the downlights shifting and swaying like lighthouses surrounded by an ocean of milk.

When I think of you, I picture the colour red. Your red dress is permanently painted on the cave walls of my memory. The red of your lips. The red of the wine in the glass held in your red-nailed fingers. And the other red of course. The red that ran and ran and ran like rivers. Rivers that ran, like I did. Between—

"I think the working are drugs," says Nisha, opening the door. She catches her error, winces and says, "I mean; I think the *working* are *drugs*." She blinks. "I said it wrong again, didn't I?"

I laugh, not knowing what else to do. The laughter fills my lungs like helium and lifts me slowly off the bed, bringing me to hover and hum about three inches above the mattress.

Nisha lies down on the bed next to me and murmurs, "Do you see the flying fish?"

I think I reply "no," but I'm not sure if the word manages to escape my mouth or just exists inside my skull.

"Actually, they are not flying so much as hovering while also existing in a quantum state of uncertain polarity. Like a piscine electron cloud?"

I answer, "only you would use the term 'quantum state of uncertain polarity' while tripping," but the words exit my mouth as matter instead of sound, turning into tiny linguistic gems that clatter onto the carpet.

Nisha stares at her hands. "Hands are really incredible, when you think about it. The things we can do with them. Little lumps of cell and skin and bone. And we can use them to give pleasure or play the piano or take a life or bake bread or build a home." She turns them back and forth, marvelling. "These opposable thumbs! They took us millions of years to evolve, and we just walk around with these incredible tools like it's nothing! But they are miracles. *Miracles!*" She lifts her hands exultantly above her head.

I'm too polite to say, but she is being very quite ridiculous. I turn a few slow somersaults in the air.

Nisha spills more words from her mouth. "Did you know that there are actually dozens of states of matter? Everyone knows about the basics, liquidsolidgasplasma, but there are sososo many more! There's disordered hyperuniformity, excitonium—I like that one because it sounds like the state of being excited—Bose Einstein condensate, time crystals. *Time Crystals!* Sounds like something from a fantasy novel! This simulation is so incredibly complex. I have to tip my hat to the architects."

I float across the room; the air feels gelatinous as I swim

through it. I place my finger on her lips and say, "ssssssssh." The sound expels from my mouth as an inky stream that fills the gelatinous air.

"Appy polly loggies. I get very philosophical when I get high. Would you prefer we just watch the fish without making word sounds?"

I still can't see the fish she's talking about but there are some very brightly coloured beetles crawling across the room that make sounds like tiny tap dancers when they walk. I start giggling. I can't remember the last time I giggled.

Nisha shakes her head and sighs, "I should have guessed. You are the sombre, brooding type when straight; it only follows that you would be the quiet, giggling type when altered."

My skin has a faint static glow, like the humidity in the air around it has become a semiconductor. Pulses of electricity shimmer in the air, electric blue charges caress my skin.

Nisha is covered in a cerulean nimbus. "Oh! We should dance!" she says, her lips sparking as she speaks. "Lessee what they have on the stereothing." She crosses the floor slowly, not so much walking as what's that word that Lewis Carroll invented, the French suitcase word? Slumping trumping…galumphing! She galumphs over to the tablet on the wall and stabs the play button with her finger. An insistent drumbeat fills the air, flourishes of guitar whorl around and behind and below it. Eyeless faces stare up at me, smiling with teeth grinding as the music shifts, doubling in speed and volume.

Nisha emits a joyous wail, her face illuminated with a manic grin, flailing in time to the ecstatic punches of trumpets and trombones. For a moment I'm so caught up in her revelry that I don't realise the song is familiar.

And then I hear her voice.

Your voice.

The sonic snare that traps me, burrowing via my ears into my brain, my skin, infusing into my molecular structure. Vibrating at a frequency that could topple golden palaces and shatter police barricades. I haven't heard your voice since Cuba (at least, not outside of my own head). My legs transmogrify into meat pudding beneath me and I collapse onto the bed, hypnotised, mesmerised, caught in the thrall of your throat. *Sophia. Sophia. Sophia. Your siren's song, luring me towards the sweet, swirling abyss.*

MI AMOR DE MIL CARAS
MI AMOR DE MIL MENTIRAS
MI AMOR QUE ES UNA COSA A LA LUZ DEL DÍA
Y OTRA ENTERAMENTE POR LA NOCHE

Sophia, your voice disembodied and transported across aeons and oceans, piercing the veils of space and time, of body and mind, cutting me like concentration camp razor wire, like the beaks of obsidian black birds who carry the name of death in each beat of their ragged wings. Sophia. Sophia. Sophia.

"Nisha?" I sit up, swallowed by sound. She's nowhere to be seen. "Nisha?"

She has vanished. Perhaps her avatar has finally escaped the confines of the simulation via a chemical variant of the Konami code. "Nisha?" Your voice fills my head. A rapturous death roll of ecstasy and anguish. "Sophia!" I call out. Your name forms a crimson cloud in the air in front of me.

"I am so sorry I'm sorry I'msorryI'msorry...." I watch my

pathetic apologies become effete grey clouds in front of my face. Your voice from the speakers is my only reply.

NO ME DISCULPES
SOLO BAÑAME CON TUS HERMOSAS MENTIRAS
NO ME PIDAS PERDÓN
SOLO MIRAGE CON TUS HERMOSOS OJOS

Viscous beads of sweat run down my face. I can't pull enough oxygen from the air to satiate my lungs. I heave frantic, manic breaths but my head still spins. I snatch up the tablet and mash the emergency assistance button. I look up at one of the cameras and wail "We need help!"

Both God and Ojal are defiantly absent. At least Ojal actually exists, she has that one up on the Almighty, I suppose. I stagger to the door, the bread pudding mush of my legs trembling underneath me. I fall to my knees, twist the doorknob open. Someone has cruelly adjusted the gravity of the room. Doubled it. Tripled it. Quadrupled it. Pen…whatever five times is. I crawl on my hands and knees through the thick plush carpet. The hall is empty and uncaring. It extends towards the infinite in either direction, a ceaseless cascade of portals to unknown terrors, delights, and purgatories.

I crawl to the door next to our room. "Ojal!" I scream, but your voice drowns mine out, just like old times. I picture you gesticulating like a conductor, spilling wine onto the carpet with one hand, the tiny orange glow of your cigarette dancing in the other.

I bang at the door, but there's no answer. I reach for the doorknob, pull myself to my feet, force my legs into begrudging submission, attempting to lower the gravitational force of the hall to standard terran levels through sheer force of will. I turn the doorknob, stumble through the door, collapse onto the carpet.

"Stand up, Anthony."

I look up and mumble a glossolalic garble of sounds in disbelief.

A rising squeal fills my ears.

The air escapes from my lungs.

My heart pounds in my chest.

Even in the shadows of the dimly lit room I can see the smile cleave across your face, which is impossibly unaltered from the last time I saw you, despite both the passage of time and the act of suicide.

"It has been a long time. We have much to talk about, no?"

20

I move closer to her. You? Her.

She raises up her hand and says, "No closer, *por favor*."

I want to ask her how is she here how is she alive if she for-gives me if I can ever forgive myself if—

"You look like a dog who has lost its bone, Anthony. Also its mind."

"It's the Abracadabra, ah, Abraxas. My head. Spinning."

She leans forward. "Yes. That is the idea."

"W-what…do you mean?" The floor is swampy beneath my knees and hands. I keep shuffling, worried that I'll be swallowed up by the carpet.

"I wanted to see you on your hands and knees." She stands up and flicks off the lamp behind her, reducing the room to shadows.

I stare up at her face, drinking it in with my eyes.

"You do not deserve to look at me like that."

"I didn't know I swear I didn't know I would never have run away if I knew—"

"*But you did run!* You did not check for a pulse. For breathing. Call an ambulance."

"I heard someone else call the ambulance. I thought it was too late!"

"You were glad to have the excuse. To run away."

"I didn't I didn't I didn't I didn't..." I can't stop my mouth from repeating these words over and over. My heart jackhammers in my chest.

"You like to pretend to be a white knight, playing saviour to a poor Cuban girl. But you took what you wanted, and you left when you were needed. This is how you Americans see the world; everything is disposable, right? Even people."

I try to stand up, and something clips against the back of my head. I slump back to the ground. A high-pitched tinnitic whine thrums in my ears. I touch my fingers to where I've been hit and they come away sticky.

She grabs my hand, examines it. "I see you still wear the ring." She fingers the wooden ring she gave me all those years ago. I can't tell if she's impressed or appalled. She drops my hand, points to the floor. "Stay. Down. You ran *como un perro.*"

The translation clambers into my mind: You ran like a dog.

"Now you will stay down, like a good dog should."

Through the ringing in my ears and the mind-altering haze of the Abraxas, I notice something strange, stranger even than my hallucinations of swamp-carpet and the fact that my skin feels like it's going to slip right off my body. I look up at Sophia. "Your voice is diff—"

"I did not ask you to speak, dog." She delivers a swift kick to my ribs. The pain is a blossoming of penance.

I want to buy her bouquets of flowers in gratitude. "I deserve to suffer. I want to atone."

She offers up a stuttering burst of laughter. "Atone?" She walks over, places her hand beneath my chin, lifts my face to look at hers. She is a goddess of destruction, wreathed in shadow. "You will have no atonement, only suffering. I will destroy you and anyone you love. Anyone and everyone you care about. Are you understanding me?"

"...everyone?"

Her red lips crawl into a grin.

"No, leave Nisha alone!"

Sophia slaps me, and pain fans out across my face. Death has made her a shadow of her former self. The Sophia I knew would never be so vindictive. "From now on, your job is to suffer, and my job is to cause your suffering. *Por todo su vida.* This is all there is, and all there will ever be. *Entiendes?*"

"Yes. I understand." I want to throw up and I want to die and I want to be forgiven and I want to suffer forever.

"It took me a long time to find you. Many years. You are good at running and hiding. But now?" She grabs my hair and yanks my head back, leans close enough that the heat of her breath warms my skin. "You. Are. *Mine.*"

"I've always been yours."

She slaps me again, this time her nails claw my face. "You are a liar and a coward. I will drink your blood with my evening wine and salt my meals with your tears." She presses a knife against my throat and through the pain and the undulating floor and the sound of the woman I once loved gleefully detailing the ways she plans to torture me all I can think is: *Do it. Draw the blade across my throat. Set me free.*

Only love can birth hate of this fortitude, this devotion, this unyielding intensity. There's a reason why the first suspect in a murder case is usually the spouse. I draw my eyes up and strain to meet her gaze. Her eyes are illuminated with unbridled fury, eyes I'd spent months staring into, eyes I would have loved to lose myself in for the rest of my days. They look different than how I've revisited them in the annals of my memory. But my memory, like the rest of me, is dishonest.

She pushes the blade closer, and my skin breaks. A trickle of blood runs over the steel. "If you try to kill yourself? I will kill *su madre.*" She drops me to the carpet. The room spins. "I found her hotel in Chicago. It looks lovely, *muy bonita.* If you kill yourself, I will get on a plane and she will be dead within an hour of my arrival. I will pluck her eyes from their sockets and feed them to the crows."

"No. I give up. I'm yours. I'm yours."

The door springs open, light floods the room and I cover my eyes. A silhouetted figure stands in the doorway. It charges into the room, unleashing a primal scream. I watch, limp and helpless, as Sophia's blade slashes against the intruder's leg. There is a clash of metal on metal. I try and raise my limbs, my voice, but my body is unresponsive.

There is another scream, Sophia's this time, as she slashes the knife again. Blood splashes onto my face and lips, the sickly sweet taste fills my mouth and I want to stand up, to fight, to run, but the messages from my brain to my body are all being lost in translation.

Nisha falls to the floor beside me. Sophia crouches down next to us, locks onto me, her eyes lit with incandescent rage. "See you soon, *mi amor.*" She plants a kiss on my cheek, her lips returning to the territory they claimed many years ago. The door slams shut behind her. She's gone.

Nisha drags herself upright, dripping blood onto the carpet. She stabs the emergency button.

Wheeeeomp! Wheeeeeeomp!

Charisma appears in the door, and her professional demeanour does a handbrake turn into crisis mode. She takes out her phone and barks, "Medical? We need you in room 23. Code red." She presses her hand against the wall, and a hidden panel pops open, exposing a first aid kit and defibrillator. "Help me get her onto the bed."

"I…I can't. My legs." The adrenaline gives me enough of a surge to get halfway upright, but no further. I collapse back onto the floor, as helpful as a water pistol in an inferno. Charisma ignores me, lifts Nisha up with a strength belying her slender frame, and inspects her wound. The world starts to slip away. "Are there any other injuries?" she asks Nisha.

"No. Did they catch her?" Nisha's voice warps and swims around the melting walls.

"Who?"

"The woman who just ran out of here carrying a bloody knife. Cuban. Tall. Pretty."

"I didn't see her. She might've escaped through the service elevator. What happened to your friend?"

"He is not injured, but he can barely move. He was clearly drugged with something other than Abraxas. You need to speak to Ojal immediately."

"With whom?"

"Ojal? Your facilitator?"

"We don't have anyone here by that name."

"Then who gave us the drugs?"

"..."

"Fuck."

21

The doctor opens the door and leads Nisha into Charisma's office, where I've been cataloguing ceiling tiles for the last twenty minutes. She hands her some medication and rattles off instructions about dosage and rest. Nisha keeps her eyes locked on me the whole time. The fading influence of whatever chemical cocktail I was given is granting her an ethereal nimbus around her head. After napping on the office for a while I seem to be gradually returning to normal, although my baseline for normal may need to be recalibrated after recent events.

"I hope I've made you as comfortable as I can while we wait for Charisma to deal with the, ah, recent incident," the doctor says, preparing to depart.

"As comfortable as one can be after being drugged and stabbed," Nisha says, rubbing the bandage on her shoulder.

"Of course. I didn't mean to be flippant. On behalf of every-one here at Level 6, I extend our most ardent apologies." She sounds like a politician apologising at a press conference. The doctor exits and the room is swallowed by silence.

"She is quite well resourced, for a struggling singer from Cuba?" says Nisha. "To travel all this way, enlist the help of an assistant, offer a bounty on the dark web?"

"I don't know how she's doing all this. She isn't the same person she was before. She hasn't aged. It's like she's frozen in time. Or she's come back from the land of the dead."

Nisha says nothing. Waits for me to continue.

"The more logical explanation, of course, is that she must've had plastic surgery after the fall. The impact may have caused permanent brain damage. Head injuries can often result in reduced impulse control, an increase in violent behavior. Twenty percent of death row prisoners have a record of severe head injury."

"What a fun little statistic," she deadpans. "There is, of course, the other explanation."

"..."

"I understand that she was your first true love, that you've spent almost a decade obsessing over the memory of her...but the reality is that you spent less than twelve months with her, nine years ago. How well did you really know her?"

"Love doesn't have a temporal prerequisite. I knew her. We were in love."

"Perhaps. Or perhaps the story you have told yourself about her is not biography but hagiography. You have elevated her from mortal to goddess in all your years of fixating on this one chapter of your life."

"You don't know what the fuck you're talking about!" I snap at her. A migraine detonates behind my eyes, rapidly annexing a

series of cerebral tracts. I lean forward, massage my temples. "I'm sorry. I didn't mean to yell at you. Whatever drug she gave me is still having a field day with my brain. How are you feeling?"

Nisha shrugs, leans back with her arms stretched above her head and taps her fingers on the wall behind her. "A slight headache but other than that I am fine. Whatever they gave me for the pain is performing miracles on my shoulder. If it was not for the bandage I would forget the wound was even there."

"You seem to have shaken the effects a lot quicker than I have?"

"She probably tailored our doses. But I also have an extremely high tolerance to morphine." I wait for her to expand but instead she makes use of the tea set Charisma's assistant prepared for us. Fills her cup, stirs in some sugar.

"Do you have a history of addiction?" Not much to gain by being coy at this point.

"Only the aforementioned issues with internet addiction. The morphine tolerance is not because of addiction. It is the result of abuse." She runs her tongue over her teeth. Her eyes move to the left as she revisits a memory. "This is why I need your help. My abuser is still—"

Charisma enters the room with her hands clasped in front of her like a statue of a twenty-first-century black-market capitalist saint. "We here at Level 6 offer our sincerest apologies—"

"The doctor already gave us this spiel," Nisha interjects.

"Of course. I will add that the intruders you have identified as Sophia and Ojal will be dealt with by our security team."

"For an establishment in the business of illegal drug distribution, you could certainly use an upgrade in your security protocols," Nisha says.

Charisma bows almost comically low to the ground, draws herself up again and replies, "You are correct. They managed to infiltrate this floor and subdue your scheduled attendant, replacing her with the woman calling herself 'Ojal.' This is com-*plete*-ly unprecedented and thoroughly unacceptable. We are going to do ev-er-y-thing within our power to make sure you are compensated. In addition, I would like to offer my *personal* expression of remorse for my failings. I am *deep*-ly ashamed of my role in this affair."

Nisha sips her tea, turns to me. "Her constant apologising is rather annoying isn't it?"

"Nisha. You're being rude."

Charisma pulls a lock of her hair behind her ear. It flops back in front of her eyes. She pulls it back again. It returns. She gives up. "We don't deal with traditional law enforcement, for *ob*-vious reasons. But rest assured our team is the best that money, *a lot of money*, can buy." She seems confident, I'm not so sure. Ghosts are notoriously difficult to throw into the back of black vans. "Of course, there is *nothing* we could ever do to adequately compensate you for what has transpired here, but we are com-plete-ly prepared to make a *very* generous offer in the hopes of making amends. Our proposal is as follows." She steeples her hands and looks at each of us in turn. "You will both be granted a lifetime of free access to all of our facilities here on Level 6—"

Nisha makes a sound somewhere between a cough and an orgasm.

Charisma allows the briefest twitch of a grin to appear on her lips before banishing it and continuing. "We will give each of you a substantial compensatory settlement. This can be provided in cash, crypto, organic material, work credits, narcotics—"

"I assume you have contacts in the black-market medical industry?"

Charisma frowns at my interruption, clears her throat and says, "We prefer the term 'post-institutional,' but yes, of course. Our resources here at Level 6 are *considerable.*"

"I need eyes."

"Meth? No problem at all! We have the *highest* qual—"

"No, not 'ice,' eyes."

"I'm afraid you may need to elucidate." She bats her eyes at me.

"They're not for me. I have a client who requires a bionic retinal prosthesis and a surgeon to install it."

She flicks her eyes up, dances her right fingers across her left palm making quick calculations. "Yes! I think that will be en-*tire*-ly possible! It will take a few days."

"I need it done immediately."

"It will take *a few days,*" she repeats, but then backs down a little. "Perhaps as few as three."

I nearly implode with relief.

"Finally, and I must emphasise that this is a *very rare* privi-lege…" She pauses for dramatic effect, as if we need any more drama in our lives right now. "Each of you will be granted access to Level 9."

"What's on Level 9?"

She shakes her head at me. "I wish I knew! Only a select few patrons of the Orrery have ever been up there. Access is by invita-tion only. I can tell you that everyone who visits that level comes back *ir-revoc-ab-ly* changed. Many of them become Pulitzer, Nobel, and Academy Award winners, not to mention those whose gifts are not recognised by traditional public ceremonies.

In exchange, we ask simply that you sign an agreement stating you will not disclose what has happened here tonight."

"An NDA?"

"After a fashion. This is both a legally and an illegally binding document, if you follow me. Given that our business here is of the *extralegal* variety, our enforcement measurements are appropriately…unconventional."

"Cement shoes?" asks Nisha.

Charisma recoils with disgust. "Not my department, so I couldn't say. But *something* in that ballpark. Yes." She hands us each an envelope.

"Do we need to sign it in blood?" I ask.

"Nothing quite so pagan. We ask simply that you spit into the provided tubes in the envelope." For a second I consider asking if she's joking but the question is clearly redundant given that Charisma appears to view humour with the kind of disdain most people reserve for telemarketing. "We use a system of DNA-supported contract verification."

"Of course, I should've guessed."

"When can we visit Level 9?" asks Nisha, near explosive with enthusiasm.

"We'll collect your contact details on the form and make arrangements. Please take these restaurant menus. They are your physical token that you'll need to present to the doorman along with a password we'll deliver to you sometime in the next twelve to seventeen hours." She stands up and smooths out her dress, despite the fact it appears to lack the physical properties requisite for folds to manifest. "If you will excuse me, I have a *ra*-ther substantial mess to clean up." She reaches into a pocket that I could've sworn didn't exist a second earlier, removes a business card, and drops it on the table. The pocket vanishes like it was never there. "I'd best start executing some plans. And possibly some employees. I'll have my assistant collect your forms shortly." She bows and exits.

⊙

We collect our phones from the doorman. Nisha exhibits an unsettling degree of joy as she snatches her phone and turns it on. The bleep of its reactivation appears to provide her with a hefty dopamine hit. I, on the other hand, feel like I'm recovering from both gastroenteritis and a minor concussion. I can't wait to sleep. We step outside. The sky is tinged with pink.

"I cannot *believe* we are going to visit Level 9! This is how Galahad must have felt when he held the Holy Grail!"

"Galahad wasn't real. Nor was the Grail, for that matter."

"Neither is any of this, doesn't mean we can't enjoy it."

I'm far too drained to enter into another ontological argument with Nisha right now. I turn my phone back on and glance at the date and time. A Rube Goldberg series of connections fires off in my brain, and I let out a terrified moan.

"What's wrong?"

"Nisha, we were supposed to be out for an hour, two at most. It's been eighteen hours. This isn't dawn, it's *dusk*." I murmur a cascade of curses as my phone collects the messages that have been flitting around in the aether waiting for its reawakening. Alerts blurt from the speaker, notifications strobing across the screen, all of them from Goldie. I open up Messages and scan the thread.

Nisha reads the horror on my face. "What's happened?"

I toss her the phone as I pull on my helmet and climb onto the bike.

She reads the message aloud:

> Just getting to know yr friend from upstairs. Get here quick
> unless U feel like cleaning up a nasty blonde mess.

22

Nisha attempts to call Goldie as we drive, but he doesn't pick up. I cut through red lights, angry drivers offering up Doppler-effected shrieks of their horns as we pass. We lean into corners so low that our knees almost kiss the asphalt, roar over hills so quickly that the tyres lose contact with the ground. Driving at this speed summons the terror-inducing beauty of the vision I had during death to press at the edges of my consciousness. Memories of *eternal ethereal transubstantiated flesh, non-Euclidean towers and spires, seas of seraphic citadels* fight to spill into the front of my awareness as I charge through an intersection, cutting through the vanishing gap between two cars approaching from opposite directions. The screech of metal against metal sings out behind us. I glance back to check no one is injured. For one fleeting moment I think that one of the furious drivers stepping out of their car is you, but the illusion quickly disappears. She is shorter, older, lighter-skinned. I look back ahead and their splenetic screaming vanishes into the distance.

We're a few minutes from home when we run into road-works, an artery clogged with cars. I cut between rows of seething motorists, arms rigid as we run close enough to skin our knees on both sides simultaneously. We reach the exit and peel off, then tear down the last part of our street and along our shared driveway. Nisha leaps off the bike and I bark, "Go to your apartment. Call the police if I'm not out in ten minutes."

"I am coming with—"

"You're *not* coming with me."

She yells something after me, but my head is too lit up with noise and light and heat to understand her. I slip brass knuckles over my left hand, grab a switchblade with my right, then try the door. It's locked. I take my keys out of my pocket and open it as quietly as I can. Nisha calls out again, and I look up at her, shake my head once, then creep inside and close the door behind me.

Goldie is there waiting for me as expected, but he's asleep, lit by the glow of the laptop screen in front of him. Clearly, he's been waiting for quite some time. He's snoring so loud I can't make out the dialogue from the film he's watching. Goldie has opened the hinged surface of the puzzle table, revealing my meticulously completed *Garden of Earthly Delights*. His laptop, crushed beer cans, and empty chip packets sit on top of Bosch's grandiose depiction of sin, sensuality, and suffering. For one bright, furious moment I'm angrier about his violation of the puzzle I've spent weeks completing than any of his other transgressions.

I snap back to my senses and skulk past, careful to avoid crunching the minefield of scattered Doritos beneath my feet.

Goldie exhibits a curiously prosaic pose; he resembles a suburban dad surrendered to sleep after a busy day driving the kids to soccer practice and shopping at IKEA.

I sneak into the bedroom, then reach under the bed to grab my bag of cash. I add in some of the money Nisha gave me to bring it up to the amount I owe, then return to the living room. My knife presses against Goldie's throat as I pinch his nose. He erupts back into consciousness. I release his nose and growl, "Don't. Move."

He takes a minute to come back to the waking world. His eyes dart around the room, waves of confusion undulating across his face. "Whattha fuck?" he yelps. His arms flail and he attempts to pull away, but I grab his shoulder and shove him back onto the couch.

"I said *don't move.*"

He does as instructed. Goldie's dumb, but he's not stupid.

"What have you done with…" I'm distracted from my interrogation by a peal of laughter from the laptop speakers. I glance at the screen. Stare at Goldie. Look back at the screen. "Are you watching *Muriel's Wedding*?"

He crumples his face in a mélange of anger and embarrassment. "What? Fuck no! It was…just on the tele."

"It's a laptop?"

"Oh, yeah, but nah. I was watchin', ahhhhh, I was watchin' a porno. Must've come on after that. Autoplay, algorithms, and shit."

It's such a ridiculous lie that I can't help but snort a laugh. I close the screen, darkness and silence swallow us. We stare at each other, faces barely visible in the shadows. I inhale and demand: "The money's there at your feet, as promised. Where is—"

"Yeah, lemme stop you right there, sport. Blondie's long gone." His lips peel into a sneer. He's replaced his signature grill, and it glints grotesquely in the half-light.

"Why? I ran every red light over here as soon as I got your message!"

"Yeah, nah, don't think so. I sent that last message a couple of hours ago. Your dear old neighbour is deader than disco. Did you have your phone off or something? Pretty sure we told ya not to do that."

Fuck. How could I be so stupid? The time stamp on the message was from when I turned the phone on, not from when the message was sent. I'm too late. "Where did you put—"

"Bathtub."

I shove him to the floor and run into the bathroom, my right boot slips upwards towards the ceiling as it slides over something wet. I look down to see dark streaks all over the bathroom tiles.

"Saklas is real serious about deadlines, Leachy. I hope I've made that clear."

I flick the light on. The trail of red runs across the floor and into the bathtub. Emily's body is silhouetted behind the shower curtain. "I'm going to *fucking kill you!*"

Goldie appears in the hallway, ostentatiously gold-plated gun pointed in my direction. "Nah, I don't reckon you will, hey? Saklas wouldn't like that. Kill me and two more take my place, like the hydrant."

"It's *Hydra*, you fucking moron."

"You sure you wanna be correcting me right now?" He treats me to a gilded grin. "Anyways. My grandad always said 'mistakes are a learnin' opportunity.' Course, he also lost all his money at the pokies, making the same mistake a couple of times a week, so maybe not the best man to take advice from. But you get the picture. Make sure the next payment's on time, or yer pal next door will be takin' a bath as well. And by 'takin' a bath,' I mean—"

"Get the fuck out of here. *NOW!*"

He flicks me a wave and says, "Righto. Catch ya soon, Leach. Have fun with the cleanup."

He collects his laptop, freezes for a moment, and studies the puzzle. He turns his gaze back to me as he lifts the table and the pieces spill to the ground. Tiny jagged-edged pieces of vice and virtue scatter across the floor. He winks, picks up the money, and departs, slamming the door behind him. I step over the bathroom tiles, avoiding the blood as best I can, then pull back the curtain to examine the second cadaver I've found in my bathtub in a matter of weeks. I lean down, brush bloodied hair away from pale white skin, then yelp and slump back onto the floor. My laughter ricochets around the bloodstained bathroom.

23

The garage door rolls up, and Nisha drives in, then steps out of the car clad in a faded Nine Inch Nails T-shirt and ripped jeans that sporadically expose the glinting metal of her prosthesis. She removes a bucket filled with cleaning supplies from the passenger seat.

"I wouldn't have picked you for a Nine Inch Nails fan." I say, gesturing for her to enter the apartment.

"What's a Nine Inch Nails fan look like?" she asks.

"I don't know. A bit more...gothy?"

She raises an eyebrow. "It has been a long time since you have been to a concert, hasn't it?"

"Nine years, give or take."

She lifts the bucket. "I brought everything on the list you gave me, except for stones. I assume we will pick those up when we go out to the ocean."

I take a pair of gloves from the bucket and head into the bathroom.

Nisha stops in her tracks and steadies herself against the doorframe. "Oh, my God…"

I'd somehow managed to forget that civilians aren't as comfortable with the sight of blood as the people I keep company with. "I'm sorry, I realise it's a lot. Maybe you should leave the supplies and let me do the cleanup? I can call you when the body is covered in plastic and ready for transport. Might be less confronting."

She turns this over in her head, oscillating between retreat and advance before saying, "No. I am here to help you. Where do we begin?"

I pass her some old towels. "You start by getting this blood off the floor. I'll deal with the body."

She takes the towels and clutches them tight against her chest. "I…think…"

"What's wrong?"

"…"

"Nisha?"

"I think I need to see the body."

I glance at her. At the shower curtain. Back at her. "You sure that's a good idea?"

"We fear the unknown more than the known. If I do not look at it, it will haunt my nightmares."

I know Nisha well enough by now to be able to tell when she isn't going to back down. "Only if you're sure."

"I am."

I pull the shower curtain back.

She takes a step forward.

Then another.

Then hesitates.

Then takes the final step to reach the edge of the bathtub.

Nisha crouches down, examines the lifeless husk. She sighs with relief. "I never thought I would be so grateful to see a dead body. Have you checked on Emily?"

"Yes. She's at her mother's place in Newcastle. She was worried Reese would try and find her, in spite of my threat. She was right, evidently."

Nisha throws a towel over Reese's ruined face. "At least she does not have to worry anymore. How did this happen?"

I empty the cleaning supplies out of the bucket onto the bench and fill it with hot water and bleach. "Once Goldie left and I'd had a minute to reassess, I went back through all of his voicemails. From what I can piece together, he came to collect payment and when he found the place empty, he decided to settle in and wait for me. Not too long after, Reese must've come round looking for me too. He was wearing leather gloves and carrying a handgun, so I can assume he wasn't here to try and have a reasonable conversation with me."

"But instead he found a bikie thug relaxing on your couch?"

"Watching *Muriel's Wedding* and chowing down on Doritos."

"He was watching *what*?"

"That was my reaction too. I'm guessing Reese must've tried to pretend like he was just a friendly neighbour popping around to say hi. I'd warned Goldie to stay away from Emily and Reese's place, which meant he mistook Reese for someone I cared about."

"When in fact, he was doing the world a favour by putting a bullet through Reese's skull."

"I'm not sure I'd go that far."

"I would. There is nothing more repellant than someone who hurts the people they claim to love."

I turn the tap off, wet a sponge, and pass the bucket to Nisha, then grab the tarpaulin and gaffer tape and start rolling Reese inside it.

Nisha soaks up the worst of the blood, throws the towels into a garbage bag, then starts on the bloodstains with the bleach. "Is it weird that I'm hungry?" she asks.

"We haven't eaten in…what, seventeen, eighteen hours? So, no, I suppose not." I stop and stare at her.

"What?"

"You're probably not going to want to answer this but—"

"Why on earth would you ask a question that you know in advance I do not wish to answer?"

"Curiosity is stronger than courtesy?"

She scrubs for a few seconds before answering, "Alright. Ask."

"Your abuser isn't looking for you. It's the other way round."

She keeps her eyes on the floor, creating ever-expanding spirals of muddy red-brown. "I assume you are aware that was a statement, not a question?"

"Right. Sorry. I meant to ask: are you looking for the person—"

"Yes. Obviously." She stops. Stares at the floor. Stands up. Sits on the bench next to the sink. "My parents divorced when I was six years old. My mother decided to take me far away, here, to Australia.

"I liked it: the heat and bright blue skies reminded me of home, but there was so much more greenery. Also, the teachers didn't hit their students. This was a major selling point for me, because I was a very smart-mouthed child. Every summer holidays for the first few years I would go home and stay with my father. My mother hated me leaving, but it was part of the custody agreement so there was nothing she could do about it. After a few years of this arrangement I became sick. I developed curious, ephemeral symptoms. I would be dangerously febrile for a week, but then recover completely. I would throw up every day for a month and then be totally fine. We saw doctor after doctor checking for allergies, parasites, and so on, but they never came close to a diagnosis.

"Eventually my mother decided that school was too much of a challenge in my condition and so I was homeschooled. Unfortunately, her idea of 'homeschooling' was to throw the occasional nature documentary on the TV. Then one year—I think I was fourteen, maybe fifteen—I decided to try and sneak out to meet up with a friend I had met online. I crept out to the garage, picked up the bike I hadn't used in years, and started pedalling down the street with what little strength I had. I heard the angry blaring of a horn behind me, and I turned around to find my mother's car charging down the street. I skidded and came off my bike, limbs splayed out on the ground. She braked, swerved, and ran over my leg, crushing it completely beyond repair. Mum rushed me to the hospital, and when I woke up, heavily dosed with anaesthetic, we saw a doctor, one we hadn't met before. He asked us a few questions, and she kept answering for me until he insisted she let me answer for myself. When she went to the bathroom, the doctor leaned in close and asked me 'Nisha, is your mother sometimes overly protective? A little too controlling?' I didn't know what to say. I only had one mother, I had no other frame of reference. He asked again and this time I saw something in his eyes: concern. But also fear."

I wind the last of the gaffer tape around the tarpaulin,

transforming Reese into a plastic-enshrouded mummy, then sit on the edge of the bath and wait for Nisha to continue.

"They said my leg would have to be amputated. I called my father, told him I was scared. He and my mother screamed at each other for a few hours, but when I told her it was my choice to go with him, she could not stop me. After the operation I returned to Rajasthan and within weeks I began to heal and change; it was almost supernatural. I grew five centimetres in just a few weeks. I went from skeletal to having actual flesh on my arms and legs. All those years, my mother had been making me sick so that she could care for me. They call it 'Munchausen by proxy' or sometimes 'factitious disorder imposed on others.' A malady born of love and control."

"Is that why you have a salt allergy, and the opioid tolerance?"

"Correct. The ancient chemist Paracelsus said that in the right dose everything is a poison. Even the world's most popular condiment can be fatal, in the wrong hands. Morphine was another favourite of hers. It kept me subdued and docile." Nisha sighs. "After I returned to Rajasthan, I never saw my mother again." She looks at the bloodstained floor, resolutely still and silent, then hops down and resumes scrubbing.

"No messages, calls, nothing?"

"That is not what I said."

"So she has contacted you."

She scrubs harder, turning the red-brown to light red and then dirty white.

"Nisha?"

"She sent me many letters over the years. I burned them all. Eventually she stopped writing. Years later I moved back here, for work and because I missed the greenery and the ocean, the space and the beaches. Perhaps a very small part of me thought that someday I'd be ready to turn up on her doorstep and try and mend things between us. But that day was always tomorrow, tomorrow, tomorrow. A few weeks ago, my father told me that an old friend of theirs who knew them when they were only newlyweds recently reconnected with my mother on Facebook. She is living in Adelaide, with her new husband, and their ten-year-old daughter April." She soaks the sponge. Scrubs like she's trying to reduce the tile to dust. "Apparently, April is the victim of a mysterious and undiagnosable illness."

"Oh, God. What did you do?"

Nisha stops scrubbing. Leans against the cupboard. Tosses the ruined sponge into the bathtub. "I hired you."

"Your *sister* is the retrieval job?"

She nods.

"Nisha, that's insane."

"Is it? Or is it insane to leave a vulnerable child in the hands of an abuser?"

"Surely there are better ways to go about this. We could contact the police?"

She laughs bitterly. "The police? You mean law enforcement or the popular rock group best known for their hit single 'Roxanne'? Either would be equally useless. You know that as well as I do." Nisha waits for a response. I offer only a confused and anxious silence. "April has a very popular Patreon account. Do you know what that is?"

I shake my head.

"A subscription support service, mostly used by YouTubers, podcasters, and such. My mother posts videos of her singing songs dressed in grotesque frilly doll outfits. April has tens of thousands of followers. Strange that my mother and I have ended up in a similar line of work, but where I am pretending to be many people, she is pretending to be only one, the loving mother of a tragically ill child. At least all of this information has made it very easy to find them. I have an address."

"When are you planning to—"

"Tomorrow. I've already started packing."

"You're leaving town?"

"Yes."

"..."

"Anthony. I want you to come with me."

"..."

"Please."

"Nisha, you don't want that."

"*Do not tell me what I want!* Aren't you tired of this endless self-imposed suffering? Sophia is alive. Shouldn't you be relieved?"

I stare at the body wrapped in tarpaulin waiting for me to bury it, trying to remember what "relief" feels like. "That's exactly it. Sophia is alive. I want to make amends. Make it work again."

Her eyes grow wide with shock and she slaps her hand to her mouth, stifling laughter. She walks over to me, places a hand on my shoulder. "With the woman who drugged you, stabbed me, and threatened to kill your mother?"

"I know it sounds crazy—"

"Anthony, you are fucking *insane*. Can you not pretend to be one of your personas with enough rationality to realise that there is no happily ever after for you and her?"

"Maybe not 'happily,' but I am hoping for an ever after."

She grabs my face between her hands. "It. Is. *NOT*. Your. Fault. She tried to kill herself. It is tragic, but it happens. And you cannot always prevent it, no matter how much you wish to do so." She releases me, leans against the wall, hangs her head.

"But I left her there."

"Yes, but you thought she was dead. I am not saying it was the *right* thing to do. But it is what a lot of people *would* do, under the circumstances. And you are wildly deluded if you believe you can start up some sort of post-trauma romance. Also?" She glances at the body in the bathtub, back at me. "She may kill you."

I think about your hands wrenching my head back, your blade pressed against my neck. "It's possible."

"I would say it is almost certain."

I shrug.

"But you are going to do it anyway."

"I have to." The memory of your skin against mine. The sound of your voice over the backdrop of drums and guitars. The smell of your first coffee of the day wafting from the kitchen.

"I *have* to. I *must*. I have *no choice*. What is this cosmic compulsion you are always talking about? What unseen hand is forcing you into these decisions?" She pokes the center of my head with her finger. "What is in here making you believe that free will is some sort of illusory, abstract concept?"

I snort a laugh. "Nisha, you don't even believe in this *reality*, who are you to talk?"

She groans and says, "Do not try to justify your death wish with ontological arguing." Nisha glares at me for a moment, but then her face softens and she hangs her head low. "Anthony. I have not had a friend—a real meatspace friend—in a very long time. I do not wish to lose you. If you go back to her? She will either ruin your life or end it. And if you are being hurt, pain will ripple out to me, because I care about you. Do you understand that? If you cannot keep away from her for your own sake, for the love of every deity in every denomination, would you do it for mine?"

I look into Nisha's beseeching eyes, listen to the sound of possums rustling in the tree outside the window. The fluorescent light emits a low, angry buzz. "I'm sorry. I can't."

She murmurs something in Hindi, removes her keys and throws them into the bathtub, then kicks over the bucket of water and storms out, calling over her shoulder: "This is one mess you will have to clean up on your own."

24

After I've relocated Reese to his final resting place at the bottom of the sea (as a real estate agent, I'm sure he'd appreciate the 360-degree ocean views), I return to the apartment block and slide Nisha's keys through the mail slot, doing my best to repress the guilt and shame I feel about letting her down. I'm barely back inside my apartment when my phone pings with a text from Charisma with details for the pickup. Even quicker than expected, you've got to love people who under-promise and over-deliver, although she does warn me that the surgeon won't be available for a few days yet. I jump on my bike and pick up the delivery from the dead drop, then race over to Saklas's. The knocker on the front door is a roaring golden lion, regal mane flowing around its neck. I tap it and imagine the wealthy aristocrats who built this house, people who probably had names like Chantelle and Algernon, dreaming of hosting garden parties and literary salons on their grand estate. How would they feel about their dream home ending up as the clubhouse for a pack of thieves and murderers?

Goldie opens the door, munching on a packet of gummy bears. "Well, if it isn't the esteemed Mr. Leach. Had any friendly visits from your neighbours lately?" he says, his mouth filled with a gelatinous rainbow mush.

"Watched any good films lately?" I reply.

The smirk is excised from his face. He tips the last of the tiny imitations of ursine apex predators into his gold-encrusted maw. "Make it quick. I'm busy."

"Yes. So I see. I have something for Saklas."

"Great. He loves somethings. Particularly drugs, cash, and women. Also podcasts. If it's any of those, hand it over. Otherwise, fuck off home."

I remove the box from my pocket and pop it open. Goldie's mouth drops open mid-chew. The sight makes me physically ill. What does it say about me that I can clean up and dispose of a mutilated corpse without gagging but poor table manners make me want to puke?

"Fuck me dead, drunk, and dizzy! Ain't that an interesting turn of events? Credit where it's due, this is a good fucken' effort! I'll take 'em right to him."

I snap the box closed and put it back in my pocket. "I'd like to deliver them personally."

"Yeah, well. I'd like a mountain of cocaine and a couple of supermodels to climb it with, but we can't all get what we want now, can we? Saklas is in a meeting with the recumbent premier."

"Incumbent."

"Yeah. That guy. And his opponent. Bit of wheelin' and dealin' and that. Real important-like. But trust me, I'll take 'em right to him." He registers the doubt on my face and rolls his eyes dramatically. "For cryin' out loud, you really know how to hurt a bloke's feelings, you know that? I get it, you don't trust me. And you're probably sore about what happened to your pal upstairs, but that wasn't personal. Understand? And anyways, if anything happened to these peepers, Saklas would tear me a new arsehole, right? So at least trust my instincts for self-preservation."

I hold the box in the air between us, then press it into his hands. "Alright. I've arranged a surgeon, one of the best in the southern hemisphere. She'll be ready to do the operation in a few days. Anything happens to that box and—"

"Yeah, yeah, I get it. Let's skip the unpleasantries and keep this businesslike. Pains me to say it, but I've got a lot more respect for you than I used to. Took you for a lightweight to start with, but you got guts of steel and balls of brass."

"It means a lot to know that I have the respect of a man of your integrity and social standing," I reply, then immediately regret it. Not a great idea to irritate the man who is holding my life in his hands. Fortunately, he doesn't seem to have picked up on my sarcasm.

He grins and says, "Yeah, cheers. Right back atcha. Alright. Give us a buzz when the surgeon's ready. Later."

He slams the door in my face, and I walk back to the bike, hands shaking with relief. I take out my keys and drop them from my trembling fingers. When I bend down to pick them up I notice something unusual underneath the seat. I reach up and pull the black box away and inspect it; a sleek, compact tracking device, spewing data back to some unknown observer. I walk the tracker out to the street, find the nearest car parked on the curb and plant it on the undercarriage.

☿

When I get home I scroll through the news on my phone, looking for traces of you. I see your face in everything; victims, perpetrators, journalists. Every woman who bears even the slightest resemblance fleetingly assumes your face…and then the moment passes, and I realise I'm looking at an elderly Chinese woman or a young Cambodian girl or any number of people who aren't at all you, and yet somehow for a handful of heartbeats they indisputably *are*.

After half an hour of this I can't bear the emotional turbulence, can't trust my own senses anymore. Not when it comes to you. Next door Nisha is slamming doors, moving furniture around to a soundtrack of LCD Soundsystem. I wonder if she'll leave most of her stuff behind for her landlord to deal with. I assume, like me, she's rented under one of her aliases. Makes it a lot easier to avoid consequences, unless of course you go constantly charging towards them.

A car pulls up outside, the engine thunderous in comparison to the late-night silence. The car door opens, engine still running. Footsteps approach my front door. I stand up, but by the time I open the door they are already retreating. A stream of long black hair trails behind the figure running back to the car and slamming the door behind her. *It's not you. I know it can't be you. It can't possibly be you I need to stop fooling myself this is an aftereffect of the drugs or the concussion or the temporary fatality but it can'tbeyouit isn'tyouit—*

The tinted window rolls down.

And there you are, as real as the unbreakable promise of death.

"Sophia!" I scream. The rest of the world dissolves into a

Gaussian blur. You reverse the car at breakneck speed. I run after you, screaming your name, but you've already pulled the car away into the night, tyres screeching.

I look around and I can see a couple of faces in windows, no doubt irritated by the disturbance. Mason is on his front balcony, the soft orange glow of a cigarette hovering in front of his face. He makes a low gargling sound, like a jungle cat enjoying the sticky warm blood of freshly felled prey. He throws me a two-fingered salute. I return the gesture and he grins, exposing a row of jagged teeth. I get it now. We're not so different, brothers of the same demented fraternity.

When I get back to my front door I realise that I was so desperate to chase after you that I completely missed the package you left on my doorstep. It's beautifully wrapped, Sophia. Crisp red paper, the same red as the dress you wore the night we parted, folded with origamiesque perfection, bound in a white silk bow. You always put so much care into the presentation of your gifts, made the wrapping into a beautiful skin that I always felt reluctant to unravel. The box is scented with the same perfume you always used to wear, Corazón Rojo. I inhale the scent, then take the box inside, close the door behind me and sink into the couch.

I slip my finger under the ribbon, untying it with the delicate care of a nurse removing sutures. Next door Nisha smashes something, screams in frustration. I tell myself I will knock on her door and help her pack. And apologise. And explain. Just as soon as I've opened your gift.

I place the ribbon on the seat next to me, then pull at the tape on the edges of the package, careful not to rip the paper itself, as though it were an artefact of tremendous historical and fiscal value, and open the box beneath. Part of me wouldn't be surprised if it contained anthrax, or explosives. Part of me would be relieved.

Inside soft red tissue paper forms the final barrier between me and whatever it is you've chosen to place in my hands. I push the tissue paper aside. A pickup truck roars down the driveway. My reflection in the black mirror of the glass screen in front of me is gaunt and cadaverous. I lift the tablet out and turn it on. The home screen is blank save for a single video file labelled with a date I don't recognise.

The truck's engine shuts off. Boots clomp across the cement.

I tumble the numbers around in my head, trying to figure out their significance. I realise I've become used to the Australian method of labelling the date: day/month/year. I flip back to the month/day/year system we use back home—and in Cuba—and the date becomes painfully familiar.

There's an angry knock at the door, followed by Saklas's voice yelling "Leachy! Open up!" He rattles the doorknob.

I hit play, and Havana springs to life in front of me. It's obviously been recorded on a cameraphone; the resolution is poor and the screen shakes constantly. I hurtle back through time and space to Calle 17. The video is centered on an alfresco table at a streetside restaurant, family and friends gathered around as a cake illuminated by candles is brought to the table and they joyously erupt into singing "Cumpleaños Feliz."

Goldie unlocks the door and pushes it open, but I've pulled the chain into place and he can't move it more than an inch. "Oi, I can fucken' see you sittin' there. *Open the door!*"

The camera zooms shakily on the young man behind the cake, the flickering light of the flames dancing across his face. One of the singing voices breaks off into a concerned murmur.

The singing stops. The camera shifts up to examine a figure in the distance, taking in the beautiful chaos of another night in Havana. It stops and centers on a young woman yelling angrily on her balcony. Our balcony.

Goldie shoves the barrel of his gun through the gap in the door. "Hey! Quit watching fucken' YouTube and open the fucken' door!"

The camera zooms a little further, the image dissolves into indecipherable pixels, then pulls back again. And there you are. It's you. Of course it's you.

The bullet burying into the couch cushion beside me snaps me out of my reverie. I look up into Goldie's furious, red-rimmed eyes. If I die, I'll never get to see what happens next. This is perhaps the only reason why I comply with his demand. I put the tablet down and open the door.

Goldie shoves me onto the couch, rips the tablet out of my hands, and tosses it across the room. It strikes the wall, bounces on the ground and lands facedown. I can only imagine this is how a parent feels when they watch their child fall down a set of stairs. I rise up out of the chair, but he shoves me back down and presses the barrel of the gun to my head. I hold my hands up in surrender, eyes fixed on the tablet.

"Eyes glued to the fucken' screen. Typical bloody millennial." Goldie murmurs as he removes a seat from the dining table and sets it up opposite, leads his boss to sit down.

Saklas sits up straight, hands clasped in his lap. Takes a deep breath. "Mr. Leach. As you're aware, I don't often personally attend to matters such as collection. But given the gravity of the situation, I've made an exception. You're late on payments. Very fucken' late."

"Mr. Saklas, I—"

He holds up his hand for silence and continues. "We've already applied the penalty fee, and still seen no improvement. Thus, we have to move to our escalation protocol. I'm here to escalate."

"I know that the last payment was late but—"

"*Last* payment? Besides waiving the first instalment due to your services on Level 7, I've not had one measly penny, farthing, sovereign, or drachma from you." He doesn't raise his voice, but it is terrifying in its concentration and composure.

"That's not tr—" the words wither in my mouth when I see the devilish grin on Goldie's face. He winks at me, then mimes taking out his eyes and throwing them over his shoulder, finishing his little act with a clownish 'where did they go?' expression.

I mouth at him: *I am going to kill you.*

He cups his hand to his ear and mouths back: *Sorry? Can't hear you?*

I take a moment to run a few scenarios in my mind; they all end in bloodshed. I just need to make sure the blood in question isn't my own. "Mr. Saklas, it appears there's been an error of communication."

"Don't you fucken' play games with me, Leach. You are well and truly up shit creek without the proverbial at this juncture."

"I am aware. And I don't think you're going to like what I have to say next."

"First true words I've heard from you thus far."

"Goldie has been letting his personal vendetta against me get in the way of your business interests."

Saklas flares his nostrils, strokes his beard. "That true, Goldie?"

Goldie winks at me again. He's been expecting this. Of course he has, he's had way more time to anticipate the responses. He stands next to Saklas, the right-hand man assuming his place. "Boss, I been working with you since I dropped outta high school. I helped you build this empire. We've only known this pommy prick a few years. Throwing alla that away 'cos of some petty rivalry would be fucken' stupid."

Saklas leans in close to me, not to get a closer look, obviously, but to intimidate me. I watch my own terrified face reflected in the twin mirrors of his sunglass lenses.

"Mr. Saklas please listen to me I can fix this I promise I obtained a pair of eyes for youIjustneed—"

"Goldie, hand me my knife. The big one."

Goldie illuminates with vile mirth as he removes a hunting knife from the sheath on his belt and hands it to his employer. Saklas takes it from him, places his other hand on Goldie's wrist. "You're right, Goldie. You were fucken' stupid." He yanks him forward and drives the blade directly into Goldie's chest. Pulls it out again.

A sputtering waterfall of blood cascades from Goldie's lips. He tips forward, striking his head on the table and then falling to the floor. A slowly expanding pool of red surrounds him. He shudders once. Gurgles blood.

Saklas cocks his head, pinpointing the location of the sound, then flips the knife over and rams the solid metal base of the hilt firmly against Goldie's head.

Goldie falls still and silent.

Saklas sits back in his chair. "Tea towel."

"I'm sorry?"

"Could I trouble you for a tea towel? This is my favourite knife. Like to keep it clean."

"Ah, yes. Of course. One moment." I stagger off the couch, move around Saklas's left side to avoid stepping over Goldie. Yet another dead body in my apartment. Looks like I won't be getting my bond back. I take a tea towel from the kitchen door, walk it back over and hand it to him. He cleans the knife with the delicate care of a luthier restoring an antique viola.

I take my seat on the couch opposite him.

He places the knife in his jacket pocket. "Righto then, where were we?"

Goldie's dead eyes stare at me. "The…ah, the payment. I gave it to Goldie. He must've been withholding it from you."

Saklas nods. "Yeah, I reckon that's about right. Dumb fucker's been skimming off me for a couple of months now. Thought just because I was blind he could rob me that way. I had to hire a forensic accountant. Didn't even know there was such a thing until I need one. Now what's this you said about the eyes?"

"I managed to obtain a pair of bionic retinal implants; these are cutting edge, best on the black market. I wanted to give them to you directly, but Goldie intercepted me. They're in a small red box, about the size of a glasses case."

He raises an eyebrow. "That so? Bloody hell. Even I didn't have the resources to track down another pair. How'd you manage that?"

"It's a long story."

"…"

"Ah, well, not so much long as it is…strange."

"Strange is part of my daily grind. Spit it out already."

"There was an incident at the Orrery, Level 6. They offered me a very generous compensation package."

"That so? They're a weird bunch down on 6, but they have

their ways 'n' means. Gotta give 'em that. Nicely done. Those eyes are gonna need finding." He takes out his phone and holds it horizontal to his face. "Call: Frankie."

"Calling Frankie," the automated voice replies.

It rings for a few seconds. The pool of blood from Goldie's head is pressing against my feet.

Frankie picks up. "Yeah, boss?"

"Frankie. I'm gonna need a ride and a cleanup crew at Leachy's place. Goldie's been retired. His truck's here, I'll need someone to drive it back to his place and then find a small red box for me. Tear the joint apart if you have to, but careful with the box. And can you quickly check in with the local sergeant? There was a gunshot here 'bout five minutes back. Double-check he knows it's the type he's supposed to avoid investigating."

"Righto."

"Oh, one last thing. Can you pop to the pharmacy and get me some Pepto? Just ate a steak and veg, and my stomach is giving me hell. Thanks, mate." He hangs up and says to me, "Should be here in a bit. Now, the place you got these eyes from, they provide an installation service?"

"I've arranged a surgeon. She should be in contact soon."

Saklas grins. "Today just gets better and better!" He leans back, crosses his arms. "Listen, all this only confirms my earlier suspicions about you; that you're more'n ready for a promotion. And as you're aware, I have a recent vacancy to fill." He tilts his head at Goldie's bloody corpse. "You know how we operate, yer smart, don't let yer personal gripes and grievances get in the way of the job. That's a rare quality in my line of work. Couldn't count the number of times one of my boys has barrelled in claiming we've gotta go to war with some crew because one of them accidentally chipped the paint on his bike or winked at his missus, some petty shit like that. Plus, you got a head for numbers, you know how to lay low, and you don't like to fight, but you *can* if you have to. You already know more about the ins and outs of our operations than most of my foot soldiers. I can't think of a better candidate. How about it, you wanna be my new right-hand man?"

"Mr. Saklas, I'm flattered but—"

"Job comes with a lotta perks. I got sway with cops, pollies, feds. You want something, I can make it happen. Whaddya chasing as a signing bonus, drugs, new bike? Girls, guys, nonbinary? I don't fucken' judge, me. Got a cousin who's neither this nor that, it's all gravy as far as I'm concerned."

"That's very generous, but I've decided to get out of the life. I'm going straight."

Saklas scrunches his face up in confusion and then laughs so hard his belly shakes. "*You?* Go legit? You're fucken' *built* for the life. I bet you came outta yer mum's snatch with a fake passport and a shank in yer tiny, thieving fingers! You wouldn't last a week as a civilian. I met plenty of blokes who went straight; they all ended up one of two places: rehab or the cemetery. Once you're in, there ain't no gettin' out." He pauses, strokes his beard. "Actually, I tell a lie. One fella did move on to a successful career in politics. Similar skill set after all, but other'n that? Bloody hopeless. Is there nothing I can offer you, new apartment? Triceratops skull? I've got a moon rock I might be persuaded to part with, if it'll bring you in?"

"That's certainly fascinating, but no. I am certain."

"Make no mistake, this is the opportunity of a lifetime."

"I'm aware. But it's not for me, I'm afraid."

"Well, can't blame a guy for tryin', eh? 'S been a pleasure." He holds out his hand and I shake it. He clasps his other hand over the top and says, "Shame about the coffee table."

"What do you—"

His left hand dives into his jacket as his right slips from my palm to my wrist, shoving my hand down onto the table between us. He raises the knife and drives it clean through my hand, pinning it to the table. I scream loud enough to rival Mason. My hand is flooded with agony, white light white heat blinding me, obscuring all thought but the pain roaring through my flesh.

"Yeah, so. When I said 'opportunity of a lifetime,' I also meant it could be the *last* opportunity of your lifetime. See, the problem is, your strength is also yer weakness. You know a lotta what we do around here. And if you're goin' straight, I can't trust you to keep that to yourself. Knowledge is valuable, and you are currently information-rich." He pulls another knife from his jacket. "I know, it's a bit much. What am I, a bloody chef? But guns aren't real useful for a man such as myself. As much as I like to say 'you don't need eyes to see, you need vision,' eyes do come in pretty bloody handy when it comes to aiming. Besides, I've always thought that if you're going to take a life, you should get close enough to feel the condemned man's breath in your face. That's just common courtesy."

"Please. You don't...need to do this. I'm leaving. For... Adelaide. You'll. Never see me. Again."

"Yeah, nah. Sorry, Leach. Can't take that risk. But I'll make it quick, eh? You want a last drink, a smoke, anything like that?"

"I can get...you...into Level 9!"

He pauses. Shifts in his chair. Twirls the knife in his hand, points it at me. "Bullshit."

"It's true! I have…an invitation. It's the Indian takeaway menu on the counter."

"The invitation to the most exclusive venue in the underground is a takeaway menu?"

"Hiding in plain sight. You need that and the one-time password: hypostasis."

"Hippo-what?"

"Hypostasis. It's a medical term. Also theological. Doesn't matter. It'll get you inside."

Saklas utters a low groan. "If you're fucken' with me…"

"I'm not. I swear!"

"Righto, then. In that case, business wise, it'd make the most sense to continue on course and just take the invite after I'm done with you. Sorry, mate. Nothing personal. Just gotta make sure I'm attending to those Ps and Qs."

He presses the knife against my throat and says, "It's been a pleasure working with you. Sorry it had to end like this. You got family you want me to notify, put 'em at ease?"

"Saklas, I'm begging you! I can—"

"Don't beg. It's undignified and ineffective. Best speak up now, where do you want yer personal effects sent? I won't skim anything off the top. You have my word."

I close my eyes. Let out a slow, long breath. I relax into my natural voice, not much point in pretending anymore. "Chicago. The Voynich Hotel, in Oak Park. Address it to Mary Voynich. She already thinks I'm dead. Send her anything of value and dump the rest."

Saklas recoils in surprise. "Fuck me! Are you a fucken' seppo?"

"You mean American? Yes."

"Full of surprises 'til the bloody end, eh? Alright. Consider it done. You might want to close yer eyes. Say a prayer if you're that way inclined."

I want to say goodbye to you, Sophia. But if I mention your name it'll only put you in danger. I'm sorry.

I'm so sorry.

I'm sorry for what I did and for running and for not being a better person to begin with. Hopefully this puts an end to it all, at long last.

A high-pitched squeal fills my ears. I close my eyes and behind my eyelids all I can see is the blinding bright light of *orphic orbs orbiting seraphic suns lighting transmundane transdimensional bridges with length and breadth beyond form and physics*... An ethereal warmth envelops me.

I slow my pulse.

Bow my head.

And wait for death.

The door opens, and before I can look up, a thick wet sound cuts through the air in front of me. When I open my eyes Saklas is eerily still. I reach for the knife in his hand, but as I do so his head tilts to the left. And keeps tilting.

Then slides right off his shoulders and falls to the floor, where it bounces, rolls, and comes to rest next to Goldie's feet. I stare at the decapitated body, leather-clad and rigid in front of me. Slowly, the room comes back into focus. Nisha is standing to my left, holding a bloody katana in her trembling hands.

25

I swallow the pain meds as Nisha bandages my head, my eyes locked on the broken tablet as she works.

"We need to get you to an actual doctor."

"No time. It'll have to wait until we're out of town or Saklas's crew will find us. We can stop somewhere on the way. Moss Vale maybe, or Canberra."

She pauses, looks up at me. "On the way to where?"

"Adelaide."

A grin splits her face and she throws her arms around me.

I wince with pain and say, "Okay! Take it easy! I figure I owe you given this latest addition to my mounting karmic debt. I'll come and help you find your sister, then figure things out from there."

"So you have finally come to your senses? You will not be chasing Sophia any longer?"

The lie almost slips from my lips, they're so permanently

calibrated for deception that getting them to tell the truth requires concerted effort. "I...didn't say that. I still need to find her. But I will help you first, I owe you that. I owe you everything."

Nisha sighs, shakes her head. "I suppose I will have to accept this as a compromise. I should warn you, I am going to continue trying to talk you out of it."

"And I will continue to be unpersuaded."

"I understand." She pulls back, finishes the bandage, kisses me on the cheek. "Thank you, Anthony."

"Anything for a friend. Also a blood debt. I'm going to grab my bug-out bag, then we need to go." I run into the bedroom and pull it out from under the bed.

"What should I do with...?" She tilts her head at the bloodied katana on the floor, as though saying its name will somehow animate it into sentience.

"Best not to leave any evidence behind. Especially given that we don't have time to clean up the bodies. Saklas's crew is already on the way."

I open the front door for her and she pauses, processes this and replies, "Right. I will bring the bloody sword that I used to decapitate a bikie gang leader then. Because it is the sensible thing to do. Apparently." She picks up the katana and examines it, dripping yet more blood onto the floor, then sheathes it and slings it over her shoulder.

I grab a towel from the linen cupboard and toss it to her. "Wrap it up, just in case someone sees us on the way to the car." She exits and I pick up the tablet and takeaway menu, shove them into my bag, and then lock the door behind me.

Nisha leads me into her garage, where her car is packed with boxes, garbage bags, screens, and cables. She runs inside to get Dante, who rushes over to lick my face with zealous affection. "I called the cops as soon as I heard the gunshot. They were disturbingly relaxed about the situation. I took the katana and stood outside the door and listened, waiting for them to arrive. When I could hear that you were in mortal danger, I had to do... the thing I dead. Ah! The thing I *did*." She laughs. "That was a Freudian slip of epic proportions."

"Thank you, Nisha. You've saved my life more than once now."

She loads Dante inside and climbs into the driver's seat. I open the passenger door and throw my bag in. Mason's tortured scream fills the night air. "Start the car, I need to do one thing before we go."

"Where are you—"

I run out to Goldie's truck and try the handle. He's left it unlocked. Funny how people in the business of thieving can be so careless with their own security. I dig around in the glove box and find a couple of knives, a revolver, a small bag of coke, and a large bag of weed. The back of the cab yields nothing save fast-food packaging and an old T-shirt. I reach under the driver's seat and my hand brushes against a familiar fabric. I pull the duffel bag out and inspect it; there's a few grand missing, but the bulk of the cash I gave him is still here. Fortunately for me, having a vision-impaired boss has made Goldie reckless when it comes to concealing his ill-gotten gain. I run up the stairs to Mason's apartment and drop the bag at the door.

Mason tears the door open before I can disappear, regards me with an angry glare. He drops his gaze to the bag. "Hrn?"

"It's cash. So you can pay for assistance, medication. Whatever."

He points at it, then at himself. "Hrn-*un*?"

"Yes. For you."

Mason crouches down, unzips it as though concerned it might contain a nest of vipers. His eyes expand with disbelief. "Hrn-*un*-nuh!" He reaches out his hand to me. I take it and he shakes my arm up and down, grunting ecstatically.

"Take care of yourself."

He grunts, takes the bag inside, and closes the door. When I reach the bottom of the stairs I can hear Mariah Carey's melismatic soprano blasting from his stereo in celebration. Interesting choice, Mason.

Nisha is idling in the driveway, I climb in and pull Dante on top of me.

"What was that about?" she asks.

"Just trying to see if it's possible to perform a good deed without inadvertently harming someone in the process." I grab the tablet out of bag. "I am going to be unbearably selfish and ask one more favor. Goldie smashed my tablet, is there any way to watch a video file from it?"

"There's a laptop bag at your feet there, and a cable and head-phones in the side pocket. Plug it in, if the hard drive's still working you should be able to copy the file."

Nisha takes corners at full tilt, cutting through red lights and weaving through traffic. "Fuck!" she yells.

"What?"

"I forgot my toothbrush. I can see it in my mind's eye now; sitting there on the fucking sink." She slams the wheel, cursing in Hindi.

"I have a spare in my bag."

She sighs with relief. "I knew there was a reason I was still keeping you around. Has it booted up yet? Okay, the user-name is atlasshrugged, all one word, and the password is livefreeordie69, also one word."

I scoff and she slaps my leg. "It is not *my* computer; it is cal-ibrated for one of my homunculi. The username and password help me get into character. Everything on there: the wallpaper, applications, and especially the disturbing browser history, is the work of Walter James Jenkins, fifty-four-year-old libertarian and father of three. I have a dozen other machines in the boot with their own fake histories."

"That's what they all say." I login and wait for the tablet hard drive to appear. When it blinks to life a desperate gasp escapes my lips.

"Cute puppy video?"

"Not quite. Give me a minute to watch this." I take the headphones out of the laptop bag and plug them in, then hit play. The scene plays out again; the birthday, the shaky zoom, you standing on that ledge. And then there I am, reaching out towards you. Even through the heavy pixellation I look younger, more naive, desperately in love.

I know what happens next, of course. We scream at each other. You smash your phone, you climb onto the railing. I reach out.

And you fall.

I watch myself, my own temporal ghost, reaching out through the abyss of time towards you. Missing your hand. Watching you fall.

And I—the "I" that is here and now—watch as the camera throws to where your body has landed on the back of that van, and the scene that I have replayed countless times in my mind unfurls in front of me. But something here is different. This is an alternate ending to the familiar tale, a director's cut, a creative reinterpretation. I watch this new, impossible ending to the story I have convinced myself I know so well and the blood drains from my face.

The video cuts and is replaced by a still image of a handwritten note:

THE ORRERY
LEVEL 9
TONIGHT

My head hammered with guilt and shame and desperate cries of "do something do something do something!" but I reasoned that I could already hear someone on their phone, calling an ambulance, what more could I do? A bystander pointed their phone at you. I had the audacity to feel disgusted that they would film something like this, as well as the obscene sense of self-preservation to throw my arm in front of my face as I passed them.

I ran out towards Avenida 23. The timbre of the screaming shifted dramatically; there were cries of "Gracias a Dios!" I turned around and there, on top of the black van, I saw your bloodied hand shoot up into the air. I stood and watched for one heartbeat. Two. Three. Four.

Then I turned, ran to the street, and hailed a taxi to the airport.

26

Nisha parks the car. Turns to me. Places her hand on mine. "Should I even bother wasting my breath?"

"Probably not, no."

Her expression is a compromise between relief and defeat. "I thought that would be the case. If I am being honest? I am very excited to finally get to see Level 9. It is a shame that we are doing it in these circumstances." We step out of the car. Nisha rubs Dante's belly and rolls the window down for him. "How long do you think she has been planning this?"

"I don't know." We walk in lockstep to the Orrery's revolving doors.

"What will you say to her when you see her?"

I stop and glare at Nisha, then turn back and continue walking at double speed.

"Sorry, I will attempt to rein in my natural curiosity. But if you must do this, I am glad to be here with you."

"Me too."

We enter the lobby and hand over our phones to the door-man. Nisha tenses and then trembles as she passes hers over. We pass the doorman the takeaway menus and his lips curl into a grin.

"Hypostasis," I say.

He turns to Nisha.

"Syzygy," she says.

His grin broadens and he throws his arms open wide. "My friends, it is my great pleasure to welcome you to Level 9! A rare honour bestowed upon only a fortunate few. Please follow me."

We follow him to the lift. He presses the call button and then swipes an RFID band in front of a hidden panel. It pops open and a tiny glass tray slides out. He takes a small white medi-cal fingerpick from his pocket and presses it against his finger, then takes the drop of blood and places it on the glass slide. It retracts and a series of whirs and hums emit from behind the panel. "DNA entry verification," he explains. It emits an affirma-tive bleep, and the elevator doors open. "It'll take you straight to Level 9. The kingdom is inside of you and it is outside of you." He waves us inside and we watch the doors close across the manic grin plastered on his face.

"What do you think he meant by that?" Nisha asks.

"I don't know. Some esoteric bullshit."

She scratches her arm and takes slow, heavy breaths.

"We won't be long. You'll get your phone back soon."

"Oh! I am not worried about that. Well, perhaps a little. But I am more concerned about the fact that we may both be about to die."

The elevator climbs with unusual torpor.

"It is a possibility, yes."

"I even set up a scheduled email to the RSPCA. If I don't cancel it, they'll get a notification in a few hours telling them to take care of Dante."

"That demonstrates impressive forethought and disturbing pessimism. But you don't believe any of this is real, in any case."

"That does not mean I want it to end."

"What do you think happens, then? You respawn in some new body, another world, another time?"

She considers this. "I think that attempting to contemplate our next form would be as difficult as trying to conceptualise a colour our eyes are incapable of seeing. We can only use the colours we know as reference points. I think the next life—the next iteration of the simulation—will be a slew of new colours, new modes of being. Perhaps in a universe unbound by the forces of this one; gravity an unknown concept, electromagnetism an improbable myth."

The elevator doors open. In front of us is a long, narrow hallway. The ceiling is bright, clinical white. To the right is a lush green wall of plants that move gently, although of course there is no breeze in here. To the left, a wall of floor-to-ceiling mirror runs the entire length of the hallway. It seems implausibly long, perhaps two or three times the width of the entire building. It's clearly an optical illusion, but it's a convincing one.

We step into the hall. Our footsteps echo cavernously around us. "This may be one of the last things we see before we die. This corridor. These walls. Each other."

Nisha considers this. "If this is the end of things, I could certainly think of less pleasing faces to gaze upon."

I snort a laugh. "I'm envious of your ability to be so calm

and rational. When my heart stopped I saw—" *Light that makes supernovas look like dim candles, a multitude of infinities held in grains of sand tumbling through*—"Things I can't explain. Saw isn't even the right word. I felt it. Or became it. I know that sounds surreal."

Nisha gestures around us. "In these surroundings? I would say it is entirely appropriate."

"I once heard a theory that the unearthly white light you see in a near-death experience is the result of your brain hallucinating due to trauma-induced DMT release."

Nisha says nothing for a few steps. The distant red door at the end of the hall seems to be moving farther and farther away. "Perhaps you were glimpsing the next level."

"Do you really believe that?"

"I read something recently about Buddhist monks who make mandala robots."

"How is that relev—"

"They used to make mandalas out of sand, backbreaking labour that would require days of work. When they finished, they would sweep up the sand and toss it into the river to symbolise the impermanence of this level of reality."

Something thuds against the glass next to us. I snap my head around but can only see my reflection. I cup my hand to my ear, place it against the glass. I could swear there is the sound of muffled laughter on the other side.

"Come on. Your mind is playing tricks on you." Nisha pulls me by the arm and continues. "Recently monks have been making robots called scribits to make the mandalas for them. When the mandala is complete they retrace their steps until their creation has been relegated to oblivion. But the question is: does the karma the robot has acquired in the act of making the mandala flow back to its creator, or is it held in this non-sentient manmade construction? What do you think?"

"I think we might be about to die."

"All the more reason to think about our possible end."

A light flickers in front of us, then sputters and expires. "When I was in India I saw prayer wheels placed in rivers, the flow of the water turning them instead of human hands. Like hydroelectricity, but for karma. I guess what you're talking about is a form of spirituality via technological interface. Digital dharma."

She smiles in approval. "That makes sense, I think. For much of human history, we have used drugs and meditation and dance and fasting and ritual to contact the divine. In an age of techno-logical advancement, it only makes sense that we would use the new tools at our disposal to do the same."

"Is it just me or does this hallway seem like it keeps getting longer?"

"We are nearly there. It's probably just a side effect of the pain meds. Hurry up!" She doubles her pace, and I follow her as we walk and walk and walk along this seemingly infinite hallway that treats the laws of time and space as though they are nothing more than the polite recommendations of a sommelier.

"How is your hand?"

"I can't feel it. It's like it's not even there." I wave it in front of me to confirm it exists.

The glass panel next to me shudders. This time I'm *sure* I hear laughter. "Did you hear that?"

"Anthony! Your drugs will wear off soon, and you will be ren-dered immobile with agony. Stay focused. We are almost there."

She runs the last few hundred meters and the door in front of us shifts from distant to arms-length in a confusingly short span of time. Now that we're in front of it, it becomes clear that the door and adjoining wall are slightly curved. Nisha squeezes my shoulder. "Are you ready?"

"I have never been less ready for anything my entire life."

"Me too. Let's be unprepared together." She knocks on the door and rather than opening inward it disappears upwards into the ceiling. We step through, and it thuds closed behind us.

27

The room is a perfect circle. Floor-to-ceiling mirrors surround us, and the inside of the door is likewise mirrored. Once it closes it becomes impossible to discern its location. Everything is a reflection of itself. An array of tentacular plants hangs from the ceiling. Nisha doesn't seem bothered by them, but I could swear they're moving, tiny verdant tongues taking languorous licks at the air. The only objects in the room are three wooden chairs.

We sit.

I've already forgotten where the door is. Nisha gazes straight ahead with the composure of a Zen master.

We wait.

I stare up at the plants, watching them shift and sway. A section of the mirrored wall slides up. I don't think it's the same one we came through, but then again I wouldn't place any bets on it.

The lights dim. The first faint murmurs of feeling return to my hand.

Ojal enters, her high heels clapping with military precision over the floor as she approaches. "So lovely to see you again!"

Nisha jumps out of her seat, but Ojal shakes her head and motions for her to sit, then holds out a syringe in my direction. "What is that?" Nisha snarls.

"A sedative. It is for you, but we would like Anthony to administer it. Understand, we do not wish for you to be hurt, but we also can't have you leave or witness what is about to transpire."

Nisha shoots me a wounded look, turns her gaze back to Ojal. "Do you know how long I have waited to be here? I was granted entry."

"You are here because we wished you to be. Now, you will be sedated because we wish you to be, or you will be dead because you refused." She pushes the syringe into my hands. "We would like you to do this, as proof of your commitment."

"Who is 'we'?" I ask.

"My employer and I."

"Sophia?"

Ojal maintains her inscrutably professional demeanour.

Nisha scowls, screams. Buries her head in her hands, then looks up at me and says, "Have I mentioned I do not like her?"

"It's come up, yes."

"Are you really going to let her do this?"

"I'm sorry. I have to see this through. Then we'll leave, together."

I place my hand on Nisha's leg, hoping she's paying attention when I dart my eyes down to where the syringe is resting. She nods, closes her eyes. I take the syringe and press it in, emptying the sedative, then hold her head as she slumps.

Ojal exits, but the door stays open. There appears to be

nothing on the other side. The light from the room blinds me to anything beyond it. It is like Ojal has entered a state of nonexistence.

I watch the abyss.

Muffled laughter emanates from the other side of the glass.

Footsteps approach the door.

You enter the room.

My head whorls with fear and confusion and love and adoration and guilt and remonstration. You press a button on a remote and the door slides closed behind you. You unsling the backpack from your shoulder and drop the remote inside. You study me with your infamously piercing glare and say a vast and hideous nothing. Then you pull your hand back and strike my face.

"Sophia…" I mumble, my tongue encumbered with drugs and remorse.

"You can stop calling me that now."

"I—"

"Do not speak until I ask you to." You throw your arms wide, proclaiming, "We are alone at last! Except for all these people who are watching." Muffled laughter emanates from behind the glass again. "Want to hear the big secret about Level 9? It is a theatre. The people behind this glass have paid a lot of money to be there. More money than anyone in Havana would make in ten lifetimes. They are right now sipping tea or champagne, snorting *cocaina*. Some of them have *putas* on their laps; some are there with notepads and pens, scribbling their little observations. Waiting to see what will happen. Because within these shiny walls? Anything is possible.

"Sometimes there is a revenge killing, or a world leader

confessing to hideous crimes. Revelations, executions, confessions. Once? A pope sat exactly where you are sitting now and admitted that he had made sacrifices to the devil on the altar at the Vatican church. You remember this thing, they called it the God particle? Higgs-something-bison? It was first revealed here, long before the world knew about it. What happens in this room is not magical, not divine. It is entertainment, like the Romans had with their colosseum. These people?" She points again at the mirrors. "Are bored, pathetic, one-percenters here for a *show*. And we will give them one, no?"

I stare at the mirrored walls surrounding us, hoping to glimpse billionaires reacting to your less-than-flattering description, but I see only my own defeated face staring back at me.

"I had to write an application. Like applying for a grant. To tell them the story of what happened, of what you did." You lean in close, lift my chin up, spit in my face. "And what I wanted to do to you."

I wipe the spit away. You always said that spitting was one of the most disgusting human behaviors imaginable, that there were cleverer and more effective ways to communicate spite.

"*This* is what I wanted to do. What I have dreamed of doing for years and years." You are close enough that I can breathe in your scent. It's all wrong. Sharper. Notes of blood and vodka. I stare into the eyes I used to know so well.

Something is wrong.

Something is missing.

"I wanted to tell you. How. Much. I. *Hate. You.*"

"Sophia, I—"

You slap me again, and this time a light buzz of pain stirs in my cheek. The wound in my hand is starting to work its way up from a dull ache, on its way to full-blown agony. You lift your shirt, revealing a flat, unmarked stomach.

I lift a trembling, drug-addled hand and point at it. "Where is your—"

"My scar? The scar she told you she got in a car accident? A scar that happened to run in a perfectly straight line across her belly, precisely where a cesarean scar would be?"

"You told me that—"

"*I* told you nothing. My mother told you a lie. One of many."

The pain in my hand is growing in intensity, like a stadium concert crowd entreating for an encore. "Your...mother?" I wonder how the billionaires are reacting to this, because I feel like the centre cannot hold.

"I am her daughter, Zoe. I look just like her, no? Identical, *mi abuela* says. Aren't genes strange? Little stories encoded in semen and blood, told and retold in new flesh and form. I am now only a few years younger than my mother was when you met her, but I have aged faster than I should. Revenge and obsession will do that, I guess. I was pulled from the scar that she lied to you about. It was the doorway that brought me into this world."

I crowbar open the connection between my consciousness and my mouth, manage to force out the words, "But...you, Sophia, didn't have a daughter?"

"She had me very young. She was only *trece*, thir-teen. Pregnancy is something of a, in English I think you would say 'occupational hassle'?"

"Occupational hazard?"

The person I believed to be you but is in fact Zoe snaps her fingers. "Yes! This one. An occupational hazard."

"For...singers?"

Her eyes grow wide with confusion and then delight. A bitter laugh escapes her lips. "*Dios mio*, no. Her other job. As *una mujer de la noche*. A prostitute."

The pain in my hand clamours for attention, but I'm currently preoccupied with the task of reeling in shock and denial.

"I never met my father, but it does not matter. He was a client, one of the many disgusting men who paid her to part her legs."

"She never told me."

"Of course she did not. But for you to not realise? You are either very stupid, or very in love. Both are possible, I suppose. Having a whining child running around is not so good for business. *Mi abuela* raised me."

She sweeps her arms in a dramatic circle. "Get ready, rich bastards behind the mirror! We are coming to the good part! I am—" she stops. Tips her head. "What's that noise?"

"What?"

"It is...a dripping sound?"

"I don't hear anything."

She looks around the room, finds nothing, continues. "I know what you're thinking. You were in *love*, truly in love! The stuff of poetry and Hollywood movies. The kind of love that ends wars, and starts them." She pats my cheek and laughs sardonically. "But by the time my mother met you she had changed her job description, just a little. She would find men, usually tourists, and swallow their hearts. Often she would have two or three at once, not just for a single night, but during the day as well. Like a girlfriend for hire. They would buy her dinners, pay her rent and her bills. Not exactly prostitution, but only a few steps away. With you, she'd all but given it up, because she was truly in love."

Zoe lets this sink in, then grabs my shirt. An impious smile forms on her lips. "But not with you. She was still in love with Carlos. He was the real thing. She never lied to him. She had promised that she would give up the life, she called it 'professional romance.'"

"This isn't true. Zoe, I know you want to hurt me. I deserve that, but these lies—"

"I am a lot of things, Anthony, but *una menterosa? Nunca.* I am telling you the truth, but to you the truth is a foreign language; you do not speak it well." She turns to the mirrored walls again. "Here it comes, *pendejos! Todos listos?*"

She turns back to me, leans in close, taps my nose. "But then you came along. You were her one last heist. A big, fat, juicy American whale. This is what they call an easy target in the con game. And you were a *very* easy target. She went out and bought a new dress, the red one you would not shut up about; cheap and red and shiny, like something a bird would find fascinating, or a very dull human man." She reaches into the backpack, removes the dress, dumps it in my lap. It is worn and tarnished. "It is a little tight on me, choked the air in my lungs. Made it hard to breathe. Sometimes women do this to themselves, take away our own ability to breathe in order to render a man breathless.

"She told Carlos, the man I hoped and prayed would be my stepfather, that you would be the last one. That she would strip you clean and send you home penniless, and we could start life as a new family together. She said she would spend some time with you, maybe six, maybe seven months, then chew you up and spit you out. Take everything you had."

"This isn't true. You're ly—"

She slaps me again.

My face stings, and the wound in my hand sends pain roaring through my body. "I need…my pills."

"You need to listen! This is your own story, but you have never heard it properly told. Eventually, she was close, she had you… I think the English expression is 'hook, line, and sinker?' She had your PIN, signature, credit card details, ID numbers, passwords, personal information. She had enough to take everything. American authorities wouldn't bother with her all the way over in Cuba. Besides, you weren't even supposed to be in the country, because of the embargo between our idiotic governments.

"But she found out Carlos had been lying. He had another woman. Yet another man who could not keep his dick in his pants. The night she found out, she went to see you. If I am honest? I think, maybe, there was a seed of real love underneath all of the deception. But this is a guess. And now? We will never know. Because that night she jumped." She grabs my hair, wrenches my head back, hisses into my ear. "And you ran and left her to *die*."

Murmurs and shuffling arise from behind the glass. From the corner of my eye, I see Nisha twitching.

"I'm sorry I'm sorry I'm sorry I—"

"Shut your mouth!" Zoe releases me, reaches into her pocket. "You left her to die. But she did not." She tosses a photo onto my lap. "Although I would not say that she is truly alive, either."

I pick up the photo with my bloodied, bandaged hand. And there you are. Really you, this time. Not your ghost. Not your memory. Not your daughter. The real you.

Your head is lolling to one side, eyes glassy and unfocused. Spittle hangs in the corner of your mouth. You are seated in a wheelchair, your dress stained with food. A deep, jagged scar runs across your forehead. A streak of grey cuts through your hair.

"She is no longer the great beauty you remember. She is like a child again. A simpleton. She knows a few basic words; *hombre, agua, kaka, madre, ida.* Sometimes she mumbles the lyrics to one of her songs. And she says your name: 'Anthony Anthony Anthony...' All day and all night I must hear this name. When I am feeding her food that dribbles down her face. When I am wiping her ass. When I am trying to get her to stop screaming in the middle of the night. And where are you, all this time? Here with the beaches and kangaroos. You were not easy to find. For a while, my uncle paid many people to try and find you, first good men who were bad at their job, then bad men who were good at their job. But you were too far away for even these ex-military types to find you. But these people did tell me about this place, the Orrery. Told me they could fund me, if they thought the entertainment was good enough. If I agreed to have my final revenge here, in this theatre." She turns again to the mirrors. "I hope you are pleased with your investment!"

Muted applause radiates from the other side of the glass. I want to smash through it and tear throats and gouge eyes, but I am spellbound by Zoe's story, the story I thought I knew.

"There was no trace of you on the internet, not after the day you left my mother to die. Until one day I found a newspaper article claiming you had died in Thailand. But I did not believe this, not for one second. I still had your name, your face, your passwords. I logged into your Facebook account: told it to tell me when new photos of you appeared. There was nothing nothing nothing for years. And then? Ping! Do I wish to tag this photo of Anthony Voynich? And yes. I wish to do this. Very much. There you are; outside a hospital, behind two self-obsessed *gringas* taking selfies. They put everything I need in this photo: the city, the name of the hospital, the date and time. Here you are, on the other side of the world. Waiting for me."

The teenage extortionists I met at the hospital must've posted the photo before I snatched the camera away, or accessed it from a cloud backup. Either way, all this time, all this work, all these cover stories, completely undone by two careless strangers.

"I figured out how to use the dark web. Posted an ad, found some lowlife scum to help us. Some man who worked with you—Goldie." She clocks the flicker of recognition in my eyes and laughs. "He was *very* eager to help. He really does not like you, do you know that?"

"Goldie's body is currently lying on my living room floor." I don't mean this as a threat, but it certainly comes out this way.

Zoe hesitates. Pulls a knife from her pocket. "You do not scare me. Nothing scares me anymore. It was a long, expensive flight here to Australia. Luckily, I have these sick *pendejos* to pay for the bill." She tips her head towards the unseen spectators behind us; an invisible Greek chorus exultant with the task of announcing my impending doom. "In this way my mother and I are not so different, taking the money of pathetic men to fulfill a fantasy. It is poetic justice that I avenge her this way." Zoe pokes at the bandages on my hand. "And I can see I am not the only one who wishes you harm." The wooden ring you gave me pokes out from under the bandages and she bursts into laughter, wrenches it from my finger. "You sad, wretched man! You kept this all these years? You know she gave these to all of her clients? Told each of them the same story—made by hand by her cousin

Maria blah blah blah. She bought them at the local market by the dozen." She tosses the ring away.

I clutch your photo in my hand. You as you truly are, rather than the deified simulacrum of you I've created. "*Mi abuela* raised her, then she had to raise me, and now she has to care for her daughter a second time. Because of you. Because you would not stay. You always told this lie that you loved her. That you would do anything for her. You have built a palace of lies, and you sit on the throne as its king. *La rey de las mentiras.*" She reaches into her bag and tosses me a manila folder and pen. "All these years, you have claimed to love my mother. Now, I want you to sign your name to this lie. Your *real* name. And I want you to leave everything you have to her. Every penny. Every shitty piece of clothing and furniture and, ah, *curiosadades*? In English, this is…"

"I understand. You want me to leave everything to her." I take a document out of the manila folder: a will and details of a bank account.

"Yes. Everything is to go to this account here. It is my grandmother's. She will use it to care for my mother." She stabs at the name: Sophia Valis Sr. The will is laughably flimsy in form, dissonantly powerful in its effect.

"Of course. I don't have much. But when I die, it's all hers. Everything." I sign the will without anything more than a cursory glance. It could be a contract for my soul and I wouldn't care. If anything I'd be giving Lucifer a raw deal, given how corrupted my spiritual real estate has become.

Zoe takes the contract. "Excellent. This brings us to the final matter." She sweeps her arms around the mirrored walls again. "Prepare yourselves, filthy perverts. We approach the grand finale!" She takes a silver flask from her bag, hands it to me. "You will leave her everything when you die. And you will die right now."

I turn the innocuous-looking flask over in my hands.

"It was a gift from my mother. I used to take it to school with me. My grandmother would make soup for me to have at lunch-time. When my mother fell, when you abandoned her? No more school for little Zoe. I had to spend my days caring for her and my nights working endless shitty jobs. I cleaned hotel rooms for rich tourists, like you. I used this flask to carry bleach, for the cleaning. It has that same bleach in it now, for you to drink."

I turn it over in my hands, wondering if the murmuring I can hear is coming from inside my head or behind the glass around me. It's such an unremarkable object, weighing little more than a paperback novel. Certainly not as elaborate a method of exe-cution as a hanging or crucifixion, but every bit as effective. It's fitting, I suppose. A quiet, simple end to all this. I can finally atone for leaving, and for lying to myself—and to you—for all these years. I can help your family, and you. Give up on my use-less, endless quest for atonement and penance.

I look at my own distorted reflection in the cylindrical silver of the flask, then up at Zoe. "You must really love her, to go to such great lengths to seek revenge. She is fortunate to have you."

Consternation washes over her face, and she casts her eyes down, mutters something to herself I can't quite hear. A prayer, perhaps. Or a string of curses. She looks up at me and says, "*Gracias*. Those are the first truthful words you have said." With the wrath temporarily absent from her face, she is truly beauti-ful. I wonder what kind of young woman she might have grown into, if not for the arrival of an errant American tourist into her mother's life. She takes the flask from me, unscrews the lid. Presses the open container into my hand. "Goodbye, Anthony. Now you can rest."

There is a clamouring of excitement from behind the mirrored walls. Rather than fear, I feel a curious exhilaration, a sort of pre-death euphoria. *Maybe, after I'm gone, you can find a way to forgive me.*

I'm sorry, Sophia.

I swill the bleach around in the bottle like I'm about to sample wine, then close my eyes. The approaching roar of the all-encompassing void calls to me, not just provisionally this time, but for a boundless, endless, formless eternity.

The room dissolves, time dilates, my mind empties.

I tip the bottle to my lips.

28

The first thing I notice is the screaming, an infernal choir of anguish and agony. Strangely, my voice is not among them. I open my eyes and see Zoe doubled over, clawing at her eyes. Nisha discards the flask she's just emptied into Zoe's face, then rummages in her backpack for the door remote. Some of the bleach has splashed on my shirt, but fortunately not my skin. The back of Nisha's pants have a wet patch where the sedative has leaked through her prosthetic leg. The mirrored walls around us are shaking, trembling. Cracks begin to emerge, glass shards fall to the ground. Fingers emerge from the gaps, scrambling to pry them wider. Blood spills against the edges of the new openings, freshly opened wounds in some strange celestial skin.

Nisha opens the door with the remote, grabs my arm with her free hand and screams, "RUN!"

She pulls me out the door. I take a moment to look behind

me, like Lot's wife glancing back at the destruction of Sodom. Zoe's eyes are clenched shut, her hands flailing blindly in front of her.

The door closes behind us, and my adrenaline kicks in. We run down the corridor and find a service elevator. Nisha hits the button for the ground floor, and we descend in a whir of cogs and gears. She watches the painfully slow descent of the indicator light, chest heaving.

"Nisha, I—"

"Why would you bother pretending to sedate me if you were just going to fucking kill yourself anyway?"

"I wanted to protect you!"

She scoffs. "Really? The man who was about to drink a bottle of bleach because he was asked to by a woman he's barely met was trying to offer protection?"

We're almost at ground level. Distant klaxons sound somewhere above us. "I wasn't thinking straight. The drugs made my head foggy." As though responding to my voice, the last vestiges of the pain meds disappear, and my hand roars with agony. I reach into my pocket and swallow a couple more pills.

Nisha stares straight ahead and says through gritted teeth. "When these doors open? We run for the car. We drive. And we don't ever look back. Understand?"

"Yes."

We reach our floor and run out into a storage area, a dank maze of boxes and broken computers and cleaning supplies. There are no exit signs in sight so we charge straight ahead, taking corners at random, shoving boxes and brooms out of the way as we run.

"Over here, I think I see an exit!" Nisha yells.

Behind us there is the clamping of boots and yelling of furious security guards. I turn the corner to find Nisha struggling to open a rusty old metal service door with a filthy glass window. "There's something blocking it from the other side. I can't get it open."

I glance around the room for something to smash the window, but it offers up only a selection of faded tablecloths and a couple of bottles of Jiff.

"What's your leg made out of?"

"...?"

Behind us, the voices grow closer. "Your leg, what's it made from?"

"It's a blend of titanium-aluminum alloy coated with—"

"That'll work. I'm going to pick you up, you need to kick the window. Then I'll push you through, and you need to land on the other side."

"I...what?"

I scoop her up, ignoring the pain in my hand and her surprised shriek, then hold her aloft. "Ready?"

"Yes?"

I ignore the uncertainty in her voice and push her forward, she draws her legs back and jabs the prosthesis out in front of her as I hurl her towards the window. It splinters and presses outwards, but doesn't quite give. A trio of security guards yells at us to stop, but before I can pull her back, she's already landed a second kick. The window explodes in a shower of glass, and I use the last of my strength to throw her through the opening, praying it's wide enough to spare her anything worse than a few minor cuts on the way out. She curses as she lands, but scrambles quickly to her feet and shoves whatever is blocking the door out of the way.

I push the door open just as hairy-fingered hands reach out to grab me, then slam it closed behind me.

"Help me push this back!" yells Nisha.

I keep my shoulder pressed against the door and awkwardly grab at the handle of the broken fridge she's pushing along the ground. We shove it back into place and watch the door shaking as the guards attempt to force it open.

Nisha already has her keys in her hand. I follow her as she dashes around the corner. The basketball court where her car is parked is perhaps a hundred feet away. I've never been so excited to see a thirty-year-old midrange sedan in my entire life.

"I'll drive!" I call out as I overtake Nisha, the faded blue of her car calling to me with the glorious promise of freedom.

"No! You are not in any condition to—"

A bullet cuts past my ear, obliterating the rear passenger window. Dante pokes his head out and begins barking. "This is kind of my forte." I insist, rounding the side of the car to the driver's side as a bullet blasts into the passenger door.

She relents and tosses me the keys. I unlock the car and climb inside as more bullets sing past us, slugging into the sides of neighbouring cars. I rev the engine and Nisha opens the door, I wait for her to get most of her body inside before slamming the accelerator. She screams as she slams the door behind her and pulls on her seat belt. Dante barks at the slew of bullets filling the air around us. The rear window disintegrates. We tear out of the parking lot, tyres screeching as we pull sharply in front of a station wagon. The man behind the wheel screams and swerves across the road, right into a Toyota pulling a camping trailer coming from the other direction. Metal shrieks against metal. I glance in the rearview mirror to see the two drivers exit their cars and scream at each other. A black Escalade emerges from the Orrery's parking lot and pulls up behind them, its progress blocked by the barricade of twisted metal scratched across both lanes of the road.

I switch gears and eat up as much road as possible. Traffic lights, billboards, buildings whir by and the wind whips through the broken windows. For a long time, the only noise is the roar of the engine and Dante's barking. Finally, he settles.

I turn to Nisha. Her hands are gripped tight to the door handle and seat, her eyes locked straight ahead. The buildings grow sparser, the billboards less frequent. The highway becomes a dark river cutting through miles of empty earth.

For the first hour or so I keep glancing in the rearview mirror, inspecting every car trailing us for adversaries, ears trained against the rush of wind for the sound of bullets. After a couple of hundred miles, the road is bereft of cars save for the occasional eighteen-wheeler. Both the front window and the rearview mirror yield nothing but the steady intervals of highway lights, and I breathe the late-night air in deep and turn and smile at Nisha. She returns my manic grin, and there is nothing but the pitch-black road beneath us and the midnight-black sky above, and we are free.

29

Hours later, when I am at last sure that Nisha is asleep, I pull into a gas station, step out of the car, and find your photo in my pocket.

30

When Nisha wakes me, the sun is high in the sky. She tosses me a pair of sunglasses, preempting my discomfort. "Where are we?" I murmur.

"Mildura."

"Where's—"

"About four and a half hours east of Adelaide. We need to sleep and get new phones, and you need to get your hand patched up."

31

Adelaide is both smaller and more beautiful than I anticipated. I stare out the window as Nisha follows the serene voice of the GPS through the city's neat, tree-lined streets. We pull up outside a condo complex, and Nisha lets the engine idle, watching for movement inside.

Almost as much to fill the silence as to retrieve the answer I ask, "Before we left I found a tracking device on my motorcycle. I assume that was—"

"Yes. It was me."

"Can I ask why?"

Nisha keeps her eyes glued on the condo window. "To protect you. To keep you safe."

A shadow appears in the window behind the blinds, too short for an adult. Pop music is blaring from inside. Nisha turns to me, eyes brimming with tears.

32

Kamasi Washington's new record—yet another one of Nisha's recommendations—sings through the foyer speakers. When I first arrived, the endless flaccid loop of classical piano almost drove me mad. For some people music is like oxygen in that they can't live without it, and for others music is like oxygen in that they pay no attention to it. Our illustrious hotel manager is from the latter camp. I was hesitant to change the music at first, wanting to avoid drawing attention to myself at all costs, but once I realised that anything short of death metal covers of the Beatles would go completely unnoticed, I started programming some playlists that were less likely to result in early-onset dementia.

Outside, golden rays of sunlight—still a novelty to me—stream over the rolling green hills of the vineyards. If it weren't for the cars idly wending up and down Tanunda's central street, you could almost be tricked into believing you were staring at a painting. I cast my eyes back down to the pages of the remarkably awful spy novel I found in room 26 yesterday afternoon: *Death Protocol: Blood and Bullets in the Bahamas*. It features gems such as "Randall hated the heat almost as much as he hated getting shot, and he *really* hated getting shot." Prose so wooden you could build a house with it. I'll pick up something else on my next day off, but for the moment, pulp like this is exactly what my brain needs.

A black BMW pulls into the driveway and a grey-haired gentleman in his late fifties steps out. I've been here almost a month without any signs of trouble, so I've started to let my guard down a little, but I still make the same precautionary risk assessments just in case. The number plate seems dirty enough to have been on for a while but not dirty enough to have been intentionally obscured. It also reads: AWSUM, far too vain and distinctive for anyone trying to keep a low profile. He's too old and slim to be any kind of standover man. A woman young enough to be his daughter's much younger friend steps out of the car. Nothing to see here, just a run-of-the-mill extramarital affair.

They enter the foyer. I put the book down and Maurice Micklewhite slips behind the wheel of my consciousness—formal, eager to please, but with a hint of snark when the situation calls for it.

The gentleman approaches the desk and says, "I have a booking under 'Burton.'"

"No problem, Mr. Burton. Lovely to have you with us." Micklewhite's clipped, posh English accent marches out of my mouth. It's an enjoyable voice to use; I get the same pleasure from bringing it out of semiretirement as I imagine musicians do when they return to a beloved instrument they haven't used in many years. "And have you stayed with us before, Mr. Burton?"

"No. This is my first time." The woman shoots him a glare. "Our first time."

"Wonderful! Could I interest you in our wine tour? We visit a magnificent selection of—"

"No, thank you."

"Are you quite sure? It really is a fabulous a—"

"Yes. I'm sure."

I tap at the keyboard, pull up his booking, make a show of being impressed. "I see you've booked our executive suite. You are in for a real treat! The view is just *stunning*. Now if I could grab your credit card—"

He hands it to me; it's brand new. The expiry date is years away and the plastic is fresh and clean. I wonder if he picked it up specifically for the purposes of this affair. I swipe the card while at the same time holding the escape key on the keypad. It beeps. I pretend to be confused and scan it again. The machine spits out a receipt which reads "user error," but I make use of a little sleight of hand and switch it out for one that displays the words "card error, please contact your bank," which I keep on hand for purposes such as these. Maurice displays his trademark look of polite regret and says, "Terribly sorry, sir. Perhaps you have another card we could—"

"We just used that at a petrol station ten minutes ago!"

"I'm so sorry, sir. Once we get that message it's out of my hands."

"I'll pay in cash then."

"I'm afraid we do require a credit card to cover incidentals, regardless. But not to worry. We'll just give them a quick ring, have this sorted in a jiffy!"

His mistress glares at him. "Our dinner reservation is in an hour, I need to get to the room and get ready!"

I pass her the magnetic key. "No trouble at all, ma'am, you head on up and make yourself comfortable. Mr. Burton and I will have this all sorted in a minute. Just head on around to your right and head on up the staircase."

She plants a peck on her lover's cheek and disappears.

I offer Mr. Burton a conspiratorial grin. "If you do have another card and you'd like the charge to be a little more…discreet, I can arrange to have it appear under the auspices of our parent company, Chatsworth and Green?"

"Yes. Good. Do that then."

"For a small fee…"

His face darkens and the number in my head immediately doubles.

"…of one hundred dollars."

His jaw drops and his face flushes red with ire. I hold his gaze and watch the cogs whir inside his head until he finally elects the path of least resistance and slams a one-hundred-dollar bill on the table.

"Much obliged, sir." I slide the note into my pocket, relishing a feeling which I would describe as "AWSUM." I finish the check-in, then turn to the bar fridge behind me and remove a bottle of our complimentary "sparkling white wine," a generous euphemism for the effervescent cleaning solvent we offer to guests on arrival. "Compliments of the house, sir. Enjoy your stay." I place the second room key on the counter. He snatches it up and storms outside to park the car.

I return my gaze to the idyllic view outside, and I'm about to resume chapter three of *Death Protocol* when Ava appears from the kitchen, lifts herself up onto the bench next to me, and plucks the book from my hands. She scoffs at the cover and tosses it to the floor, swinging her legs as she says, "I saw you chasing that bribe, Mo."

I tug at my collar in mock consternation. "Oh, golly, Miss Ava! Please don't tell the boss. Why, I'd be in all kindsa hot water!" I pick up the book, place it on the bench. "Also, I've told you I don't like the nickname 'Mo.'"

"Give it time. It'll grow on you."

"I'm betting you won't tell Frank anything, given that I elected not to mention the time when you came to work stoned."

"Which one?" she laughs and punches me gently in the shoulder. She's been here a few months, clearly running from something. I haven't completely figured out her story yet, but the wedding band tan and the faint scarring on her forearm where she's had a tattoo removed are large pieces of the puzzle. "Hey, my buddy Charlie wants to know if your friend is single. What's her name again, Nusha, Nishi?"

"Nisha. And, yes, she is single. She's also a lesbian."

"So's Charlie. I'll let her know. Thanks." She slides down off the bench. "Dating opportunities aren't exactly limitless in a little tourist town like this. Gotta chase those leads when you got 'em." She picks up one of the chocolates from the bowl on the counter, unwraps it, pops it in her mouth, shoves the wrapper in my jacket pocket. "Janie managed to liberate a few prime bottles from the cellar, we're gonna take 'em down to the firepit on the Lindsworth Vineyard tonight, have a little payday party. You should tell Nisha to come along."

"She's in Adelaide right now, but I think she was planning on being back tonight. I'll let her know."

"Oh, yeah, what's she doing in Adelaide?"

Reconnaissance, research into sedatives, assessing security systems, studying juvenile emancipation laws. "Planning a family reunion."

"Cool. Well, tell her Charlie's keen to get to know her. But no pressure, it's a casual deal."

"Like everything around here."

She laughs and says, "Yeah, that is the default setting, more or less." She starts to walk away, then half-turns back to me. "Hey, I heard that when the two of you arrived in town your car had a bunch of busted-up windows. That true?"

"Absolutely. And we had a boot filled with cocaine and diamonds as well."

Ava snorts a laugh. "Yeah, got it. Fucking rumours in this town, right? When there's not much to do but eat, drink, and be merry, people tend to make a little drama just for the fun of it." She starts to walk away, but calls back over her shoulder. "Oh, and, you could make an appearance tonight, too, if you wanted. Provided you can tear yourself away from *Death Protocol*."

She disappears into the kitchen, humming to herself. I take out my phone and log into the bank account I've created for Maurice. It's quite a change, being paid on a regular cycle by a single legitimate employer rather than receiving sporadic sums of both blood and bloodstained money. I run some quick calculations to figure out how much I'll need to pay expenses for the next couple of weeks. Living at the hotel means I have free rent and a near limitless supply of buffet food, easily pilfered wine, and crappy paperbacks from the book exchange, so I don't need much. I could probably make the hundred dollars sitting in my pocket last for weeks if need be.

My first paycheque went to setup costs—mostly clothes and new ID for Maurice. This time I just need to set aside a little bit for essentials. I take out the scrunched-up piece of paper with Sophia Valis Sr.'s bank details I've been keeping in my pocket these last few weeks. I enter her name and account number into the banking app, and create a perpetually recurring transaction. I type in the transaction label: *Penance*.

33

I pull the work van up outside Nisha's new house, a quaint, one-storey place a few minutes' walk from the main street. It looks like it belongs in a miniature train set. I ring the door-bell, and she answers wrapped in a towel. "I am so sorry. I lost track of time! Strange how the hours seem to slip away from you here. Come in and have a drink, say hi to Dante. There's wine and a present for you on the kitchen bench." She runs into the bathroom.

Dante runs over and envelops me in a canine tornado of fur and affection. I rub his belly then head into the kitchen. I pick up the box on the bench and turn it over. "Where did you get this? I've been looking for one of these forever." I marvel at the three-thousand-piece puzzle depicting M. C. Escher's mind-bending *Metamorphosis II*.

"I know, you mentioned it a couple of times," Nisha calls out from the bathroom. "I have a client who deals in vintage puzzles and games who got her hands on it for me. I thought I could help you put it together one evening."

She's greatly underestimating the time it takes to assemble three thousand pieces, but the gesture is truly humbling. It might be the most thoughtful gift I've ever received. I open the bottle of wine and pour a glass. Wine is everywhere in this vineyard-ensconced town, it seems to simply appear on benches, like ants in winter. I sit down on the couch. The sound of Neko Case on the stereo is drowned out by Nisha's hair dryer. She's kept her new abode a little neater than her old place; only four computers and six screens on display on the trestle table in the living room, practically a digital detox by Nisha's standards.

I poke my head around the corner. Nisha displays a near supernatural ambidexterity as she blow-dries her hair with her left hand while applying lipstick with her right. I sit back down and sip the wine. It's unreasonably delicious. I put the glass down and glance up at the smoke detector where I installed a camera a few weeks ago, then sit down at her main laptop and type in the password I've watched her use on the video feed.

"What time is it?" she calls out from the bathroom.

"7:48."

"Ah, I am so late! I am sorry."

"It's okay. I'm in no rush."

"What is she like, this Charlie? Do you know anything about her?"

"No. But Ava seems like she keeps good company. I suppose that counts for something."

She shuts off the hairdryer and I snap the screen closed. Her face appears around the corner, plastered in a red-lipsticked grin.

"What?"

"You talk about her a lot, you know." She disappears again, closing the door behind her.

Dante pads over, plants himself at my feet.

I open Signal and scan the conversation logs.

34

"You are very quiet this evening, Anthony."

"Just tired. Long day of being Maurice Micklewhite."

"Yes. I like this one better than your old personas, I have to say. Maurice is very charming, as one would expect from the artist better known as Michael Caine."

I pull the car up at the end of the road. "It's a nice night. I thought we might walk the last little stretch through the forest."

"That sounds wonderful. The full moon is marvellous."

We step out of the car, each clutching a bottle of wine. Leaves and dirt crunch beneath our feet. "I'm glad she got the first payment okay."

Nisha stops in her tracks like she's been hit with a tranquilliser dart. "I am afraid I do not know what you are referring to?"

I twist off the top of the wine bottle, take a swig. "You should know by now that I can tell when you're lying."

Her expression shimmers from surprise to confusion to

defeat. "Yeah, well. I could bloody well say the same about you, couldn't I?"

I throw my head back with laughter and pass her the wine. "*Australian*, really? All this time you were putting on that incredibly precise global blended accent, and your real voice is fucking *Australian*?"

"One of the hardest accents to fake, yeah. I moved here young enough that I lost my native accent. The rest of the story I told you is true, it's just that my parents came over here together initially." She swigs. "This wine is fucking great. All the wine here is fucking great."

I snatch it back from her. "Is Zoe satisfied with your services, Nisha?"

Her eyes drop to the ground. "Actually, it's Deepika."

"Deepika." I repeat, tasting the sound of it in my mouth. Now, at long last, we know one another's true names.

"When did you figure it out?" The con artist formerly known as Nisha asks.

"I knew something was up when I got a glimpse of the video feed of my apartment on your screen when I came to visit your place. You turned it off quickly, but I'd already seen it. Rookie mistake."

"Shiiiit. I was worried you'd seen that. Yeah, well. I mostly had those there for your safety. I was worried Goldie would put an end to you. Should've been more careful, I guess."

"Probably. I installed cameras at your place too, when we arrived. Watched you type all your passwords. Guess we're even there. I also thought it was odd you recovered from your injury so quickly when Zoe attacked you."

"We used a squib."

"...?"

"Standard film effect device. Little bag of fake blood that bursts open on contact."

"Ah, makes sense. But I wasn't completely sure until after we went to Level 9. Some of that 'bleach' you threw in Zoe's face splashed on my shirt, but it didn't fade or discolour. Then when we got the car repaired, I doubled back to the mechanic's after you'd left and found a rubber bullet in the backseat. It was strange enough those goons had such terrible aim, made a lot more sense when I figured out they never meant to hit us in the first place. And when you were in the bathroom earlier, I checked the conversation logs in that Signal app you told me about. I saw all your messages with her; how she set up everything up with the staff on Level 6 so we'd be invited to the top floor."

Deepika rubs her neck. "That's actually how I came across the job in the first place. I was looking for information about Level 9 when I saw Zoe's post."

"How fortunate that I was able to assist you on your voyage of discovery."

She winces. "I was asked to try and appear as though I was keeping you away from her, from danger, to add to the authenticity of the whole charade. But when we were cleaning up the body in the bathroom and I pleaded with you to forget her and run away, to come with me and start somewhere new, I was being sincere. I was hoping I could persuade you to stay away from her. But as we both know, you're not an easy person to persuade."

She kicks at the dirt. A bat drops out of a tree and flaps its leathery wings above us. "Well. Whaddya wanna do now? I'm pretty much ready to get April back. Just need a couple of days to pack up and find someone else to help me retrieve her, and then you won't ever have to see me again."

"That part was genuine?"

"Like you said; the best lies are always built on a foundation of truth."

"But Dante really does like me, right? Tell me that part's true, at least."

"Of course he does! He adores you. Even though…"

"Even though what?"

"I only met Dante just before you did. I picked him up from a shelter to help accelerate our connection. Animals are very effective social-engineering aids. But I have grown to genuinely love him. *And you.*"

We study each other's micro expressions, tells, eye movements—mining for reams of emotional data until at last I break the silence by saying, "Yeah. You too." I'm almost as surprised to hear the words come out of my mouth as she is. "Are you supposed to do anything else, besides keep an eye on me?"

"Just ensure that you continue to make payments. A trusted friend nudging someone to do something is usually more effective, long-term, than standover men making threats. It's a pretty standard long con technique. And I can understand why she wants insurance, but I think I know you well enough by now to be sure you'll keep your word anyway."

"I will. But I'd like you to stick around in any case."

"…?"

"I'm serious."

"Can I ask why?"

I turn and start walking towards the fire. The sound of laughter echoes through the bush. She grabs my arm and turns me around. "Hey! Anthony. C'mon, answer me. I can't ever forgive myself for what I did to you, and I don't expect you to forgive me either, but it really was all so that I could get my sister back. I needed the help, and I needed the money. But I wasn't lying when I told you how much you mean to me. Believe me when I say that I hate myself more than you ever could." Someone throws a new log onto the fire, sending sparks sailing into the night sky. We watch them rise, spin, and fade into nothingness.

I swig more wine, pass the bottle to her. "All of this self-flagellation really isn't a good look on you, you know that?"

She takes the bottle, stares at me as she drinks. "Touché."

"Let me know when you're ready and we'll do the retrieval job."

"...are you sure?"

"That's what friends are for, right?"

"Anthony, I don't know what to say."

I take the bottle back from her, hold it by the neck, assessing its adjusted weight. "Save it. We've got plenty of time." I toss it into the air, catch it behind my back.

"Cute trick."

"Ava taught me. Broke a few dozen bottles before I could nail it."

"Is that the only trick she's taught you?"

"So far, yeah. But we'll see what happens." I gesture towards the fire. "We shouldn't keep Charlie waiting. I understand she's eager to meet you. Or a version of you, at least."

Nisha/Deepika nods. "Alright. We'll finish this discussion in the morning then. Besides, I've got this bottle of grenache that I'd like to share with you. It's older than I am. Or at least, older than I *tell* people I am. I've been saying I 'just turned' thirty for the last couple years." She places her hand on my cheek. Her smile is luminous in the dark. "Promise you won't tell?"

READ ON FOR AN EXCERPT FROM
ANOTHER EXCITING MYSTERY
BY J. M. DONELLAN

KILLING ADONIS

1

Cakewalking

"I hate this song."

"Freya, you didn't answer my question."

"I'll take a Moscow Mule. Cheers."

A disapproving frown fills Jane's face. "I didn't ask if you wanted another drink, Frey, I asked if you're serious about this."

"Yeah, I heard you. I was hoping I could change the subject. Look, I don't want to think of it so much as 'giving up on my lifelong dreams of working for the Red Cross in East Timor' as 'embracing my backup dream of sitting on the couch getting fat watching *Seinfeld* reruns.' East Timor will still be there in a year or two. Unless Indonesia forcefully reclaims it, I suppose."

"But this is what you've been working towards, what you *always* said you were going to do…four years' experience in a local hospital, then a job in East Timor. You bored us all to death talking about it. I get that you're upset about what happened to Valerie…."

Freya winces at the mention of Valerie's name, images of blood and steel ricocheting through her head. "No. You don't get it at all. If I had a religion to lose then, I would be losing it right now. What happened to Val was…Christ, you know what? We've been over this. If I start talking about it again I'm just going to end up the weird girl crying in the bar that everyone looks at. Let's talk about something else. You want another drink?"

"Vodka and Coke, easy on the vodka."

"Got it." Freya moves through the crowd of bleary-eyed early evening revellers. The air is a sweltering haze of foul-smelling smoke and ear-wrenchingly bad American electro-noise. It sounds like a drunken tattoo artist singing karaoke over the glitchy bleeping of an ancient Commodore 64 computer.

On nights like this the clouds of colour swimming in front of her eyes are usually more a source of entertainment than annoyance, but right now their buzzing and bouncing greatly vexes her. She ignores the "little Kandinskys" dancing in her vision and walks inside.

She passes through the doors of Ric's for, what, the ten-millionth time? How many hazy drunken nights has she begun, regretted, and then repeated here? Too many to count. She checks her reflection in the glass and is as satisfied as she ever allows herself to be. A curtain of crimson hair frames her elegant cheekbones and kryptonite green eyes. She would like to be a little thinner, she supposes. Her tight red dress, paired with matching red gloves, displays her curves that are teetering between "femininely seductive" and "a little more to love." But if she lost any more weight she could hardly criticise the waif-like creatures on TV and, more to the point, filling this bar, with half as much vitriol. And she enjoys doing that.

She stands at the bar waiting for the Barbie doll ahead of her to finish her mating dance with the bartender. When the girlish tittering and batting of eyelids goes on for too long she says, "Hey, Twinkle Toes, when you're done staring down at that fake blonde's fake breasts you want to rustle me up a couple of drinks? I'll take a Moscow Mule, heavy on the Moscow, and a vodka and Coke, heavy on the part that isn't Coke."

"Hey, sweetheart, I'll serve you these but, after that, you'd better slow down."

"Sorry Nosebleed, I have a strict policy of not taking advice from anyone who has brand-name tattoos on his neck."

"Nosebleed? Shit! Is my...?"

"Not yet. It's a preemptive nickname. Call me 'sweetheart' one more time and it'll suddenly be highly applicable."

"Jesus, I was just being friendly!"

"You and Merriam-Webster have very different interpretations of 'friendly.' Now hurry up with that booze. I've got a future I need to avoid thinking about."

The bartender complies with a grimace. Freya grins at him and walks back outside, holding the two glasses as proudly as a hunter bearing fresh kill.

Jane's brow is still furrowed with the same endearing yet irritating concern. She takes the drink from Freya's hand, nods appreciatively, sips it, then says, "Christ! Freya, are you sure you asked them to go easy on the vodka? This is like making out with Dostoyevsky!"

"Yeah, pretty sure," Freya lies. She's a good liar. It's a skill she prides herself on. The clamour of the bar rushes in to fill the silence between them. Finally Freya says, "Listen, I know I'm getting a little worked up about this. I don't mean to be a bitch. I just need a year in a cakewalk job before I get back to saving the world one penicillin injection at a time.

"After what happened to Valerie, I need some time out. Or off. Or maybe in. I won't spend the next ten years as a guilt-ridden workaholic until I get knocked up by some surgeon who decides two weeks before the baby's due that he's staying with his wife. I need one lap around the sun. To paint, eat, drink, live, love, drive to the beach. Then I'll get back to turning into the person I've spent the last quarter-century trying to become."

"But it's crazy to give it all up. All through university, you worked twice as hard as any of us. Even if Karen had slightly better grades…"

"Karen had slightly better breasts, too, and a tendency to display them to any tutor with questionable morals. I'm happy to take second place with my integrity fully intact."

Jane sighs, leans back into her chair, and takes another swig from her allegedly half-strength vodka and Coke. "Okay. Fine. Are you really serious about wanting a cakewalk job?"

"I just want to go cakewalking for a year, I swear."

Jane nods begrudgingly. Freya can see the disappointment in her friend's eyes, but she has more than enough guilt to wrestle with on her own, let alone deal with someone else's. "Jane? You've got that face on. That face you get when you're trying not to say something you really want to say, like when you found out that the girl Mark left you for was admitted to the emergency room after the collagen in her lips exploded…."

"Alright, alright, alright. I do have something and, from the sound of it, you'd be paid really well to do almost nothing, plus the job's right here in Brisbane."

"Are you kidding me? Why the hell have you been holding out on me?"

"Well, the whole thing's a little...unusual. But if you really want to put your work in East Timor on hold for a year, well, I know how goddamned stubborn you are."

"Like a mule, Jane; an adorable mule."

"Alright, but don't say I didn't warn you. I have this little 'help wanted' card that a weird rich lady gave me at that fancy benefit at the Tivoli last week."

Jane reaches into her handbag and removes a pristine white card that's more like a wedding invitation than a job advertisement. Freya inspects the front.

WANTED: NURSE
(a proper girl, not a silly male)
PRETTY (but not too pretty)
CLEVER (but not too clever)

"Hmm. Not big on tact, these people, are they? Certainly sounds weird enough to be interesting. Now, can we leave the serious talk 'til tomorrow when we're chronically hungover, and start getting properly drunk?"

—

Three, or maybe four, or maybe sixteen hours later—it's hard to tell after inhaling heroic quantities of booze—Freya finds herself at a bar she swore on her mother's grave to never enter again. She mumbles an apology to her dearly departed and downs the last of her drink.

"Callum, do you think I'm a fuck-up?"

Callum sips at his whisky before answering. "Freya, I think that even da Vinci would be asking that if he was as drunk as you are now, although he might phrase it differently."

"Everyone's doing…like…amazing things…and I'm not. I want to find out about the world before I try to save it. And maybe date someone close to normal before I start collecting caesarean scars, a mortgage, a husband who resents me for letting myself go too quickly and a little house on the prairie."

"Jesus, has Jane been drilling that stuff into you again? Why'd she go home so early, anyway?"

"She has to do some disgustingly wholesome activity tomorrow morning, like bake cupcakes for the homeless whilst running a marathon to raise awareness for canine epilepsy or some crap. That girl is always so da–*Oh my God, I love this song!* No… wait…fuck. I love that David Bowie song they sampled to make this piece of shit. Now everything's going all purple. I *hate* when everything goes purple. You know what I mean?"

He smiles and shakes his head. "Rarely, if ever. But, yes, I understand. I'm hardly the poster boy for the Suburban Australian Dream."

"Oh yeah, I forgot. Hey, everybody, look at Callum…he's a boy who likes boys. Isn't that so different and *interesting*?"

"Frey, if I didn't love you to death I would beat you to death with this bar stool."

"I wish you were the first person to tell me that. Tonight. And Jane's not so bad—I shouldn't be so harsh. She just makes the rest of us look like jerks because she's such an overachiever. She found a job offer for me. Says it's easy and the pay is good, but it sounds a little weird."

"You gonna check it out?"

"Sure, why the hell not? I've got the card in my—" Freya's sentence aborts in midair as she begins madly hammering Callum's arm with her fist.

"For the love of God, Freya, what the hell is your problem?"

"Look!" she whispers in reverential awe, pointing at the street outside. "It's her!"

"What the hell are you whispering for? Her who? Oh, *her*! Yes, she is something, isn't she?"

They watch as the "her" skilfully navigates obstacles presented by the drunken horde as though she were in a platform video game, dodging multicoloured projectile vomit, flailing limbs, lascivious leers, and glasses smashed haphazardly on the pavement. She glides through each of these minor perils with the unwavering grace of a Russian princess. Her eyes are focused straight ahead, each step is poised and dainty. She is dressed, as always, in an outfit so grandiloquent that it very nearly defies the laws of physics.

A feather boa curls around her neck like a flamboyant serpent, her dress clings like a second skin, and her bright red heels clack heavily on the concrete like a war drum. She ignores the heckles thrown her way—not so much with silent defiance as the imperious manner that shows responding is completely beneath her.

"She is *so* amazing!" Freya sighs in admiration.

"Really, you don't think she's a little strange?"

"Obviously, but that's the whole point. She is what she is and she doesn't care what anyone else thinks. She's so *enigmagnetic*!"

As though she can hear Freya and Callum across the crowded street, she turns for one brief moment and glances their way.

Marilyn Monroe locks eyes with them and treats them to a dazzling, confident smile, then disappears into the throng.

Freya smiles at the space where Marilyn once stood, before staring drunkenly into Callum's handsome brown eyes and murmuring, "If you weren't my best friend and annoyingly gay, I would definitely take you home with me."

"Thanks, that's the best offer I've had all week. One last round?"

"Please, madam, you are talking very loudly! I must concentrate my driving."

"Yeahyeahyeah, very, you know...studious of you or whatever. I guess they raise 'em good in Tajikistan."

"As I said before, I am a proud son of Turkmenistan."

"Right! I knew...I knew it was one of the 'stans. Pakistan, Uzbekistan, Kurdistan, Cantunderstand. Ha! Lil joke. You like that one? No? Nothing? No dice? Doin' the ol' stare straight ahead and pretend you can't hear me, huh? You know what, I'd probably do that too if I was driving around some drunk idiot who didn't know how to tell the difference between countries. Fair call. Hey, you know once when I was on holiday in Fiji I met this American guy who wouldn't stop staring at my chest and he was all like 'I love the choc-o-late from your country.' And I was like, 'Are you talking about *Austria*?' I mean, Christ, how can you be so ignor—Wait, this is my house! Okay, lemme...I gotta find my...Oh fuck..."

"What is problem?"

Freya rummages through her handbag. "I think...I think I lost my purse in the Beat...or maybe the Bowery."

"Madam, I must have my pay."

"No but, see, s'okay cos I keep a twennie in the letterbox for this 'xact reason."

Freya tumbles awkwardly out of the cab with an impressive lack of grace. Her bare feet collide with the cold cement of the footpath, painfully alerting her to the fact that she has also lost her shoes. She snatches the twenty-dollar bill she keeps hidden in an envelope beneath a rock behind the front fence and hands it to the taxi driver.

"Peace out, brother," she slurs, holding up two fingers in what she imagines is a magnanimous display of cross-cultural solidarity, but more closely resembles the gesture of a pop star posing for the paparazzi on her way into rehab. The driver considers demanding the extra dollar-twenty-five she owes him, but thinks better of it and speeds off into the early morning, where a microwave dinner and his long-suffering wife await him.

Freya struggles with the lock on the door and bursts inside with a series of crashes. She stumbles up the stairs to her apartment, opens the door, and hurls her handbag against the wall, where its contents spill out like the organs of a goat beneath a voodoo knife. In the rubble of makeup, aspirin, and fast-food vouchers is an extravagant white-and-silver card that she vaguely recalls Jane giving her, somewhere between their fourth and fourteenth Moscow Mule.

The card lies there, incongruent with its squalid surrounds. If the card had a voice, it would no doubt be a royal accent lamenting the agony it was enduring among this trash and riff-raff. Freya giggles at the thought of a talking business card, then picks it up and whispers, "Sssssh, sssssssssh." She squints to discern the words hiding within the grandiose flowing font. She realises that she has not yet read both sides of the card. Through the thick clouds of her drunken stupor she can barely read the contact information accompanying the message:

APPLICANTS WITH AN EXCESSIVELY CURIOUS
AND INQUISITIVE NATURE
ARE DISTINCTLY NOT WELCOME.
LIGHT DUTIES. LARGE PAY.
NO QUESTIONS ASKED OR ANSWERED.

Freya lacks the mental energy to be sufficiently confused by the strange cluster of words printed in embossed silver on the card. She carries it over to her desk, opens her e-mail, attaches her CV, and clicks send. Precisely two seconds later she is struck by the horrific realisation that there is no "undo" function on her e-mail and her CV is now recklessly hurtling through cyberspace. She is about to perform some sort of panicked dance that will involve manic arm-thrashing and an eclectic collection of yelping noises, when the extraordinary quantity of alcohol rushing through her bloodstream overpowers her and she passes out on the keyboard with a satisfyingly heavy clunk.

ACKNOWLEDGMENTS

I wrote much of this book during a pandemic, so I have a lot of people to whom I owe a great deal of gratitude. First and foremost, everyone, everywhere who put themselves on the line keeping the wheels on for the rest of us: childcare workers, grocery store staff, nurses, doctors, teachers. I know that thanks is not enough, but while I'm yelling into the void for structural change, I might as well yell my admiration in your direction as well. To the people and the city of Havana, *gracias por todo*. Huge and squishy hugs to everyone who worked on and listened to *Six Cold Feet*. Jess McGaw, Mel Zanetti, Robert Zosars, Elizabeth Best, Damien Campagnolo, Hayley Francis, Kate Logan, Jenna Saini, Liam Soden, Helen Stephens, Tom Yaxley, Scott Mercer, Adele Pickvance, and Ash Shanahan, you are all bright and shiny stars in the firmament of the creative cosmos. Shoutout to everyone in the *#audiodramasunday* crew.

Huge thanks to Tristan Barr, Kate O'Sullivan, and Luke Arnold for help and advice with the film script version (fingers forever crossed). Thank you to the Francis family for your constant support, care, and assistance, especially with all your help making our house into a (possibly haunted) home. Thanks to Cindy Bullard at Birch Literary for making more than one dream come true this year. Dad, Mum, Trent, and Louise, you are the glue that keeps my googly eyes from falling to the floor; you all deserve eternal medals and gold stars for putting up with me all these years. I am forever indebted to Diane DiBiase for championing this book and helping bring it into the light. You, Beth Deveny, and the whole team at Sourcebooks have been a joy to work with. Dave Clarke(y), thanks for the pic. Also for many years of friendship, not necessarily in that order.

Naïm Paddington, thank you for giving me such a warm and welcoming place to write, work, and relax. Your incomparable coffee and company fuelled many of these pages. Thank you also to the Queensland Writers Centre for providing a quiet writing space as well as creating the excellent Adaptable program, which has opened some very exciting doors for me. Millennial Pink Book Club: I couldn't wish for a kinder, smarter, funnier group to yell about books with on a regular basis. Honestly, I probably care more about your opinion of my work than just about anyone else's.

Sandie Fraser and the team at Speakers Ink, you have provided so many opportunities to spend my days sharing ideas, techniques, and jokes of dubious quality with a plethora of wonderful people. You help keep my writing life much more kinetic than hermetic. Angela Peita, it is such an honour to work with you on so many fun and meaningful projects; congratulations on the ongoing success of your cult. L. E. Daniels, thank you for being such a supporter of my work for so long and for your insights into the early draft of this book; your guidance was invaluable. Liesel Zink, thank you for being a dream collaborator. Of all things I've worked on in my life, your projects have been some of the most delightfully revealing and reward-ing. Mike Willmett, Alana Sargent, Ashleigh Musk, Lauren Carr, Katina Olsen, Michael Smith, Erin O'Rourke, and Erica Field, thank you for bringing *Awesome: A State of Wonder and Fear* to life and giving me the opportunity to have my poems fact-checked by scientists (a sentence I thought I would never write). Dr. Kate Jardine, thank you for your medical advice and insight. I'll make sure to never be clinically dead for more than four minutes, now that I know the risks.

I have innumerable people to thank for all their help before, during, and after the birth of our daughter while I was also writ-ing this book. Listing them all here would require this book to double in length, but please write your name here and know that I love you with all of my heart and most of my liver:

_____

Thank you to Tilly for reminding me about the things that truly matter: staring at rocks and leaves, spiders, laughing, reading, and painting on windows. Welcome to the world, it's a much better place now that you're here. Lastly, thank you to my wife, Hannah. Listing all your virtues, kindnesses and insights would mean this book would quadruple in length *and* have to be printed on Bible-page thin paper, but I couldn't do any of this without you. Thanks for being my everything.

ABOUT THE AUTHOR

J. M. Donellan is an author, musician, poet, podcaster, and teacher. He was almost devoured by a tiger in the jungles of Malaysia, nearly died of a lung collapse in the Nepalese Himalayas, and once fended off a pack of rabid dogs with a guitar in the mountains of India. He has performed at the Sydney Writers' Festival, TEDxBrisbane, the Sydney Opera House, Brisbane Festival, and some very prestigious basements.

His writing spans a range of genres and formats in a manner that is either highly impressive or, in the words of his accountant, "irritatingly convoluted and frankly quite annoying." He has won and been nominated for numerous awards but refuses to list them all here, because no one likes a braggart. He lives in Brisbane with his wife and daughter, who are both wonderful, thank you for asking. Most of the rumours you've heard about him are true, except for the one about the werewolf, which is merely a half-truth.